The Investor's Wife

The Caregivers, Volume 5

Rose Fresquez

Published by Rose Fresquez, 2022.

---

1.   https://www.myidentifiers.com/title_registration?is-bn=978-1-961159-04-4&icon_type=New

To Joel, Isaiah, Caleb, Abigail and Micah. I love you so much and I'm so blessed to laugh and cry with you every day. Thanks for being my inspiration.

ACKNOWLEDGEMENTS

I want to thank the Lord, my Savior. Without you, Father, there's no point in trying to do anything at all. It's my prayer that I can honor you with my words. I thank you for connecting me with an amazing group of people who helped support me in accomplishing this novel.

To my husband Joel, who works so hard to provide for our family, so that I can stay home and take care of the kids. I'm so blessed that we get to journey through life together.

To my children Isaiah, Caleb, Abigail and Micah, you fill my heart with joy. Thanks for the giggles, laughter and encouragement.

Unending thanks to my editor, Deirdre Lockhart. Your insights and wisdom have helped shape this story.

To my insider team, thanks for always suggesting the coolest ideas.

Jerri Hall, Thanks for your support and encouragement always. You're such an inspiration

To Nicole, Deb, Melissa, Marie, Nancy, Linda, Katherine, Elizabeth and Trudy. You ladies are so amazing for the time you invested to brainstorm, beta read and critique my manuscript. Thank you from the bottom of my heart.

CHAPTER 1

Liberty Solace sat before a long folding table while addressing her team of ten employees. Three of them were jotting notes on sticky pads while the others had their focus intent on her—as if she held the key to their success. But that wasn't the case at all. She was still learning the ropes of running a home-care business while taking care of her daughter, Myra.

"Just like I mentioned in the email." She peered at her laptop to check the copy she'd included with the backup caregiver contacts. Even with all the effort to get backup fill-ins, she couldn't guarantee they'd be fully staffed throughout the weekend. "Try to call any of these subs in case you can't make it."

The silence stretched on as one of the girls stared at the lit Christmas tree aglow in the corner of the small lobby. Perhaps everyone was ready to call it a day.

"Any questions?"

Abeba, the least outspoken, rubbed at her forehead, looking frazzled while opening and closing her mouth. Liberty understood her well since her mom had the same quality—a trait she admired after reaping the consequences of walking away from her marriage. "What's your question, Abeba?"

Abeba scratched her ebony cheek, her skin slightly darker than Liberty's. "Can we call you if none of the subs work out?"

Liberty must have forgotten to add one tiny, but crucial detail—the lack of service where she was headed for the weekend. She tucked a loose strand of her hair behind her ear before glancing out the window.

More darkening clouds blanketed the west than had been there earlier. Unease chilled her. *Did* she want to be out of reach for an entire weekend? Frowning, she refocused on her employees and Abeba's question. "You can call Rhonda."

Her mom knew Liberty's friend who worked at the job center. Now and then, temps were available. However, Liberty would rather not have Mom dealing with scheduling while taking care of Myra. "Only if it's an emergency."

"Drive carefully!" Dag lilted in his Norwegian accent, shaking his unruly dark hair away from his face. "I hear we're getting a snowstorm this weekend."

"I have a decent car." Her Subaru Impreza could get around in town, but if the weather got out of hand, would it handle the mountain roads in the snow?

The time on the corner of her computer warned her it was three already, and she had lots to do before the one-hour drive to meet her friends at the cabin.

"You guys are awesome!" She clasped her hands. "Don't forget to stay and enjoy the Chinese dinner I'm having delivered in thirty minutes." Once a month, she ordered dinner for her employees so they could share a meal and connect.

"When is the Christmas party?" asked another guy.

Liberty spread her hands. "You'd best check the calendar. I'm afraid we had to reschedule the party to the third." After the New Year. She pushed back her chair. "I hope everyone has a wonderful weekend, and I'll see you on Tuesday." She gave each of them a smile before striding to her office, her daughter's temporary bedroom on days Liberty didn't work from home.

The business hadn't been her original career plan, but God presented it at a time when she needed it. Although challenging at times, the flexibility allowed her to stay with Myra throughout the day.

Myra stirred in the portable crib, snuggling her plush teddy-bear blanket to her chest. Liberty's heart squeezed at how precious a gift God had given her. Eighteen months had gone by in a blink, but she could hardly remember what life was like before Myra.

Except Myra reminded her of Bryce whenever she smiled. Her curls were a mix of Liberty's black and Bryce's copper-brown hair.

In a few years, she would start asking about her dad, and Liberty dreaded telling the story. She showed Myra pictures of Bryce so she could know what her daddy looked like.

Myra was the main reason she thought of Bryce at night, whenever she couldn't sleep—scratch that, she thought of him for herself too. She moved to her desk to put her laptop in the carry bag and struggled not to stare at Bryce's photo on her desk while she was thinking of him. How she longed to hold him in her arms again.

Did he ever think about her? A pain shot through her at the reality of the answer she knew well. He already had a woman who took care of him. His mom.

Love was brutal at times. It left you no choice in who you fell for. Liberty ached and prayed for Bryce to share in the joy of her new-found faith—for him to come back to her, to them—and not just for Myra's sake.

Having been raised by a single mom and admiring the dads other kids had, Liberty wished Myra could have two parents in her life, parents who loved each other and loved her too.

Bryce probably had no idea Liberty's heart still belonged to him, just like he didn't know he had a daughter.

She rubbed her fingers, stopping at the lightness of her ring finger. She gasped when she lifted her hand. Where was her ring? The indent on her finger marked the place where she always wore the ring.

"Oh no!" She patted the pockets of her red denims but didn't feel anything.

Her body rushed with adrenaline as she tossed her hand to her messy ponytail, pacing around the crib, her mind playing out how long it had been missing. "This can't be happening."

She rarely took it off, unless she was cleaning with bleach. Rarely did she leave the house without it. But that depended on how fast she left the house while trying to remember all Myra's baby food and diapers and, well, you name it.

"Mama!"

The sweet sound of her daughter pulled her back to the present, and the tension seeped from her shoulders. Myra was sitting in the crib, rubbing at her groggy eyes.

"I'm so sorry I woke you, my starlight." Liberty crouched, scooped her up, and planted a kiss on her amber cheek. It was so soft, and she still had that sweet baby scent. "I hope this nap won't interfere with your sleep tonight." She shifted Myra to her chest. "You need to be good for Nana."

"Nana." Her little fingers traced Liberty's neck when she wrapped her arms around her.

"Yes. You're staying with Nana for three days, okay?"

Liberty's chest tightened. Saying it aloud made three days seem too long. She'd never stayed the night away from her baby.

Ever since Liberty weaned her from breast milk, Myra seemed flexible hanging out with Nana for a longer time. No doubt, Mom would do a great job taking care of her grandchild, and Liberty just needed to let it go. Embrace the idea of hanging out and having fun with the girls.

She lifted Myra to sniff her bottom. She didn't reek from a poopy diaper, so no need to change her.

After getting her sippy cup from the small fridge in her office, Liberty shoved it in the side pocket of the diaper bag on her chair. Keeping Myra on her hip, she slugged the bag on her shoulder and grabbed her computer bag.

On the way to the parking lot, Myra bubbled while Liberty hoisted her to her hip. It was harder to understand Myra's nonsensical words with the whirling wind blowing light snowflakes in their faces.

Fully strapped in her rear-facing car seat, Myra was content drinking her milk. Bible jams blasted in the car as Liberty drove out of the parking lot.

Between her ring missing and the snow falling, a sense of dread for the trip fell over her.

Turning her phone on speaker, she called her friend, Iris Stone.

Iris answered on the first ring.

"Are you ready for the trip?" Her chipper voice rang out over the "Jesus Loves Me" song.

It's good for Myra to get used to other people when you're not around. Mom had reminded her several times over the last three weeks since Liberty found out about the getaway.

She let out a dreadful breath as she came to a stoplight. "I don't know...."

"You can't back out now. Tessa and I will run out of things to talk about."

Iris had become friends with Tessa through Liberty.

"Aren't your sisters coming?" Perhaps Liberty could back out and not feel guilty.

"They'll get here on Christmas Eve." So, Liberty better not back out. "Can you believe that?"

The light turned green, and she let her foot off the gas as she contemplated all her reasons to postpone the trip. "I still need to run to the store and get a few groceries for the cabin."

"Sabastian called the cabin maintenance and had them stock up with everything we needed."

Sabastian was their family chef.

Although wealthy, Iris and her family kept their status from hindering their relationships with people in different income brackets. Unlike Bryce's mom.

Iris and Liberty were both thirty and had been friends since nineteen. They met at the Stone reunion where Liberty had been working for the catering company. She rarely saw Iris now, though, since her friend only came to town twice a year. If Liberty canceled the cabin, she may not see her until next summer.

As she turned on the road toward her mom's neighborhood, the wind whirled a piece of cardboard over her windshield, and she cleared it off with the swipers.

"I might be late. I'll drop off Myra first." Uneasy about the ring's disappearance, she twisted her hands on the steering wheel as she told her friend about it. "It would feel like Bryce and I had never happened."

Iris was quiet before she sang out. "I think you accidentally put your ring in my duffle bag this morning."

Whew! Peace washed over her, calming her nerves. "Thank you... thank you so much!"

She'd forgotten about taking off her ring when she met with Iris at the recreation center that morning. Liberty had taken Myra swimming, so she could spend time with her before the trip. "I'll bring it tonight." Iris then added, "At this point, you should never take it off your finger. Then you won't worry about getting it lost."

Iris didn't need to remind her. Liberty had learned her lesson and intended to keep the ring on her finger at all times from now on.

Mom's housing community came into view. Single homes with different color siding, all close to each other. She was proud of Mom for finally having her own space. It wasn't a dream house by any means. But it was hers, and she deserved it after all her hard work and sacrifices to pay cash for it.

"You're ready to see Nana?"

"Nana... Nana." Myra's voice rang out as her little hands tried to clap.

I'm doing the right thing. Liberty had to remind herself since Mom had encouraged her to take the trip and have time away for herself.

One weekend with the girls wouldn't hurt. Especially at a cabin that held precious memories.

CHAPTER 2

Bryce Solace tossed his duffle bag in the back of the Wrangler and closed the door.

One step away from a fun-filled weekend, except for the slight mountain in his path. *Mom.*

He'd tried to bring up the subject last night upon his arrival, but she was more excited to talk about today's party. It might have been better to tell her then than to surprise her today, but then she might have talked him out of the trip.

He drew out a breath and stepped from the garage. He wasn't looking forward to this encounter, but he couldn't drive away without letting her know.

The savory smell of grilled meat and food beckoned him as he crossed the white marble floor in the front room.

The house buzzed with uniformed workers—black shirts and trousers for house employees and white and black for the caterers. Weekend parties were a norm in his childhood home, especially in December. Mom's favorite thing about Christmas was hosting parties at the house. She got carried away at times, but it didn't matter what Bryce or his dad thought.

A massive Christmas tree with sparkly garlands and ornaments nestled by the staircase, its glittering lights gleaming on the mahogany handrail and spindles.

As he approached the kitchen adjoining the front room, the clatter of lids came while their house manager opened and closed one lid after another on the row of food items lining the kitchen island.

"Hey there, Rita."

"Mr. Solace." She nodded a respectful greeting, then brushed something from her black dress. Rita was the only employee allowed to wear a dress if she felt like it as long as it was up to mom's standard in color and dress code. "Can I get you a snack?"

He patted his flat stomach. "You made me that late lunch two hours ago, so I'm good. But you could tell me where Mom is."

He would've looked for Mom by himself, but in the spacious three-level house and basement, he might need another thirty minutes to find her.

Rita's smile was kind as she peered down the hall further from the kitchen. "She's in the banquet room."

"Thank you."

It was a shame a woman as old as his mom addressed him formally, but Mom would fire her or any staff who didn't abide by her rules of adding formalities to house members—meaning him, Mom, and Dad, who was rarely home for more reasons than escaping his wife.

He could hear Mom's screech coming from the banquet room, yelling at someone for putting the wrong color linen on the tables.

When he made it to the entrance, she was standing by the white artificial Christmas tree, her figure in its beaded black cocktail dress reflecting in the tree's green, red, and gold glass ball ornaments. She had one hand planted on her hip while pointing with the other to the corner as she gave instructions. When she shook her head at something someone did wrong, her auburn hair swished across her black dress.

Silverware clattered against the tile when one of the women dropped a tray on the floor.

Three more women and two men deftly moved boxes, while others filled water glasses and folded napkins. He didn't recognize their faces, which wasn't unusual. Mom hired and fired employees on a monthly basis as if it were her full-time job.

As Bryce approached her, he took in the room with floor-to-ceiling windows. The tan linens looked presentable with the pine centerpieces and red LED candles. With such a strong smell of pine in the air, the centerpieces must be fresh in stark contrast to the fake Christmas trees.

As he passed a woman pulling back the chair, Bryce slowed to encourage her, in an attempt to smooth over Mom's harping. "The room looks great."

The woman gave him a fleeting glance and mumbled a thanks before stripping the fabric from one of the tables.

If only he had the guts to argue with Mom about certain things, he could save the workers a great deal of time.

"You're running a tight operation." He spoke when he got within Mom's earshot.

At his voice, she turned around, and her wrinkled brow unfolded with her smile, warming his heart. She fanned herself with her fingers. "There's my dashing son."

"Hi, Mom."

Her smile slipped back into a frown as she surveyed his outfit. A vest jacket worn over a black Henley shirt and jeans.

"People will be here in less than an hour. You should get dressed."

Here we go. Bryce gripped the back of his neck. Talking to her in front of the staff might be better than a private discussion. "I'm going skiing with Logan and his brothers tonight—for the whole weekend." He had to be specific.

Her wrinkles were more visible when her frown returned, deepening, before she managed, "Definitely not." She took a step back and scowled. "You can't abandon your family."

By family, she meant her. Dad was on a business trip in Rhode Island for another two days. "I'm not abandoning you, Mom." Not when she would have a bunch of her socialite friends and their families at the party.

She threw her hands up. "You just got here."

He was thirty-two, a grown man. So why did he still feel small around her? Always torn between doing his own thing and doing whatever she planned for him to do.

"I'll be back on Monday. In plenty of time before the Christmas party on Friday."

Then he'd spend Christmas day on Tuesday with her and Dad. He'd taken two weeks off from work so he could squeeze in the ski trip with the guys.

Mom sucked in a breath and stared at him with sorrow-seeped eyes. "I can't believe you're just telling me this now."

He kneaded the back of his neck, but the muscles were so knotted nothing would help now. So he peered out of the window. The wind curled the snow in swirls, whipping it against the glass.

She followed his gaze. "You can't go in this weather. Driving in that wind is dangerous."

He had great tires, four-wheel drive, and high clearance to drive through several inches of snow. But reasoning with her had never been easy. "If I leave now, the weather won't be a problem."

There'd been a projected storm later that evening, but if she hadn't heard about it, he didn't intend to update her.

They argued as she expressed all the reasons he shouldn't go. Her usual trick to guilt him into staying almost worked.

"What's the point of this party if you're not here?"

It wasn't any different from all the other parties. To make Mom happy, he entertained the idea of canceling his plans. But this time, the need to prove to the Stone siblings that he wasn't Mom's boy was stronger than the need to please her.

Conflicted, he rubbed his thumb over his fingers, the ring on his finger scraped against his flesh.

"I'm sorry for letting you down this one time. "

Her gaze darted to his ring finger. "You're forgetting you haven't gotten rid of that stupid ring."

As she'd asked for the last few years since his wife left.

His body jerked, and his jaw twitched. The ring had been a battle, and he'd fight for it all over. Mom must have noticed his internal conflict because she gave him what seemed like a sympathetic look and conceded with an embrace. "Keep your phone handy."

There was no cell service where he was headed, now that Mom brought it up, but maybe he wouldn't give her the cabin's landline. A weekend without her calling him might be good for both of them.

"All right, Mom."

When he stepped out of the embrace, she touched his chin. Her brown eyes always radiated with warmth toward him. "Have Rita pack you some snacks."

"The guys have it covered." Or so Logan had said when Bryce offered to bring some food.

Mom's lips pressed into a thin line before she insisted he call whenever he got to the cabin.

Moments like this made him realize how she could be stifling without meaning to.

With no time to get into why he wouldn't call, he made his way to the garage and into his Jeep.

Free at last, he fired the engine and turned on Taylor Swift's pop music from his playlist. "ME!" blasted through the Bluetooth speakers. As he drove the paved road and out of sight from his childhood home, he drummed his hands on the steering wheel, his tires trudging smoothly through the snow.

Maybe it was because he was headed to the cabin where he'd had his wedding night or because Liberty always enjoyed Taylor Swift's music, but he felt as if Liberty was singing to him. Especially when the song ended with the promise that nobody was going to love him like she did.

He ground his teeth to stem the regret flooding him. Still, a sense of unease followed as he took a mountain road further west. Liberty had loved him unconditionally, and he'd taken her for granted.

He never believed in God, but he knew people who believed in Him and credited God for the miracles in their lives. If there was a God of miracles, Bryce needed one of those miracles. If given a second chance with his wife, which seemed impossible, he'd do whatever it took to be a better husband.

Things had always been easy for him since his childhood. He'd grown up in a privileged home and gone to luxurious schools. Even when he'd switched from law to business, before he could graduate, Logan's brother, Eric, was available to train him on the ins and outs of trading and investments. Having mastered the skills fast, he'd scored big-time financially without much effort.

He'd assumed his marriage would be the same. No need to work, but still reap a great return on investment. Man, was he wrong!

This time, he was on his own without anyone to train him to be a husband.

He drove past more mountain homes spread acres apart from one another, pines and fir trees bending in the wind, their boughs waving him on. With the wind blowing snow on his car, the wipers swished nonstop, their steady *thwump-thwump* now too loud for him to hear and enjoy the music.

He took in the snowcapped mountains the further he drove. Then he started to climb from the valley and twisted along a narrow mountain road. The wind whipped at the pines. Limbs fell on his windshield but were instantly swept away.

Bryce gripped the steering wheel while navigating the narrow switchback turns between leafless deciduous trees and sweeping evergreens. If the wind wasn't so gusty, he'd open his window to breathe in the fresh mountain air.

After seemingly forever, the two-story stone cabin came into view, nestled in the trees. Even with the snow covering the path, he remembered the wide flagstones along the pathway to the driveway.

The last time he'd been here, the trees were the color of fire, and in an instant, memories of that day became clearer.

Liberty's tears... His anguish over her sadness on their wedding day... Their hotel reservations had been messed up. Logan had come to the rescue and asked his brother for the cabin on Bryce's account. They'd only needed it for a couple of nights before heading off on their honeymoon trip.

It wasn't until they'd driven to the cabin and Bryce carried her inside that the tension evaporated from her shoulders. He remembered setting her down on the couch and her looking at him with a longing that took his breath away. His heart had been so full of love for her, and as he kissed her face and neck and nose, he'd sworn to never be responsible for her tears again.

He'd failed. Mom's unwelcome opinions in their marriage, her constant interference, was his responsibility. Yet he'd done little to shield his wife from that.

He rubbed the ring on his finger. One of the few battles he'd won with Mom. He'd had lots of opportunities to move on with someone else, but how could he when Liberty had ruined him for other women?

He'd been in love with Liberty since she came into his life during his early twenties or even before. He'd fallen in love with her when they were together, then fell deeper in love with her in the years they were apart.

Regardless of her absence in his life, she would always be his wife. She'd never sent him divorce papers, but if she ever did, he would be ready to fight for another chance.

He swung open the door and walked to the garage, then punched in the code.

The wind howled, flinging wet snow droplets in his face, and he squinted, wiping the snow with his hand as he made his way back to the car and drove it into the three-car garage.

With no other cars parked there, he must be the first to arrive.

Good. He had first pick of the rooms. He knew which he wanted.

He planned to play in the snow with his friends during the day and lay in bed during the night, surrendering to memories of what he'd lost.

Leaving his dripping boots in the garage, he walked through the side door, his socks slippery against the hardwood flooring, and the cozy cabin warmed him while the utmost quiet greeted him. Restive. Peaceful. As if the high ceilings absorbed all sound.

Snowy evening light whispered cool and gray through the triple-pane European windows. Besides the lit Christmas tree in the east room, everything else looked as he remembered it from three and a half years ago.

When he made it upstairs, he rolled his luggage to one of the four bedrooms, the master bedroom where he'd shared his wedding night.

His stomach growled, and before he could take in the room, he stepped out. The hardwood stairs creaked as he took two stairs down at a time and veered to the kitchen off the left.

When he swung open the refrigerator, the variety of food options overwhelmed him. He could wait for dinner to spare himself the energy of making a sandwich. Or he tapped his hand on his chin, contemplating a soda. A seltzer, ginger ale, or Pepsi. Liberty's favorite. He glanced at a three-tiered storage shelf on the black marble counter loaded with snacks, then closed the fridge, and rummaged through the goodies before snagging some beef jerky.

The front door jerked, and someone scuffled inside, lugging something. He couldn't see the hallway from the kitchen.

Odd that the boys came through the front door instead of the garage.

Ripping open his beef jerky, he walked toward the hallway, then stopped in his tracks. The air left his lungs as Liberty set her luggage on the threshold. The beef jerky slid out of his hands and plopped onto the hardwood floor. His breathing quickened when she twisted her neck to his side and saw him.

She blinked, her eyes widening as she took him in.

For a long moment, all they could do was stare at each other without moving. It took all his strength to keep from wrapping his arms around her and kissing her the way he longed to.

When his tongue managed, he called her by the nickname he'd given her—Dimples.

Her hand flew to her heart, and her lips parted as if she were going to say something. But she didn't.

The snow dusting her dark hair started to melt into her messy ponytail, and her jaw slacked as she stood there. But she didn't have to smile for him to know she had the deepest dimples he'd ever seen.

Her confused expression mirrored his jumbled feelings. He had so many questions on why and what she was doing here, but the desire to touch her, to feel her soft brown skin was so intense. He needed to know that he wasn't hallucinating.

CHAPTER 3

Of all the people she'd expected to encounter this weekend, Bryce was the last person to cross Liberty's mind. They continued to look at each other in silence as the questions on his face seemed to ask what she couldn't bring herself to voice.

A burning pain bubbled in her chest, stretching into every sleeping corner. Their time apart had aged him a bit. Was that sadness etched around his mouth and eyes and in the hollows under his cheeks? Or was she only aching to see that he'd hurt as much as she had? Still handsome with his copper-brown hair, clean-shaven square jaw, and broad chest stretching out his black long-sleeved shirt, he sent her insides swirling.

He breathed her nickname again. The sound, so soft and perfect, compelled her to take a single step toward him.

"Bryce?" Her voice quivered. No doubt, she was dreaming. She'd walked away from him and switched her phone number just over two years ago. Not staying in touch while he lived in New York had been easy. And during his short visits to Pleasant View, his mom, Wendy, never let him out of her sight.

With slow steps, Bryce moved closer, too close.

So she stepped back. She wanted to embrace him, touch him, yet run away from him at the same time.

One side of his mouth lifted. "It's me, Dimples." He breathed out the tender words, reaching up. His fingers grazed against her hair, down to her neck. His familiar touch left a trail of goosebumps on her body, awakening every nerve that had been dormant in his absence. "I can't believe you're here."

Me too.

Her tongue was frozen. But tears stung her eyes, and she brushed the side of one eye.

He captured her hand and closed his eyes, then lifted her hand toward his mouth like he was about to kiss it, but she pulled it away and stumbled a step further backward.

There were a thousand reasons he couldn't be here, reasons she'd walked away from him, and even if she wanted him back, they had a lot to resolve. First things first.

How did he get away from Wendy, unless he'd come here straight from the airport? "Did… um… the girls invite you here?"

"I'm meeting the guys."

"I'm meeting the girls."

"That doesn't sound right… unless it's a joint party?" Bryce glanced to the side by the open space of the living room where three black leather couches cozied in front of the fireplace. "There's enough space for all of us."

She slapped a hand on her forehead. How could Iris not tell her Bryce, of all people, was coming? "Iris… must have forgotten to tell me."

He crossed his arms and nodded meditatively. "Logan didn't say anything either."

Logan was Iris's brother and Bryce's best friend. Was it a coincidence that the siblings would invite Bryce and Liberty? To the cabin where they'd stayed on their wedding night?

"Let's call Logan and find out." Bryce interrupted her thoughts, and she left her luggage to follow him into the living room. Her sock feet padded the polished hardwood floor.

It felt warm—warmer given the circumstances. Good thing she'd left her jacket and wet shoes by the mud pan in the hallway when she'd entered the house.

Bryce sank onto one of those couches before the stone fireplace. He then reached for the phone on the table.

While he punched in the numbers, Liberty sat across from him, struggling not to stare at him. Instead, she took in the three abstract paintings on the wall next to the fireplace. On the mantel was a photo of Eric Stone and his wife, Joy. Liberty had heard a lot about Joy through Iris but didn't know her personally.

Bryce must have put the phone on speaker because a deep male voice sounded through. "I see you made it to the cabin already."

"Where are you?" Bryce rubbed his long fingers on his jeans, and the ring on his finger flickered in the light.

Afraid to get caught staring, she looked away, sitting stiffer in her seat. Was it the same ring from their wedding day, or had he gotten a different ring?

No way could he marry someone else since they hadn't gotten a divorce. But his conniving mom could find a way to marry off her son to one of the wealthy girls in their circle. Wendy would rather not have Bryce interact with Liberty, even if it meant he was looking for her to sign divorce papers.

"Are you the only one there?" Logan's jocular tone came across casually. Not like someone driving through the snowy mountain road.

"Dimples... um, is here." Bryce managed a glance at her, and his softening eyes made her squirm on the couch.

"Good."

"What do you mean—good?" Bryce's shoulders stiffened as he turned his back to Liberty, then dragged the phone cord as if needing to say something to Logan—something he didn't want her to hear. He instead let out a frustrated groan.

"It's gonna be the two of you, man." Laughter carried in Logan's voice.

Oh my! Liberty's neck heated, and she understood why Bryce sounded frustrated. She, on the other hand, had no idea whether she was happy, sad, or frustrated.

The two of them in a secluded house was equally thrilling and dangerous. When her gaze drifted to him, he was staring at her, and his eyes filled with questions yet something else she couldn't read. Was he glad to run into her? Was he not? Maybe he was just as confused as she was.

She'd been sure of wanting him back in her life, aching to have another chance, but this unexpected intimate proximity sent an adrenaline rush of panic through her body. A lot could happen in one night, let alone three with the man who dominated her heart.

As if sensing her internal struggle, Bryce stared at the phone again. "Can you put Iris on the phone?"

Liberty's breath whooshed out. At least, she could talk to her friend.

Then Logan responded, "We got things going on."

The line went dead followed by the phone beeping.

Bryce rubbed his hands over his jeans, then lifted his hands in question. "I guess you heard the conversation?"

She nodded, and her palms sweat against the leather cushion. Despite the thrill to spend time with him, to reconcile, she knew what she had to do.

As she looked at the big living room window, daylight was vanishing, and snow was thickening. With more snow expected tonight, she needed to leave before it got late. "I should get going."

Like the snow enveloping the roads, his gray eyes seeped into her—his gaze freezing her in place and melting over her all at once. "Please stay."

The genuine plea tugged at her heart, but being alone with him would make her forget all the reasons they could never be together. Unless something had changed during their time apart. So she had to ask one question.

"Does your mom know you're here?"

He closed his eyes, then gripped the back of his neck. The flinch was the answer she needed. It wouldn't surprise her if Wendy had put a camera on his car or wallet to spy on his every move while he was away.

Driving in the snowy night was terrifying, but staying with him was scarier for more reasons than just Wendy. He had so much power over her emotions, and the last thing Liberty needed was chaos added to her already complicated life.

Her shoulders fell as intense loneliness blanketed her. She hated leaving before they had a chance to talk, but she had to go. She pushed to her feet. "Sorry. Good to see you."

She would call Iris the moment she had cell service and hound her over this unexpected reunion.

When she started to walk, Bryce snagged her hand and tugged at it, and she stilled, exhaling while she savored the warmth from his touch. But she didn't dare look at him. She might end up melting into him instead.

"I'll leave. Please stay." His voice was gentle, tempting.

She had to ease her arm out of his hold and walk toward the hallway.

Grabbing her luggage, he fell in step with her. He continued to plead with her to stay while pointing out the dangers of driving on the icy mountain road in the snowy darkness.

She ignored him while she slid her arms into her jacket and her feet into her tennis shoes. She'd left her boots at home in the other suitcase she forgot to bring, but the Stones had boots in the house somewhere if she'd planned on staying and sledding as she'd intended.

Her heart was heavy when she met Bryce's downcast eyes. She lifted her hand to wave before she turned for the door and swung it open, and he held it for her.

"Thanks," she said, then reached for the heavy screen door and was whipped by snow and wind.

Since the daylight had vanished, she was grateful for the porch light as she scraped snow that had piled on her Impreza. The wind blew icy prickles in her face and her ears. Her fingers numbed without gloves, and the cold seeped through her shoes. She was way underdressed.

As soon as she finished cleaning her car, she hopped in and fired the engine, then blasted the heat.

It was only six. She should be home in plenty of time to put Myra to bed.

As she drove down the winding road, her body tensed on the slippery path. In the time she'd been inside, the thick flakes had accumulated on the road fast, burying her tire tracks from earlier. Now her tires ground through the unplowed road, snow scraping the undercarriage of her Subaru. Come to think of it, she'd never driven her car in the mountains during winter.

She breathed in, then out. "I can do this."

She could handle her car attempting to slide, but the branches falling on her windshield sent her heart racing.

"Lord, please let me be safe." Myra was too young to lose a mom, should anything happen to Liberty on this trip.

She jerked when a loud crackling sounded a few yards away. The headlights lighting her path highlighted the huge pine collapsing across the road.

Her hands tightened around the steering wheel. Her heart in her throat, she slammed on her brakes so hard the car jerked, skidding on the icy surface. She gripped the steering wheel tighter, despite having no control as fear pulsed through her. Was the car going to roll down the hill and into the fallen tree?

Then the movement stopped. Just stopped.

Her body shook, and she could barely pull the steering wheel into park. So relieved she could park it, she peered into the expansive forest. The rapid racing of her heart broke the silence. "Thank You, Lord, for saving my life."

Myra came to mind. Her sweet baby. Liberty hadn't filled in the power of attorney for guardianship should she die or have something tragic happen. Mom would take care of her granddaughter and let Bryce know he had a daughter. But was Bryce ready to have kids? They'd always talked about starting a family much later after his career took off.

Through the rearview mirror, she could still see the cabin's light. Something was moving, perhaps a night creature.

On second thought, being stranded with Bryce wasn't so bad, now that she'd come close to death.

As she put her car in reverse, the tires wouldn't budge. They spun, squeaked. Great, so great. She dragged the gear shift into park and rested her head on the leather steering wheel.

"God, what a way to teach me humility." With her tennis shoes, trekking back to the cabin was going to be interesting.

She closed her eyes and exhaled. She needed to calm her racked nerves and process what she would be talking to Bryce about before making the climb. She needed to tell him about his daughter. But what if he was getting married and had initiated this get-together so he could have her sign divorce papers?

She shuddered at the possibility. Either way, despite his relationship status, she didn't want her daughter to grow up without a father like Liberty had. She'd desired a dad mostly when she was a teenager. She'd even bugged Mom when she got serious about tracking her dad down, but Mom insisted it was best not to have him be a part of their lives.

Thankful for the heat blowing in the car, she squeezed her eyes tight and prayed for Myra to always feel loved, no matter what.

What if she told Bryce and he told his mom? They could take her daughter away from her.

She was shaking, not from coldness, but from the outcome of her honesty.

Had Wendy changed? Her mind wandered to a time far away. And the day turned into ten years ago when she fell in love with Bryce.

THAT SUMMER, LIBERTY put her nursing course on hold. Mom was struggling to make ends meet while keeping up with all the other bills. Since they lived in a tourist town, the main jobs in Pleasant View were at the ski resorts or hotel and service industry jobs.

Working at a resort wasn't an option for Liberty during the off-season. She'd been contemplating applying at one of the boutiques on Main Street when Mom presented her with a different opportunity one Wednesday evening. Liberty was folding laundry and watching a reality TV show when Mom walked in from her job as a caregiver with the Solace family.

"Remember how I told you Bryce got injured?" Her voice rose over the TV noise before she reached for the remote and pressed the mute button.

Bryce probably had all sorts of medical staff tending to his bicycle injury. What could Liberty do for him? The summer dress in her hand dangled when she lifted her hands. "Mom, I'm missing the good part where people are running through the snakes."

Ignoring her protests, Mom sank onto the coffee table, blocking Liberty's view of the TV. "He's been grumpy, and Mrs. Solace requested you keep him company."

Liberty winced, thinking of Bryce in pain during his summer break, but she wasn't a physical therapist if that's what Mom meant.

She folded the light dress and set it on the pile of folded clothes she'd stacked on the carpeted floor. "Why me?"

"She wants someone he knows, someone his age to tend to him."

"I thought his mom didn't want him to talk to any girls who were"—she made air quotes—"'hired to help.'"

Mom's ponytail danced over her black blouse when she shook her head. "Another reason she wants you. You know the rules and won't fall in love with Bryce."

Liberty had always thought Bryce was strikingly handsome, but he was too sheltered. Not her type.

He'd been twelve, and she'd been ten when Mom started working for his family. Mom did all sorts of jobs for them, including housekeeping and taking care of Bryce's grandma who had dementia. Several times, she'd taken Liberty to work when they needed an extra hand during house parties, so Liberty knew Wendy wasn't the kind of boss she could work for long term.

Having a second home in New York, the Solace family mostly used their Pleasant View home during the summer months. So Liberty rarely saw Bryce.

The times they'd run into each other over the years, he'd barely spoken to her longer than five minutes. The longest they'd talked was six years ago when his dad, Charles, had invited Liberty to join him and Bryce in a game of chess.

Liberty had won, despite her newbie skills, and Bryce accused her of cheating. Two days later, she'd seen him throw a baseball in the air and try to catch it with a baseball glove. She'd felt bad for him and offered to throw so he could catch, but he'd ended up questioning where she learned to throw so terribly.

After those incidents, the summer pool parties with girls vying for his attention and the constant servants on hand whenever he needed something further convinced her Bryce was spoiled. But now she was twenty, and he'd be twenty-two, so surely, he'd grown up and changed for the better.

She sat a bit taller to clarify with Mom. "By company, you mean babysitting him?"

Mom shrugged. "Not exactly, but if that's how you put it, you'll make some good money."

Liberty needed money to pay her way through school so Mom could save hers to buy a house someday. She hadn't told Mom her plans to pay for school yet, but even if it may take another two years or longer to save up, Liberty would eventually get there.

"So?" Mom lifted her brows, waiting for her response.

"When does she need me to start?"

"Tomorrow."

When Liberty showed up with Mom the next day, the house cleaner told her where to find Wendy, and Mom left for the cottage to take care of her patient. On her way toward the back room, loud voices snapped at each other. And Liberty halted, then angled her ear down the lit hallway.

"Don't you get it, Mom?" a male voice shouted. "I'm not a child anymore!"

"You'll always be my child," the female voice, probably Wendy, screeched. "I have to take care of you—"

"I don't want you to."

Liberty considered backtracking and returning tomorrow when their anger had subsided. Sometimes she felt bad for Bryce because of how much his mom was in his business. Maybe because Liberty's mom was single and had no time to hover around her, but Liberty wouldn't trade places with him.

Then it went quiet enough to hear heels click on the tile. Liberty adjusted the ruffles on her olive-green dress, then gripped her shoulder bag and lifted her chin, taking a step forward.

Two more steps ahead, Wendy emerged, holding a full glass with green liquid.

"Good morning, Mrs. Solace." Like her mom would do, Liberty gave a polite nod.

"He's in there." Wendy waved with disinterest, pointing to the room with French doors, then handed Liberty the reeking medicinal drink. "Give him this."

Liberty stared at the drink in her hand, unsure if it caused the fight between Wendy and her son. Then she looked to Wendy for answers on how she was supposed to force a grown man to drink whatever he didn't want.

With her face flushed, Wendy was dressed in a navy suit and obviously on her way out. A black Mercedes with a driver had been waiting in the driveway.

"What exactly do you need me to do?"

"Read or figure it out." She waved painted fingers at Liberty. "I don't care." She blew out a frustrated breath, and her shoes clicked when she left Liberty standing with the drink.

So Liberty passed through the open French doors into the spacious room with big windows overlooking the rolling mountains. Towering bookshelves stood side by side on one end of the immaculate room, its ash-gray floors and white walls so subtle the room seemed a mere frame for the massive windows. Bryce was lying down in the sitting area, hands crossed over his chest, earbuds in, and bandaged leg propped on the edge of the plush gray velvet couch.

With him staring through the back glass door, she took a moment to take him in. He'd changed in the years she hadn't seen him. Still handsome with coppery brown hair. Although, now his jaw was more chiseled and covered in a day's worth of scruff. Even lying down, he seemed taller and broader. His hair was longer, his bangs dipping down nearly to his eyes.

Her lips parted to call him Mr. Solace as Wendy required, but it didn't sound right.

"Hello, Bryce." She spoke louder. Touching him might startle him. She crossed the ashy wood floors and called him again as she set the drink on the gray marbled coffee table. No way was she going to command him to drink it.

His body jerked, and he turned to face her. His mouth opened, and his eyes widened as he studied her as if seeing her for the first time. Okay, he'd always had the most mesmerizing gray eyes.

He took out the earbuds and tucked them into his cargo shorts.

"Liberty." Her name slipped off his tongue in a whisper, and the amazement in his eyes made her heart race.

She straightened her stance, dismissing her odd reaction. He wasn't her type. Their worlds were so different. Plus, he was off-limits.

"I hear you're in need of a babysitter," she said, trying to keep her voice relaxed as she lowered herself to the curved armchair across from him.

He winced, his lips twitching into an almost smile. "I didn't even know I was hiring."

He didn't sound at all like the man she'd heard yelling earlier. Maybe Wendy ignited all that anger in him. Liberty didn't want to say she'd heard their fight, but she needed to know if he wanted her here. "I take it you've had too much of your mom hanging around?"

He rolled his eyes. "My mom would still be tucking me in bed every night, if I let her."

She giggled under her breath. "Now that's going a little far."

His sheepish grin was warm and adorable. "Try living in my shoes."

Liberty pointed to the drink on the table. "I'm not going to make you drink it, but she requested I bring it over."

"Seems you already disobeyed her on day one." When she frowned, trying to understand what he was saying, he raised a brow. "You called me Bryce instead of Mr. Solace."

"Shh..." She put her finger on her mouth, then peered toward the entrance and back to him. "Don't tell anybody I did that."

He chuckled as he struggled to sit, and she was at his side, holding him by the hand so he could ease his foot on the soft rug between the couches. His hair looked damp, and he smelled of a fancy conditioner. He must've just had a shower.

"There." She slid one of the fluffy white accent pillows under his foot, then returned to her chair.

He drummed his fingers on his shorts. She'd never seen him nervous before. "Sorry you got injured." She said to clear the tension between them. "As long as you had fun though."

"It was so worth it." His eyes sparkled when he talked about the stunts he'd done with his buddies on one of the steepest hills in Pleasant View. "I've never done something that insane before, and now Mom is determined to see I never go biking again."

With all the money and power she had, Wendy found it easy to control everyone. "I know she means well." Liberty crossed one leg over the other. She'd had her fair share of rebellion, which made it hard to understand his submissive part. "What do you think?"

He shrugged, and his face fell as he stared at the enormous fresh bouquet—white roses and dahlias offset by silvery thistles and trailing plants—on the table by the window. "Your mom knows how my mom operates."

A control freak, but Liberty couldn't say *that*. So she tapped one of the crystals embedded on the side of her chair and steered the conversation elsewhere. "I hope this injury won't interfere with school."

"I have six more weeks on break, thankfully."

They talked freely that morning as if they'd needed to catch up on all those years they'd walked past each other without interacting.

He was in his third year of law at Harvard and wanted to do trading and investment, but his mom wanted him to be a lawyer.

Liberty sank back into the armchair, her dress catching on the velvet as she repositioned herself and crossed her legs at the ankles. "This is your career, not your mom's."

His gray eyes clouded over. "Mom would go ballistic if I switched." He went on about the bar exams he'd be taking next summer. Then he asked about her, and she told him about her nursing career and her break from school. She didn't tell him her struggles financially, but rather her need to work a bit.

When the chef served them breakfast—well, brunch by then—Bryce wanted to eat on the patio. So she offered him his mom's juice, and he winced. "No thank you."

She handed him his crutches, and they made their way to the back patio where a white wicker table waited on smooth flagstones. Climbing white roses spilled off the trellises against the wall. The midmorning sun warmed their faces, and the air smelled of fresh-cut grass and spicy roses as they talked over breakfast. She asked about his grandma and her dementia.

"She's fond of Rhonda."

"My mom enjoys taking care of her too."

After they'd eaten and the maid cleared the dishes, Bryce asked if Liberty had any plans to get out of the house that afternoon. He clasped his fingers together in a pleading gesture. "If I stay in the house any longer, it'll send me into a worse mood."

"Maybe you should pick up knitting."

He stifled a laugh. "I didn't realize you're so funny."

"Me neither." She rubbed her arms. "I have to confess I had a terrible attitude toward coming here today." Her lips quirked as she looked away, then braved meeting his eyes. "I kinda thought you were spoiled."

"I could be a brat sometimes. But I also used to be nervous around you."

Not believing him, she dismissed him with a wave as she steered toward the day's plans. "Do you have a place you want to go in particular?"

He rubbed his forehead. "Any place where I won't run into Mom or her friends."

In other words, not a country club or wherever the rich people hung out. "That won't be a problem."

Pleasant View had a few fun summer events. Come to think of it, the fair started today. Would that be a good place for him to walk with his crutches? She glanced at his leg and felt the need to humor him.

"I've never babysat an adult before. You'll have to be patient with me."

He shrugged, ducking his head, and a bashful smile crinkled up his cheeks. "If I'm going to hang out with a beautiful babysitter, I'm willing to be as patient as possible."

Her cheeks heated at his sincerity, and unsure of what to do, she pushed back the wicker chair to stand. Bryce just called her pretty. Ignoring the compliment, she smoothed down her dress. "When would you like to leave?"

"Whenever you're ready." He ran a hand through his spiky hair. "I've looked at the backyard gardens long enough."

"I'll go and brainstorm where we're going first." Otherwise, she'd end up drowning in those gray eyes. Either he was bored to death, or he sort of liked her as a friend.

But as Liberty took him to the town fair, he was light-humored as they rode the Ferris wheel and carousel. She avoided the bouncy rides so he didn't get injured, and it saddened her that he'd never ridden a carousel or any of the rides before. She knew people who hadn't been, mainly because they didn't have access to rides or didn't want to, but he enjoyed it.

They shared a funnel cake, and he complained about the grease and stickiness.

The next day he wanted to come back to the fair, saying he'd seen a harmonica he wanted to buy his grandma, and when they returned, they played toss the bucket and other carnival games. They came back the following week during the remaining three days the fair was in town. On its last day, they shared a plate of chili cheese fries, and Bryce surprised her when he touched her cheek. "You have something...."

She thought her heart had stopped beating when he gently brushed his thumb across her cheek, lingering on her skin.

"You're so beautiful, Liberty."

Suddenly too warm, she batted his hand away when she remembered all the girls who used to vie for his attention around the pool. "You probably say that to every girl."

"That's not true. You're different." His admission seemed genuine when she looked at his drawn brows. "You're always so confident and sure of yourself. I've always felt so small around you."

"Did you just accuse me of being proud?" Okay, so she was loaded with insecurities she'd taken on growing up in a single-parent home. "Too bad I fooled you."

She asked about the girls who came to all his parties, and he said they were family friends. He confessed that his mom had pushed him into dating one of them, Ashley, and he tried. But they broke up before he went to college.

"I like you."

She was sort of falling for him too, but it didn't matter how she felt. "Wendy would fire my mom if I went out with you."

"She wouldn't fire Rhonda when Grandma likes her."

When she drove him home, he reached for her hand. "This has been my best time in Pleasant View."

"If you think that was fun, then we need to do more fun things before summer ends."

"Deal." He gave her that steely gleam that made her want to break all the rules of why she shouldn't be with him.

That had initiated a summer of many fun days together.

A knock on the car window sounded, and she lifted her head from the steering wheel, jerking her neck. She made out a form from the shadowed light of her car and his flashlight. It had to be Bryce since it was just him and her on the mountain property.

CHAPTER 4

As soon as Liberty had left, Bryce had returned to the garage to retrieve his boots and keys to drive behind her and ensure she made it safely down the path. He'd just stepped into his boots when he heard a snap and creaking, followed by a crashing thud that couldn't be anything other than a tree falling.

As his chest tightened and his heartbeat increased, he slid on his coat and grabbed a flashlight from the hall table. Liberty was in danger.

It didn't take long to sight her car down the road. She hadn't gotten too far, and as he flashed the light toward the car, the beam bounced off the fallen pine right in front of her Impreza.

Relief swept through him, and he let out a breath. His boots padded in the snow as he approached.

Her car was still running, and the headlights were on. So he bent to the driver's-side window, making out her head resting on the steering wheel. Surely, she hadn't hit her head when the car stopped? With that thought charging through him, he failed in his effort not to startle her with his gentle tapping on the window.

He stepped back as she jolted and swung open the door, and when he flashed the light for her to see where she'd be stepping, the beam highlighted her wide eyes and trembling lips.

"Are you okay?" He stopped short of reaching out to take her hand when he remembered how she'd stepped away from his touch earlier. Good grief. He'd come close to kissing her knuckles then.

"Looks like God has different plans." Still seated in the driver's seat, she wrapped her arms around herself.

She'd never been against God, but he rarely heard her talk about Him the times they'd been together. Either way, Bryce could never live with himself if anything had happened to her. He shuddered and shook his head to keep his mind from rushing to a dark moment. "You could've... been hurt." *Or worse.*

Apparently not interested in his sympathy, she rubbed her arms. "My car is stuck too."

"I'll get it out tomorrow." Anticipation coursed through him at the mention of tomorrow.

They had tonight, stranded together. His heart began racing as his mind worked on how to utilize this one night to fix things. One night wasn't enough, but it *was* a start.

"Thanks for coming to check on me." She acknowledged, a bit breathless as she pulled her jacket zipper up to her neck.

"Ready to walk back?"

She nodded and then turned off the car. She put one foot out and planted it in the snow, then the other, and her legs sank into the snowdrift nearly to her knees.

"Good grief, you wore tennis shoes up here?"

"I didn't expect my car to get stuck in the snow." She slammed her door closed.

His blood rushed faster, and something quivered in his gut over what he was about to do. "Do you mind holding the flashlight?"

She looked down at her feet, wincing, before taking the flashlight from him. "Sure."

Before she could register why he was leaning into her, he swept her off the ground.

"What are you doing?" Her breath warmed his neck, and even if he hadn't started walking yet, his heart rate kicked up double time.

"You can't walk in your tennis shoes." His voice strained past the tightness in his throat as he kept his chin up. If he lowered his chin, he'd be tempted to sneak a chaste kiss on her lips.

"I'm missing a shoe."

"I'll come back for it later."

He wanted to tell her to point the light in their path, but he doubted his tongue was capable of composing such a long statement. Not when the familiar scent of her therapeutic conditioner teased his senses.

His body tingled like it was on fire when she curled a hand behind his neck. No doubt, she'd forgotten her job to light their path.

The rest of the trek was accompanied by noise from the howling wind that flung snow in their faces and clattered tree branches, and the thumping of their hearts against each other.

As they neared the house, the porch light sparkled off the snow on the rest of their path. Then, when he got to the house, he set her on the porch to open the screen door.

"Thank you." Her voice was a gentle wisp against the wind.

"Any time." He swung open the door. Unlike their wedding night when he'd carried her into this house, tonight she walked past him as if to signal nothing about tonight would be like that night. But they were here. Together. And he couldn't ask for more right now.

In the hallway, she took off her damp socks and tossed them in the small bucket. The light caressed her beautiful face, and she yawned, her eyelids droopy.

"Let's get you to the fire."

"I'll take a shower first." She then grimaced and spoke through gritted teeth. "Can I borrow your boots to go get my luggage?"

Didn't she know he'd do anything for her? Maybe not. Not after the things he may not have done or paid attention to while they were together. Now that she was here, though, he'd do whatever it took to have her back. "Go on and shower. I'll bring up your luggage."

She opened her mouth as if to object, then closed it, and dipped her head in a slight nod. "Thank you."

What he needed was a headlamp as he walked toward the car. He might need to use both hands if she had two pieces of luggage.

The yellow Baby on Board sticker on the back of her Impreza caught him off guard. But he still hadn't expected to encounter a stroller when he opened the trunk. He lifted the stroller and moved it in case it was on top of the luggage. Instead, a loud ABC tune erupted, and he jerked backward, nearly slipping in the thick snow.

He flashed his light in the trunk, scanning a pink electronic pad with the alphabet embossed on it. A pink shopping cart nestled in the far corner, and a mesh bag filled with toys left him wondering if she ran a daycare center.

There was no luggage in the trunk. He closed it and opened the back door. He pulled the purple travel bag off a plastic flat seat. Again, the nature of the seat screamed baby, just like the colorful mirror hooked to the back of the passenger seat.

Instead of dragging the luggage, Bryce carried it to keep it from getting wet in the snow. He paused, ignoring the wind, so he could take a few deep breaths and deal with the questions now dancing in his mind. He stood there, breathing in crisp air that smelled of pine, just the smell of Christmas.

When he got upstairs, he didn't have to wonder what room Liberty had chosen. He could hear the water running from one further down the hall from his.

With the door slightly ajar, he pushed it open and set her luggage inside, announcing that he'd brought her luggage and was stepping out. He closed the door and tried not to remember the times he'd stepped in the shower with his wife, rubbed her back with bath soap.... Shaking his head free of any wandering thoughts, he dashed down the stairs. Those days were gone, and thinking about the past wouldn't do him any good.

BRYCE WASN'T A COOK by any means, thanks to the abundance of chefs and employees he'd always had tending to him throughout his childhood.

The cabin fridge had plenty of options—lunch meats and sandwiches, salad kits and fruit platters, you name it. With all the food supply they'd stocked up, Logan and Iris seemed to have had a deliberate plan to keep Bryce and Liberty stuck here for at least a week. Unless more people were coming to the cabin after they left, they'd have plenty of food for the two of them.

Intending to fix Liberty something to eat, Bryce washed his hands and pulled out slices of bread, which he stacked with salami and turkey. From the counter, he reached for the box of tomato soup and cooked it with the help of the instructions on the back of the carton.

It wasn't hard when he poured it into the pan and turned on the stove.

Footsteps padded on the hardwood floor. His body stiffened, and his heart quickened when he turned and saw Liberty coming down the stairs. She was dressed in a familiar, overly worn red sweater, one he remembered so well. The first winter in their marriage, she'd loved the softness of the material. So did he. He could almost feel it beneath his fingers.

"Last thing we need is a kitchen fire to add to the blizzard."

The lightness in her voice made the stiffness in his shoulders evaporate. He winked in return. "I think I can pull off soup."

Hope flowed through him as he reached for two bowls from the cupboards and ladled the soup into the bowls.

"Can I help?" She wasn't too close to him when she leaned against the counter across from him, but her soft scent of rain and her sweet presence filled the kitchen.

"I think I've got it." He handed her a bowl, and their fingers brushed. He ignored the zing as she appeared unaffected when she carried her bowl to the table.

"This smells good."

"Wait till you try my gourmet dinner." Bryce carried his soup to the well-polished, though rough-hewn pine table, then returned for their sandwiches. He sat across from her.

She looked at her plate, then him, her eyes widening. "You made this?"

"I don't have a maid in New York, you know." Surely, she knew he still lived in New York.

Her brow lifted, and her face glowed beneath the pendant light. "I'm sure you order takeout every day."

Why would he cook for himself? "You know me so well."

Her dimples peeked at him even with such a fleeting smile. "I know you don't believe in prayer and faith, but if you don't mind, I'm going to close my eyes and thank God for this food."

"You can pray aloud if you want to."

Bryce had never been interested in religion, and although Liberty's mom had always been spiritual, Liberty had never followed in her mom's footsteps. Instead, her confidence and mischief had drawn Bryce to her.

With her eyes closed, she uttered words like *blessing* and *grace*, which were foreign to him.

His mind wandered to all sorts of places. Had she moved on with someone else? Did she have a kid, or did she babysit someone else's child? He'd wanted to ask Iris several times what Liberty was up to, but he'd feared receiving more harsh lectures like her best friend had given him the first time he'd inquired about Liberty.

"Amen."

That must mean it was time to reach for his sandwich.

They ate in silence, her scooping her soup and him chewing his sandwich. With so many questions dancing through his mind, he had no idea where to start.

"What have you been up to?" she asked, breaking the silence.

He set his sandwich on the plate. "Same stuff. Stock trading." He was steering away from the risky trade. He'd made a lot of money at a fast rate whenever he predicted what the stock market was about to do. Not only was he a venture capitalist, but he was also almost in a good place with his investments to make some changes.

"You still do day trading?"

That had been for fun, but he didn't have time for it anymore.

"No." He reached for his napkin and dabbed his mouth. "Remember the software company I invested in four years ago?" She should, even though they hadn't been married yet.

She nodded, and a sadness drew out beneath her eyes. She'd always been his biggest support, whether he acknowledged it or not. "I remember."

"I'm two shares away from having the controlling interest."

"From holding the largest percentage?" she asked, reminding him how intelligent she was.

"That's right."

"Congratulations!" The genuineness in her smile and tone made him blush. "God has given you such a talent. I'm glad you scored the right investments."

"It helps when you're doing what you love." His tone warmed, gratitude pumping through him. After all, she'd inspired him to pursue his passion rather than please his mom.

"How's your dad doing?"

He understood why she didn't ask anything about Mom.

"He still enjoys traveling." He managed pharmaceutical companies around the country. "He comes to New York to visit whenever he's in the area." He tended to come on days he was sure Mom wasn't anywhere close to New York.

"He's a good man." She bit into her sandwich and covered her mouth, then spoke through a muffled voice. "This is not bad."

"You're just being nice." He didn't do anything extraordinary, except for putting the cold cuts in the bread. Not a skill at all.

"It's the thought that counts the most."

She'd always given him more credit than he deserved. Food forgotten, he asked about her and what she'd been up to.

"This and that... I started a caregiver business two years ago."

His heart soared that she was an entrepreneur. "Not nursing?" She'd finished nursing while they were married.

She shrugged. "I almost worked at Pleasant View Hospital where I was training, but life happened."

Leaning closer, he asked about her business, needing to know if she enjoyed it, and her eyes glowed until she told him the challenges of scheduling employees, especially when last-minute cancellations happened. "It can be draining, but taking care of people is rewarding. It also pays the bills."

He was proud of her independence. It was no surprise since she'd always been a go-getter.

But that didn't answer why she had baby items in her car. Unless it was a friend's car. He scratched his jaw. How could he approach this subject? He had to take things slow, but he also had to know if he still had a shot with her.

"Sorry about your car getting stuck." He moved his spoon in the no longer steamy soup, probably cold by now.

"It's a good car. I've never tested it in this much snow though." She let out a breath. "Not on mountain roads anyway."

So it was her car. How could he frame his next question?

She tugged off the bottom crust of her bread and edged it to the side of her plate. "Ever come here since—"

"Our wedding night? No." His chest constricted, and suddenly, he had to know if she'd ever brought anyone up here. "You?"

She chuckled, but her eyes dulled as she shook her head. "This is my first outing in like forever. Seriously, I don't know how long—"

"I'm sure running a business takes up a lot of time."

"It does." She pressed her lips together and peered at the pine centerpiece on the island. A moment of silence passed before she spoke again. "Seems like your business didn't stop you from moving on."

Her sudden statement had him blinking. "What do you mean, moving on?"

She gestured to his hand. "Your ring."

His stomach bubbled as he laughed under his breath and she rolled her eyes.

Her seeming bothered by her assumption that he'd moved on without her was a good sign. Maybe he had another chance with her, after all.

Without bothering to remind her she was the only woman who dominated his mind, he placed his palm on the table, right in front of her.

She was quiet as her gaze swept over the ring before stopping at the inscription on the band—*B & L forever.*

She touched his ring finger and rolled the ring around. Her fingers rubbing against his sent a familiar electrical sensation through him, and he longed for more when she let go of his hand.

"You kept it," she whispered, keeping her gaze on the ring.

"I wear it every day." He wanted her to look at him so she could see he meant it when he said she'd ruined him for other women. "It was the only piece of you I had left."

Tears gleamed in her dark eyes when she gazed at him with a tenderness he recognized so well. "What does your mom think when you wear it?"

"It's the second battle I've won with her." The first one was when he switched majors for his career.

Her lips lifted, and those deep dimples appeared. "I would've loved to see that."

No one should've had to see that. "Mom sobbed over the issue and claimed I was going to give her a heart attack if I wore a ring from a woman who'd broken my heart."

"I hope you don't blame me for everything." Liberty swiped at her eyes. "I broke my heart too."

The pain in her vibrant eyes painted a picture of how she felt. His action was automatic when he stood and made his way around the table to her side.

When he opened his arms, she surprised him by standing and throwing her arms around him in a forceful embrace and nuzzling in as if she needed the contact as powerfully as he did. The soft fragrance of rose petals and summer warmed his senses, reminding him of their first days together and all that followed. Her smell meant home to him. They held each other tightly as she nestled her head against his neck, and they stayed like that for a long time while her shuddered breaths tickled his neck and sent a zing through his body.

After a while, she stepped back and stared at him with tears brimming in her eyes.

Bryce entwined their fingers to answer her earlier question. He didn't want her taking any blame for his actions.

"It's my fault." For not siding with her on a lot of things, for not standing up for her whenever Mom interfered with their lives. Now that they were going through some sort of confession, it was the best time for him to bring up the subject. "I saw baby items in your car. Did you move on?"

She closed her eyes and sucked in a breath. When her lips parted, then closed, dread chilled him. Did he want to know?

The phone rang, interrupting a unique moment. Good grief, who could be calling right now?

It had to be Logan, Iris, or the cabin maintenance. He'd make it brief or hang up on them so he could hear whatever dark news Liberty was about to share. "I'll get it."

He missed the warmth from her hands the moment he left to take the call in the living room.

"Why didn't you tell me there's no cell service at the cabin?"

Mom's voice pierced his ear, and he eased the receiver farther from his ear. His gut knotted. Of all the days he'd put up with Mom's calls, today he was tempted to hang up and cut the dangling cord off the phone.

His body stiffened. "How did you get this number?"

"I couldn't get ahold of you or any of your friends. I called the Stone residence, and their chef gave me the number."

Bryce threw his head back and dragged a hand through his hair. Mom's persistence. If she hadn't gotten ahold of him, she'd end up driving over. Fallen tree or not, she was that determined.

"I saw a storm warning and trees falling all over the mountains."

He appreciated her concern, but still.

"I'm fine, Mom." Wanting to keep her off his case for the rest of his stay, he said, "You'll not get ahold of me for the next two days."

"Why are you being so curt?"

Because you're ruining my life once again. "We're going to be on the slope for the rest of the trip."

He still intended to take Liberty on a snowmobile and play in the snow as long as the tree was still on the road.

"Call me tomorrow night. Otherwise, you will hear from me again."

Heat roiled through him. Not caring to say goodbye, he hung up. Just because he was her only child and he'd almost died at birth, didn't mean he always had to pay for her panic over what might happen to him.

He was too stiff to walk back to Liberty. Needing to compose himself, he looked at the white paper taped to the receiver—the cabin maintenance's number.

When he dialed it, a man answered, and Bryce informed him about the tree in the road. The man said he would call tomorrow and let the national forest know.

Almost relaxed, Bryce returned to the kitchen. Liberty had her back to him while she put their leftover sandwiches into Ziploc bags. Even wearing sweatpants with her hair dampening her sweater, she was the most beautiful woman he'd ever met.

Ten years ago when she'd shown up to "babysit" him, as she'd put it, the air had left his lungs the moment he saw her. She'd changed, grown more rounded and curvy, and her face had become radiant. He'd always admired her spunkiness and confidence he lacked, but that summer, he'd known he wanted to spend the rest of his life with her, even before he had a clue how to go about things.

"How's Wendy?" she asked without looking at him as she opened the fridge and put away the sandwiches. Something had shifted in her voice. Curt and cautious. Which was understandable given the circumstances.

"I didn't give her the number to the cabin."

But Liberty didn't seem to be in the mood for his details. She put the bowls and plates in the dishwasher and dried her hands with a kitchen towel. Barely meeting his gaze, she walked past him. "See you in the morning."

Bryce's chest heated, and he kicked his socked foot in the air. Mom's boy—Iris and Logan's nickname for him—taunted him, and his mind spun. Was this what it meant to be mom's boy?

Argh! He screamed inside. It was going to be a long night. He'd taken one step closer to winning his wife back. Then Mom pushed him four steps backward.

His marriage felt like a bear market—losing its value fast. Even in a bear market, a bit of buying and trading always went on, but his marriage was far from starting over.

LAYING DOWN THAT NIGHT, Bryce folded his hands behind his head and peered at the open-beamed ceiling, thinking of that first summer. If anything, he might pretend he was twenty-two again, young and stupidly in love.

During the two weeks after the fair, he'd looked forward to seeing Liberty. Maybe it was because she didn't seem to be as interested in him or because she had a wild side and the confidence he wanted and admired, but he'd been drawn to her.

Liberty the thrill-seeker, so loving in nature, impulsive, and exciting. That first summer, he learned so many new things, ventured outside his cloistered environment, discovered a zest for life.

She'd taken him to places he hadn't been to before in town. Outdoor summer concerts, boat races, bike competitions... even to a meadow to pet horses. He shifted on the bed, turning to face the direction of her room.

One afternoon, they'd driven past a random farmhouse, and she'd wanted to stop and ask the owner if she could meet the horses. The friendly older couple told her to come by any day she wanted to. It seemed no one could tell Liberty no—well, no one, but his mom.

Not one to come near manure, Bryce had greeted the horses with her, even braving touching one while she laughed at his trepidation. Then she'd helped clean the couple's stable and groom the horses. Bryce, still hobbling on crutches, had watched while he breathed in the barn's stench. Yet watching Liberty had fascinated him. How could anyone be so bold? So willing to do anything, go anywhere, approach anyone. All such rare qualities in the girls he encountered.

Besides biking and discussing numbers, he had taught her how he did online trading. Though it wasn't something Liberty, who loved things more hands-on and in-person contact, preferred to do, she'd tried it and praised him on how intelligent he was.

Many times, he tried to hug her, kiss her on the cheek, give hints he was in love with her, but she focused on not wanting her mom to lose her job.

As the days neared the end of his summer, Bryce didn't use his crutches anymore but still wore a boot.

One of the Saturdays when Liberty didn't work, Bryce's friend, Logan, was in town and they went to watch race cars outside Pleasant View. After the car races, they'd headed to Logan's house to watch the baseball game. And that's when Bryce saw her.

Beyond the floor-to-ceiling windows, she emerged from the pool. Her modest yellow-and-pink striped swimsuit showed off her slender body, and while it wasn't right to look at her, he couldn't tear his gaze away, not when he was frozen in the chair and his heart was racing a mile a minute.

"You want to tell me why your jaw is hanging open?"

Logan's voice brought Bryce back to the baseball game, but his friend looked through the window.

"Oh, man." Logan shook his head.

"Do you... know her?" Bryce could barely manage to form the words.

"Iris's friend—"

"Liberty, yeah." Bryce finished for him and rubbed his sweaty palms over his pants. "How do they know each other?"

Logan frowned, narrowing his gaze on Bryce. "How do *you* know her name?"

"Her mom works for us." No reason to mention her "babysitting" him these last weeks.

When Iris and Liberty walked through the sliding door, Liberty, threading her arms through her yellowy swimsuit cover-up, almost jumped. "Bryce?"

Unlike her, he'd never been peppy. Now, instead of responding, he fidgeted with the remote and accidentally changed the channel to some foreign language as Logan pointed out.

Much later that evening, he'd lingered so he could talk to her alone and suggested they walk down to the creek.

"So you hang out here sometimes?" he asked as they strolled past the flower garden, the roses scenting the air.

"Sometimes I come and swim with Iris."

So she liked swimming. "What else do you love doing?"

"A lot of things, but I like scrapbooking."

Whatever that was. From her description, it involved putting photos in a memory book and adding embellishments. He rubbed the back of his neck. "Like a craft?"

"Different, but to make it easy, it's like a craft." She paused, plucked an aster, and twirled it between her fingers, her gleaming eyes peering up at him. "Tell me something else you like to do. Something your parents don't know about you."

How did she know he had something nobody knew about him? "I like to play the guitar."

Those dark eyes danced, and with the big orange ball sinking through the trees, she blended in with the picturesque scenery. "Can you play for me sometime?"

He shrugged. The strings on his guitar got ripped, and he hadn't fixed them. "I don't have a guitar yet, but I'll get one."

"I can't wait." When her eyes shone like that and those deep dimples flashed, his whole body lit up. As they approached the creek, he curled his hand around her neck and kissed her. She kissed him back, her lips tasted like cherry, and it felt magical with the water trickling in a musical rhythm in their background.

After he'd kissed her, it became clear that Liberty was the woman he wanted to kiss every day for the rest of his life. He then touched her cheek, his fingers trailing across delicate skin. "When I think about you, I remember your dimples."

"You think about me sometimes?" She bit her lower lip.

"Whenever we're apart." He let his index finger glide over one of the dimples that appeared with his words. And from then on, he'd called her Dimples.

Since then, whenever she showed up at the house, Bryce created opportunities where they could be alone and he could kiss her. Outside by the ash tree on their property, in the hallways, but mostly in the car whenever they drove somewhere with loud music blasting. They would park on the side of the road and kiss.

He always felt free away from the house where security cameras weren't putting him on display.

A week before he had to leave for school, they watched a movie in their home theater.

He was already dealing with the emotions of leaving her, so they spent most of the time kissing instead of watching whatever movie it was.

"What do you think you're doing, Liberty?!" When Mom shrieked louder than the tires in the car-chase scene, Bryce tore away from Liberty.

Liberty touched her lips with one hand, then squeezed his hand with the other. "I hope I didn't get you in trouble," she whispered as Mom stormed toward them. Her flats padded the thin carpet, and when she stopped in front of them, she turned off the projector, becoming little more than a shadow hovering over him in the dim recessed lights.

"You, of all people, know employees don't associate with my son." Mom glared at their entwined fingers. He stiffened, almost afraid, but Liberty's stillness motivated him to speak.

"Mom, it was my idea—"

"Shut up!" She wagged a finger at him. "Is this why you won't get back with Ashley?"

Mom had been pushing for the reunion with Ashley for three years now. If Bryce succeeded in dodging the meetings, any chance Mom got, she was setting him up with another bimbo from her elite circle.

Bryce ground his teeth and tightened his hold onto Liberty's now damp palm. But there was no sense in saying anything while Mom was ranting at ten thousand words a minute, accusing Liberty of all sorts of things.

Liberty stiffened, raising her chin. "You're making it sound like I assaulted—"

"Get up." Mom's nostrils flared as she pointed toward the door. "Out of my house."

Torn, fearful even for what Mom might do to Liberty, he stood with her.

"You do not come back here. You're fired!"

Liberty slid her hand out of Bryce's and stood, then strode up the aisle between the seats.

"You can't fire her."

But Mom ignored his weak voice and added words to Liberty's back. "I'll send your check to your mom."

"I don't need your money." Liberty faced her with her head held high, her eyes aglow, her confidence radiant. "I mean no disrespect, but don't you think Bryce is too old not to make his own decisions?"

Was he? Mom always made his plans for him. Liberty switched her gaze to him, and he nodded as her confidence surged through him. Then he'd made the mistake of looking at his mom, and her glare had him coiling, his tongue freezing.

After Liberty left, Mom's lecture began. "It's either Ashley or you can date Courtney."

Another socialite in Mom's circle. Bryce crossed his arms. "I can date whoever I want."

He may have spoken the words low and quiet, but speak them he did, taking his first stand against Mom, his first stand for himself. But how could he not? No one, not even his dad, spoke to Mom the way Liberty just did.

"If you know what's best for you, you'll leave Liberty alone." After those warning words, Mom left him in the theater with a shattered heart.

Rebellion surged through him, and he fisted his hands as if he could hold onto it, harness the force of it, even as his heart ached. He *would* make things right with Liberty. He couldn't let her leave like this, not without him standing up for her.

On one of their afternoons, she'd driven him by her neighborhood, and even if they never entered her house, he remembered the road she'd taken there. Twenty minutes later, with the evening light fading over his shoulder, he rasped his knuckles on a weathered door of a rental bungalow Liberty had said was affordable for them.

Her mom opened the door and gasped. "Bryce! What are you doing here?"

Liberty said she'd already told Rhonda about their attraction to one another. She was transparent with her mom unlike him with his mom.

"Is it okay...?" His shoulders felt stiff. He ducked his head and rubbed the back of his neck, unsure why he'd shown up. "Can I see Liberty?"

Rhonda hesitated as she held onto the doorknob. Her skin was the same brown as her daughter's, and despite her reserved nature, in her kind brown eyes, he saw much of Liberty. Rhonda then ushered him in. "She told me what happened."

"Thank you."

The house smelled of homemade food and Liberty's soft scent of rain. She was scooping ice cream in a bowl when he walked into their cozy kitchen.

"I showed up at a good time." He couldn't help grinning, and when she lifted her head and saw him, her genuine smile melted the tension from his shoulders.

"How did you know where I live?"

"You showed me."

She blinked, setting the scoop back into the tub of vanilla ice cream.

"You remembered?" Her dimples winked, and her dark eyes flashed. "Wow. You must have a good memory." She lifted the bowl and handed it to him, then ushered him to sit on one of the two chairs at the kitchen table. "Let's have some ice cream."

Surprised she wasn't mad about the whole incident with Mom, he pulled out a chair and balanced on its edge as if waiting for her to lash out, make demands, try to control him.

"Here's a spoon for you." Rhonda handed them two spoons and tucked the ice cream container back in the freezer before joining them at the table.

And he waited. But neither put on the guilt.

Was this what other women were like? Other families? Something opened up in his chest, a hollow aching to be a part of a world and place so calm, and he let himself settle back in the battered wooden chair.

Floral magnets pinned photos to the refrigerator, which he intended to study later. No doubt, Liberty was in one of them.

Liberty slid him over to sit on his chair beside him while Rhonda pulled out the chair across from them, her face slightly guarded as she clasped her hands together on the table.

Bryce took Liberty's hand from under the table and entwined it with his, then whispered to her, loud enough for Rhonda to hear. "I'm sorry I got you fired."

Liberty squeezed his hand back. "I'll find another job. You're leaving next week anyway."

"Your mom will not like the idea of you and my daughter together." Rhonda's brows drew together, but even yet, not a word of criticism nor any type of demands spewed from her. She seemed more concerned than critical.

A jolt charged through him. Surely, she wasn't worried for *him*?

She shook her head. "From the first day I worked for your family, I learned Wendy has big plans of finding a perfect wife for you."

Liberty's hand stiffened in his hold, and he leaned in to kiss her cheek. "That's unfortunate for her because I already found my perfect future wife."

As Liberty's breathing escalated, he slid his arm around her waist. The wooden chair was hurting his bottom, and even if he loved having her close, it was too small for the both of them. He was tempted to pull her on his lap, but he had no idea if it was safe to do that in front of her mom.

"You're young," Rhonda continued, shaking her head again, "and someday you might end up realizing Liberty is not in your class."

"Mom?" Liberty held up her free hand then. "Maybe Bryce and I will love each other forever, but your job—"

"Mom knows how good you are with Grandma." Bryce reminded Rhonda of the political career Mom was building and how that kept her too busy to have time to take care of Grandma by herself. Although Mom seemed to load up on criticism for everyone around her, even Dad, she raved about Rhonda and how good she was with Grandma. "She won't fire you."

"You kids don't worry about me." Rhonda stood, and the hair spilling around her shoulders seemed to drag her posture down, unlike her usual perky ponytail. "I can find another job."

She then excused herself, saying she needed to shower.

Alone with Liberty, he felt self-conscious, and when he glanced at her, she pointed to the melted ice cream. Neither of them had eaten yet.

But he hadn't come for ice cream, so he pulled her closer and kissed her. Her soft lips melted against his, sweeter than ice cream with their cherry flavor. She ran her fingers through his hair, and as she kissed him back on the tiny chair, he stood and pulled her up with him without tearing their lips from each other.

They made out like nothing had interfered with their day.

The rest of the week, he saw her every day. She held off on her job search until his departure, saying she wanted to spend time with him, and he couldn't agree more. He picked her up at her house before noon for lunch, then took her on spontaneous outings.

One day, they went to an outdoor music festival. Another afternoon, they found a movie festival. They also drove around the nearby towns.

She would ask what his mom was like during his high school days. But he hadn't wanted to revisit those taunting memories of his mom always being the one to chaperone the school dance or any event where he had a chance to be free with his friends.

"She probably didn't mean it for bad." Liberty had looked at him with such optimism. "She thinks she's protecting you."

On their last day together, they'd driven without a destination in mind and had ended up parking by a national forest. They'd run through the meadow, hand in hand, as the summer afternoon breeze blew her long hair.

When she stopped running, he did the same. "I'll miss you," she said, looking at him with a longing that took everything else away.

It was another moment with Liberty he never wanted to end. He pulled her into his arms and kissed her softly on the lips. "I love you so much." He realized then she was the first girl he'd confessed his love to and he meant it.

"I love you too."

Running his fingers over her soft jaw, he promised her then. "I'll come and visit you."

She chuckled. "What excuse will you give your mom?"

"She won't know I'm in town. And you'll have to visit me on campus. I'll buy your tickets." He tapped a finger to her lips, silencing her as she parted them to argue. "Plenty of money goes into my account every month—money mostly from Dad since he has a stable job—so I can afford your plane tickets."

The protest drained from her, and she nipped his finger with a soft kiss, her cheeks flushing. "I'd love that."

Oh, man. He drew her closer. They'd make it work. They just had to.

And they did for a long time. Until one time Mom didn't know he was in town and she found him and Liberty perusing the shops in downtown Pleasant View. She'd warned she could make Liberty's life miserable if she didn't leave Bryce alone, but Liberty said she wasn't afraid of her threats.

They continued dating on and off, breaking up whenever Mom got the better of Liberty until Bryce would fall apart and ask for Liberty's forgiveness on his mom's behalf. And she always took him back. That went on and off for years before he married her, a wonderful experience that lasted a little over a year.

When she'd walked away from their marriage, he'd called it a bluff and assumed she'd be back in his life. But she'd changed her phone number after she broke her phone during their final argument.

Bryce must have finally drifted off to sleep because he woke to the sound of soft Christmas music somewhere outside his room. He yawned, shaking off the reality of last night's events. He had a morning—maybe even a whole day with Liberty. And he intended to start over as if last night never happened.

CHAPTER 5

Mama's boy will always be Mama's boy. Liberty turned to her side, facing the window where early morning light streamed through the slanted blinds. She reached for her phone from underneath the pillow. Six forty. Even with no cell service, out of habit, she kept her cell phone handy in case she needed to call 911 for an emergency.

After scrolling through her playlist for some Christmas music, she tapped play, and the strings of "O Holy Night" started. The song put Myra to sleep ever since Liberty started playing Christmas music after Thanksgiving. Not only did the song hold a lot of meaning for the holiday but Liberty also found it relaxing.

Shifting into the smooth bed sheets, she couldn't believe she'd almost been fooled into assuming Wendy had backed down on interfering with Bryce's life. Wendy's call last night was a brutal reminder of her control over her son's life and another reason for Liberty to keep her mouth shut over Myra.

As her mind wandered to areas where she could draw the line, memories of last night danced as clear as day. Bryce had been so sweet to carry her through the snow so she didn't have to trudge through it in her tennis shoes. His closeness as she inhaled his scent had temporarily made her forget all the reasons she'd walked away from their marriage.

His bland sandwiches had tasted decent. Perhaps, overcome by his fixing her a meal, she would've eaten anything he fixed for her. Cooking was never his strong suit. The only time he cooked was when she cooked with him.

All those little things he'd done last night had triggered things she liked about him, reasons she'd fallen in love with him. Besides his intelligence and tenderness, he'd always done small things, even rebel against his mom for her sake—something that would have been too hard for him to do if he didn't love her.

Liberty had always felt special whenever he looked at her, like the best thing that ever happened to him.

When they dated, he'd leave school and visit her on weekends. His sleeping on the living room floor, while he could've slept in a fancy bed in his childhood home, had proven how serious he was with her.

Confused with mixed emotions, she turned to her back as "O Holy Night" ended while "Go Tell It on the Mountain" started.

Unsure of how to approach the day, she closed her eyes and prayed for God's peace. She prayed for Bryce. His pained face last night flashed in her mind. He'd tried to explain that he hadn't given his mom the cabin's number, but Liberty had walked away instead.

Of all people, Liberty should know Wendy always found out where her son was. She was designed that way. "Lord, I pray for Wendy too. She's lost." And although Liberty didn't have a personality similar to Wendy, she had traits Wendy didn't like.

Having a crazy control freak for a mother wasn't Bryce's fault.

"We're stuck together, Lord, so please I humbly request that You help me. I want to be a good wife." Like she'd been praying after Myra's birth.

Till death do us part... Like a gentle whisper, the words snuck into her mind, bringing to memory those deep gray eyes she'd looked into almost four years ago while saying those words.

She'd been confident his mom wouldn't come between them. But then Wendy had her tactical ways and had gotten to Liberty's mind, hence leading her to break those vows.

Bryce was still her husband, the father of her child, and nothing was going to change that. He was the love of her life, and she still loved him. He loved her too. She could see it in his soul while searching his eyes.

Instead of hopping out of bed, she listened to "Silent Night," another soothing song that lulled Myra to sleep. Did Myra sleep through the night, or did she wake up screaming and asking for Mama?

Liberty could call Mom from the landline and find out, but then she might end up needing to leave. The massive pine tree still blocked the path, so leaving wasn't even an option.

She'd come to play in the snow and soak in the hot tub while catching up with the girls. The girls weren't here, but Bryce was.

They could go snowshoeing together, sledding, and maybe getting out of the house to talk and breathe in cool air would help them ease into things.

After breakfast, maybe she could present the plan to Bryce.

She hadn't had the time to peruse the fridge for breakfast ideas. So she hopped out of bed with a renewed plan to fix breakfast before he woke.

Starting by taking a shower, she brushed her teeth and changed into a red V-neck sweater and dark sweats. She could've packed some designer outfits if she'd expected to run into Bryce, but this would have to do.

A burnt-bacon odor hung in the air as she took one step at a time down the stairs. Smoke saturated the kitchen, and she covered her mouth, stifling a laugh while Bryce fidgeted to slide open the window.

"It's not nice of you to laugh at someone making you breakfast." With his jaw set in hard lines, he reached for a dish towel and swung it up to chase the smoke toward the open window. His rumpled hair clumped up on one side, and a dusting of flour smeared his navy T-shirt.

"Last night, you said I was nice." After all, she'd complimented him for his sandwich. She reached for a piece of his burnt bacon from the pan and took a bite.

He scowled at her. "You're going to get a tummy ache."

Not wanting his efforts to go to waste, she chewed the burnt meat. "Wouldn't be the worst thing to happen to me." She wiped her greased hand on one of the damp napkins on the counter.

He sure made a mess. Turning to face him, she noticed remnants of flour on his cheek too.

It was automatic for her to reach out and touch his cheek, brushing the flour with her fingers. "What's with all the flour... on you?"

Her fingers slowed, lingering at the familiarity of his skin. The overnight scruff on his defined jaw prickled her flesh.

He shuddered, and the movement of his jaw had her pause her hand. He was taller than she was, and even if she was purposefully staring at his jaw rather than his face, she could feel the intensity of his gaze on her.

With her pulse racing, she slid her hand away from his cheek and sucked in a breath, then walked over to lean against the counter, crossing her arms. "Sorry... I—"

"You don't have to apologize." His voice strained, coming out almost a growl when he brushed remnants of the flour from his T-shirt.

"My attempt to make pancakes." He motioned to the silver trash can in the corner. "The trash is happy to savor them."

He'd done all this for her? Her heart squeezed. She looked at the black marble counter and the box of pancake mix among the many other mixes.

"Maybe we can fix breakfast together."

He blinked, his gray eyes darkening. "Just like we used to."

"Yes." With her voice barely a whisper, she struggled to maintain eye contact. Then she turned to the counter and opened one cabinet, closing and opening the next until she found a mixing bowl.

"The instructions on the box required two eggs." A thrill rang through his voice as he opened the fridge and pulled out a tray of eggs.

Liberty scrubbed the griddle he'd left in the sink, covered in sticky flour and the remnants of his earlier pancakes. As she cooked the sausage and alternated slicing the fruit, he flipped pancakes and presented her with the day's plans. "I thought I'd bribe you into getting on a snowmobile."

"I would love that."

He looked at her, one brow rising as if he hadn't expected her to agree.

"That's if you'll drive." She'd seen those mobiles, but she'd never ridden one.

"As long as you behave on the slopes." He grinned, seeming more relaxed when he turned and flipped the pancakes. "I'm sure they have one that carries two passengers."

"If they don't, I'll have to watch you, instead."

"Since when did you start being nervous to try something new?"

Since Myra. She refocused on cutting strawberries.

Through the corner of her eye, she could see him watching her, so she spun around to face him. "If I remember, you were always the one who got me in trouble."

"Me?" He squished his face, pointing the spatula toward her. "I was a rule follower until I met you."

He was a rule follower because of his mom, and she should've known better and kept her mouth shut whenever Wendy interfered with their business. The times she'd argue with the woman never ended well.

"I better make us some coffee." She would need it after such a restless night. She wanted to blame it on being away from Myra rather than being riled over Bryce's mom—the source of their problems.

When they sat at the table for breakfast, she said her prayers, and they ate.

"I forgot how fun it can be when I tag around in the kitchen with you," he said before forking into his pancake.

"I couldn't forget." It had been one of her favorite times they shared.

During their breakfast, he brought up Eric, the cabin's owner, and his wife, Joy.

"I never told you this, but when Eric was ill and I visited him, Joy, his caregiver at the time, made me think of you."

"Oh."

"Point is, he was so in love with her, yet he didn't have hope he'd live." Bryce swallowed, then frowned at his half-eaten pancakes. "I thought to myself—What if I got ill, like Eric? Got hit with a chronic illness before I had a chance to share my life with you. That's why I rushed you into getting married."

"You didn't rush me." They'd dated for years, except his mom, as usual, had come between them during their engagement.

Her uncle had visited from down South, and Liberty took him out for coffee. Somehow, a photo of her uncle kissing her on the cheek was taken and submitted to the local paper. Bryce called with accusations about the photo his mom had sent him.

Creeped out by Wendy stalking her and angry over him believing his mother's accusations without coming to her first, Liberty broke off their engagement. "Even though we got married, my uncle has never forgiven you for that accusation."

He blushed. "I could put up with your uncle if we were still together."

She pressed her lips together, wishing the same. At least he wanted her as much. Perhaps they could work out their problems during this stay.

After putting away their breakfast dishes, Liberty was grateful the cabin had all the gear—from clothing and snow pants to boots, ski shoes, and all necessary equipment—for their outdoor adventure.

Once fully dressed and geared up with helmets, she and Bryce went to the storage shed in the back.

He drove out the snowmobile, and then she climbed behind him on the seat. They were comfortable in their shared silence as the engine revved. She'd been hesitant to wrap her arms around him until he drove up a path on a steep climb.

Even through his ski jacket, she could feel his muscles flex under her arms as he wove around a canopy of trees.

The further they went, the more his tense muscles relaxed, and she felt herself relaxing too.

"Whoo-hoo!" he shouted over the engine roar.

"Yay!" Liberty felt like a child again, forgetting all the day's worries as they zoomed back and forth until he wanted her to take a turn driving them.

It wasn't much different from riding a bicycle when Liberty sat behind the wheel with Bryce's helpful instructions. She tried to exhale several times while pretending not to be affected by his warm breath against her neck or his arms wrapped snugly around her waist as he rode in the passenger seat.

When they had a late lunch, they shared fond memories of their time together. "That first summer with you, I can never forget." Bryce set his sandwich down and stared at the frosted window while reminiscing on the summer they'd fallen in love. It wasn't the first time he'd pointed it out. "You were a breath of fresh air, and that day, I believed in angels."

He'd always said she'd been his angel who appeared to him that summer. But honestly, that had been her favorite summer too—at least she'd said so before. Now, she laughed, looking back. "Being young and madly in love with someone who was forbidden was so thrilling!"

But he was shaking his head. "It was more than that."

And he was right. When his gaze met hers, the softness in his eyes almost had her dizzy with longing.

This only confirmed what was in her heart. She'd never stopped loving him.

The cabin was getting warm with a familiar tension and awareness buzzing between them. Thankfully, Bryce must have sensed it too, because he suggested they go back on the slopes.

"Let's try sledding." Liberty was ready to try a simple activity, and he didn't seem to mind it either.

They rode separate sleds down the hill, leaving trail marks over the soft snow where their sleds pushed it down the hill.

The workout to climb the hill made Liberty regret suggesting the activity.

Only three runs and she was panting and resigned. "I'll go and make dinner." After all, she needed an excuse to have some time to herself to think, but Bryce, not seeming to understand the need for space, offered to help her cook.

With his help, she cooked beef stew. Then they both left for their separate rooms to shower before they met downstairs at five thirty to eat.

The savory scent of stew hung in the air, and the house smelled like home.

"I've missed this stew." He stirred through his bowl.

"Thanks to whoever bought the groceries." They'd stocked an impressive variety of options, mostly their favorite food and beverage items.

"Our best friends' planning—"

Sudden darkness cut off Bryce's words.

"Oh no!" Liberty tried to strain and widen her eyes, but she couldn't see anything in the darkness.

"I don't want you tripping." He reached for her hand from across the table. His chair scraped against the tile while he kept his hand on hers. Then his steps neared as he moved around the table toward her.

"Here you are." His other hand patted her shoulder, then stopped on her face, and she choked a nervous laugh. He pulled her to him, his strong arms wrapping around her waist, and sweet anticipation warmed her.

"There are lamps around. Let's go find them," he said. But he didn't move, and she felt her arms shaking, her heart thudding against his.

"We better turn on some lights." Her voice emerged a bit squeaky, but thankfully, his hands dropped from her waist.

He still took her hand while he walked and patted on the marble counter. "I remember seeing one here earlier."

Her tongue was frozen, and so was her mind. She'd seen a lamp somewhere, but now she couldn't remember.

"This is it." Bryce declared, and when he dropped her hand and pressed a switch and light ate up the darkness, she managed a shuddered breath.

The humming refrigerator registered now that her thundering heart had subsided. She walked over and swung it open. The light came on when the fridge was opened, so it was operating just fine. "Shouldn't this be off if the power has gone out?"

"Oh yeah." Bryce nodded as if aware of something she wasn't. "Logan said there's a solar-charged battery connected to the refrigerator."

Right. Iris had mentioned the solar they'd installed in the cabin two summers ago. Liberty understood the need for a battery backup to the fridge since there wasn't enough solar energy for the rest of the house.

They walked around the house finding battery-operated lanterns and turning them on, including the two on the fireplace mantel.

After they polished off their dinner, Bryce suggested they sit by the fire to warm up.

"It's a good thing the fireplace is gas-operated." She sat on the couch facing the fire.

He sat on the couch to her right. She wished he'd sat with her, but being too cozy while alone could be a disaster. So she reached for the throw on the edge of the couch and covered her feet. For a few moments, they sat in silence, listening to the crackling flames.

Bryce, obviously uncomfortable, began bouncing his leg and rubbing his hands over his sweats.

Her mind wandered off to Myra, and she tried to count the days backward to remember what day it was today. Saturday.

She was supposed to return home on Monday night. What was she going to do about the tree? She'd had so much fun today that she hadn't thought about her car stuck in the snow or the solution to get the tree out of the way. Clasping her hands together, she let out a long, low breath, then voiced her concern.

"The maintenance man didn't get back to me yet." Bryce crossed one leg over the other, still seeming jittery, but looking comfy and at home in his socks. His slightly damp hair glowed more copper than brown beneath the dim lanterns.

"I need to be back to work on Tuesday." Mainly to Myra. If she could connect with Mom and find out if none of the workers had bailed, it would put her at ease.

"If nobody shows up by noon tomorrow..." Bryce rubbed at his forehead, his brows drawing together. "I'll spend the rest of the after-noon cutting the tree."

He would end up slicing his fingers off, and his mom would blame Liberty for it. "I'll wait."

Until maintenance showed, she hoped.

During her silence, Bryce raked a hand through his hair, casting a glance at the fire. His lips parted, then closed. With his brows drawn, no doubt he had something on his mind. She knew his struggle to voice his concerns on the things that mattered most.

"Go ahead and ask.

He didn't need more prompting when he leaned forward and braced his elbows on his knees, fixing her with a serious stare. "I want to know why you carry baby things in your car."

"Oh." She clasped her hands together, and her muscles tightened. The warmth from the fire seemed to lose the heat when her body started shaking.

"I didn't know you were still thinking about that." She needed to stall, to gain time to compose herself.

The scorching look of desire and longing he gave her made her feel squirmy. She pulled the throw all the way to her legs.

"If you haven't noticed, I've never stopped loving you." His voice rumbled low, seeming to come from deep within him. "I think you still have feelings for me too, but I want to make sure you didn't replace me with a single dad."

He was the single dad. She pressed a hand to her throat, struggling to speak over the lump forming there. "I'm still married to you."

She looked anywhere but at him, the mantel with Eric and his wife, a dark-skinned beauty, and their kids. They looked happy with the kind of family Liberty always longed to be a part of while growing up. Instead, it had always been her and Mom. Nothing wrong with that. She had an incredible mom, but that hadn't stopped her from dreaming about a family with two parents.

Was it always going to be her and Myra? What if Myra had the same longing for a family that Liberty always wanted?

"I couldn't get my heart to move on." That was a start. "I've been busy with work and taking care of our daughter."

She felt the burden lighten on her shoulders, but with its release came a discomfort over Bryce's silence. When she managed a glance at him, his brows had furrowed, and his jaw hung open as if he was still registering what she'd just said.

"You have a daughter?" he asked after an unbearable silence.

"Mine and yours. Yes."

Silence stretched as he rubbed a hand over his chiseled jaw, then furiously raked through his hair.

Her body broke into a sweat as if the fire decided to kick up the temperature.

Please say something.

CHAPTER 6

The clarity of her words sent adrenaline thrumming through Bryce's body. He felt his brain expanding, his temper simmering like a volcano dangerously close to exploding. Not knowing what to do, he stood and walked across the dimly lit room, then back toward the sitting area. This wasn't happening!

If they hadn't met today, when was she planning on telling him? Why did she keep it a secret? A hundred questions he wanted to ask roiled him, but he couldn't with this bubbling anger expanding in his chest.

He paced back and forth toward the seating arrangements, trying to open and close his mouth, raking through his damp hair as if pulling at its roots could bring blood to his brain.

"I'm so sorry I didn't tell you...." She repeated the words over and over, but that only boiled his blood faster. He stood a few feet from her. She was still on the couch with drooped shoulders. The emergency lamp illuminated her wet and shiny eyes. At least she appeared regretful for what she'd done to him.

He didn't like her right now.

Drawing out a breath, he had to know if she ever loved him, the way she'd said before. "You hate me so much... that you kept my daughter from me?"

She stood and faced him. Her lower lip quivered. "I don't hate you.... It's—"

"Then *why*?" The growl emerged from deep in his chest. What could justify *this*?

"I love you." Her voice cracked. "It's your mom."

She always stood up to Mom whenever it came down to it, and this was a legitimate reason for her to do the right thing. He sucked in a breath, barely able to calm himself down. "Don't use my mom as an excuse."

She went around the couch moving closer to him, but he took a step back.

"You think your mom would let me keep the baby if she knew I had a child with you?"

His brows drew so tightly together, the space between them pinched. He rubbed at the dull pain. "Why would she take a baby away from her mother?"

She groaned as if *he* was the one being unreasonable. "You're forgetting the woman who blackmailed me, got me thrown in jail, and plotted several schemes to tear us apart."

"No. I'm remembering the woman who ignored her threats." Liberty had been so strong. She'd stood through it all and never broke up with him—well, until the end.

"You know what hurt the most?" She leaned against the back of the couch and crossed her arms, ripples of dark hair shadowing her face from the dim light. "Whenever you sided with her." She shook her head, her eyes glossy as she went off topic. "Many times you never believed me when I told you about her verbal abuse." Her voice rose, and her index finger jabbed his way. "I don't think you believe she manipulated our wedding. Forcing me to wear her gown..."

Forcing her? He nearly snorted. Liberty had simply refused.

"Taking over our hotel reservations, then"—she made quotations with her fingers—"forgetting them."

His anger dissolved slightly when her words started coming out in gasps when she listed so many things his mom did to tear them apart. Issues he'd not see then—or hadn't wanted to believe his mom was capable of doing.

"Are you even forgetting why I left?"

How could he? That day she'd been the angriest he'd seen Liberty.

"You sided with your mom when she took over our house plans." She took a step toward him, then jabbed a finger in his chest. It didn't hurt, but he could sense the force in it. "Don't even get me started about your mother. You're the only one who can't see how devious and controlling she is!"

She stormed out of the room toward the hallway.

Speechless after the confidence and truth in her words, Bryce felt his chest rise, then fall.

Great! So much for working things out. He gripped the back of his neck, his chest tightening. As long as she didn't intend to walk back to her cold car and stay there, he could change the course of their evening and bring them back to the progress they'd almost made.

He didn't hear the door opening, so that was good.

He sat on the couch she'd vacated, staring at the dancing flames behind the glass of the fireplace. He wasn't sure if he was going to burst into tears or collapse on the floor. Either way, he felt unstable while processing everything.

Liberty was the only person unafraid of bringing to light Mom's personality. Yet whenever Liberty was with him, she focused on him and talked about the things they could do as a couple. Not a word about Mom, except for the times Mom ambushed their cottage and blurted something Liberty didn't agree with. Okay, sometimes she'd tell him a scheme Mom plotted, but he didn't think Mom would go as far as doing the unrealistic things Liberty assumed. He kneaded his fingers deeper into his neck, cringing that he hadn't sided with her all the way.

After Liberty walked away from their marriage, Bryce let his mind wander to all the times they'd broken up. Mom had always been the reason. Liberty, always forgiving, had always come back to him. Even when she left that final time, he'd assumed she'd come back in a matter of time.

He should've seen the signs, especially when they broke up during their three-year engagement.

When his mom flew to New York to show him a community newspaper of Liberty with some guy at the winter festival, he'd confronted Liberty over the phone. She'd lost it and broke up with him over the accusation. Through Liberty's mom, he'd found out the man was Liberty's uncle, Rhonda's brother, and he'd pleaded for forgiveness. But Liberty was determined never to date him again, saying he was crazy like his psycho mom and telling him not to bother her ever again.

Then, much later, Bryce visited Eric when he was ill.

He'd thought of Liberty and decided to show up at her house one evening. He gave her all the reasons he'd fallen in love with her and convinced her to take a drive with him. Then he'd driven her to all their favorite places that summer they fell in love. It had taken a lot of work on his side to convince her how much he wanted her in his life. When proposing again, he'd told her he didn't want to spend another day without her, and she'd flung her arms around him, crying and repeating, "Me too."

Terrified of losing her again, he asked if they could marry within a month. She'd agreed.

With only one month to plan a wedding, Liberty didn't care about the planning time frame. She'd been too thrilled they could spend the rest of their lives together. So had Bryce. But once he told his mom, she'd taken over and wanted to be in charge of everything from planning the menu to the venue.

"This is our wedding, Wendy," Liberty had said, refusing to wear Mom's wedding dress as Mom suggested. "I want to have my own dress."

"It's my wedding too. You're getting married to my son." Mom narrowed her gaze at him, but since Liberty always knew how to stand up for herself, he just watched. "He's my only son, and I can't sit there and do nothing."

Liberty elbowed him for intervention. "I'm sure Bryce agrees with me."

He opened his mouth, but the words died the moment Mom gave him that I-dare-you-to-go-against-me look.

"If you can't let me help with the wedding dress, then I'll be in charge of food and your hotel."

"We're flying out for our honeymoon," Bryce said, trying to stand up for them. "But we haven't booked anything for our wedding night and the day after."

"Fair enough." Mom pressed her lips together as if she'd won half the battle.

Bryce had taken Liberty's hand in his. "Right, honey?"

"Whatever." Liberty's response had seemed more to move things along than from her choosing. And that could've been a time to stick up for what Liberty wanted rather than give in to Mom's demands.

On their wedding day, more things went wrong, but the biggest was walking into a hotel exhausted from the crowd and excited to be alone, but then discovering there were no reservations in either of their names. They'd given Mom's name and any name Mom could've used, but the hotel didn't have their reservations or any vacancy that night.

"She did this to us." Liberty had broken into sobs, her shoulders shaking as she fanned herself. "She didn't want us... us getting married."

His heart sank over having her crying on what should be the happiest day of their lives. While he drew her in his arms, he called his mom, who claimed to have been so busy planning a wedding she must have forgotten to make the reservations. "Come stay at the cottage."

One look at his bride, and he'd known that was the last place Liberty wanted to be. So he'd said they were good and hung up and called his best man, Logan.

He'd suggested Eric's cabin since no one was using it.

Still, their marriage only lasted for a year or so. He'd listened to Mom's advice and moved into the family cottage with Liberty while they made plans to build a house.

Yet at the same time, he'd just started with Bloom, the venture capital firm he'd started with four business partners. He was forced to spend most of his time in New York then. At times, Liberty came with him, but most times, she stayed in Pleasant View since she was training at the hospital.

On the few times they had together, Mom stormed into the cottage whenever she pleased.

A choked cough and sniffles coming from the hallway reminded him of his responsibility. He'd sworn to love and protect her when they got married, but he'd failed. He'd better not fail now.

He walked toward the hallway, and the lantern illuminated Liberty's hunched form against the wall. With her legs pulled up to her chest, she had her face buried in her hands. His heart squeezed, and his eyes suddenly felt dusty.

How could she have had a baby when she looked as slender as she'd been before?

He lowered himself, and the cool from the hardwood floor seeped into his sweats when he sat next to her. He slid his hand around her slender waist, the softness of the sweater teased his fingers, and he pulled her toward him.

She stiffened at his touch, not even bothering to acknowledge his presence.

How could he blame her? He leaned in and kissed at the tendrils of hair on her forehead. The soft fragrance of rose petals warmed him.

Then he cleared his throat. "I'm so sorry, Dimples, for losing it." He was a father. He had no clue what the first thing about parenting was. Trying not to voice all his fears at once, he continued. "I didn't know how to process the news."

She shuddered, and he rubbed her back, moving his hand in circles in an attempt to soothe her. What he wouldn't give to see her dimples! When she lifted her head, she wiped at her tears, the tension loosening beneath his hand.

"Please forgive me."

She nodded, and when she leaned in and pressed her cheek to his chest, he let out a breath. Whew, she still trusted him enough to rest her head there.

Shifting, he drew her even closer, inhaling the familiar scent of the woman he loved. Despite everything, he felt more in love with her now than he was then.

"I'm sorry too." She surprised him with an apology. "I should've told you instead of fearing your mom's reaction."

His mom could be cold, but he doubted she'd be mean enough to take a baby away from her mom. Still... "I now understand that my mom has a lot to do with our problems."

"What has changed for you to believe that now?"

"When you left me, I had a lot of time to reflect on the details I missed."

She was shivering. With the power gone, the fireplace offered their only source of heat.

"Let's go back by the fire."

She nodded, and he stood, taking her with him, fighting the urge to carry her in his arms. Would she be okay with it? He'd better tread lightly.

♥

CHAPTER 7

"Tell me about our daughter." He kept her hand clasped in his, not even wanting to ever be a whisper apart from her ever. Heat warmed them, and he was appreciative of the couches being so close to the fireplace.

"She's so beautiful."

He rubbed his thumb against hers. "She gets that from her mother."

"She has your eyes." She nestled closer into him, her head snuggling against his chest. "She's so happy and easygoing."

A cloud of sadness blanketed him, and he sucked in a sharp breath, suddenly wanting to know everything about her. "How old is she?"

"Eighteen months."

A year and a half. He'd missed so much. "What's her name?"

"I call her Starlight." She then explained why she'd come up with the nickname. Like the guiding star in the Christmas songs, the baby had lit Liberty's path to her faith in God. "Her name is Myra."

"Like Grandma."

"She meant a lot to you... to me and my mom too."

Rhonda had quit working for Bryce's family as soon as Grandma died. "She loved you so much." Although her memory hadn't been fully there, she lit up whenever she saw Liberty.

"Does Myra walk yet?" It might be a silly question, but he had no idea what age babies did things.

"She's been walking for the last four months...." For the next few minutes, Liberty gave him a detailed update about their daughter.

They both laughed when she shared Myra's cute sayings and do-ings. Tears lodged in his throat.

He'd missed out. He would've liked to have been in the hospital when she was born. He doubted he would be a great dad, not when he had insecurities about his capabilities, but that didn't stop his heart from aching and longing to love the daughter he just learned about.

"Do you have any pictures of her? Maybe on your phone?"

"Yes." She eased out of his arms. "I'll go get it upstairs."

As if she may not be fast enough, Bryce stood with her and clasped her hand, reaching for the lantern on the mantel. They crossed the living room, and he took the stairs two at a time. Liberty kept up with his pace right until they entered her bedroom.

Her white handbag was on the nightstand where she retrieved the phone. She shivered. "It's cold in here. Can we go back to the fire-place?"

He responded by walking out of the door and leading the way back downstairs.

"Let's start with a video," Liberty said after they sat and she scrolled through the photos on her phone. While he leaned into her, she tapped her phone, and the baby's scream from the video filled the cabin. His heart constricted as he watched the most fascinating scene—a dark-haired woman dressed in scrubs, handing a baby to Liberty. The tiny peanut had a head full of dark curly hair.

Liberty was laying down, her hair rumpled, eyelids heavy with exhaustion, but happiness radiated in her face as she took the baby.

Bryce slid his free hand around her waist, snuggling her closer to him. His heart expanded, almost exploding with love for his wife. Even if he wanted to share how he felt, he didn't trust himself to speak with his throat so tight from emotion.

"I didn't want Mom to record me during the actual birthing process." Her voice was hoarse. "I hope this is okay."

He wouldn't want anyone seeing her if they weren't pulling out a baby. "Are you kidding me?" He kissed the top of her head, the familiarity of her soft skin played out like déjà vu. "I'm glad I got to see this."

When that video ended, she clicked the next video of Myra's first day at home. She had her eyes closed in the car seat. Her tiny fingers curled into a fist. He shuddered, overcome with tenderness for his little girl, and tears blinded his vision.

He watched more videos of her firsts like her real smile. Liberty explained each video as she scrolled to the next of Myra rolling from tummy to back and back to tummy, her babbling dada, her first time eating, using a sippy cup, and all sorts of firsts that had his head spinning.

At that moment, he didn't care if he ever made a single penny in his life. He wanted to spend each waking day with his wife watching his daughter grow.

Once they watched all the videos, he went through the recent photos of Myra. She looked happy, the most beautiful baby he'd ever seen. "I can't believe... she's ours." He gasped on a shudder. He didn't remember ever sobbing, and he had no idea why tears were gushing through the side of his eyes.

Liberty set the phone to the side and reached out to wipe tears from his face.

"It's okay." Her voice shook as she fought tears too.

"I wish I'd been there."

"She still needs a dad."

A glimmer of hope beckoned in her response. And he dove for the opportunity while it was there. "Will it be okay if I come and see her?"

"Yes." She turned to face the fire as if realizing she'd given the wrong response. "As long as you don't tell your mom... Not yet at least."

Mom had always wanted a daughter, but she couldn't have any more kids after Bryce. However, Bryce had to play by Liberty's rules if he wanted to see his daughter. "I understand."

They shared a silence while he ran a hand over her back. "I'd give anything to be with you and Myra."

"Me too, but... things are complicated."

Because of him and his mom. "I know." He'd probably be a terrible father. He'd already failed at being a husband, and now he'd have two people to take care of. But that didn't hinder him from wanting to try. "Please tell me what to do."

"We would need some counseling." She let out a breath before she leaned in again and rested her head on his shoulder. That had always been her favorite thing to do when they sat on the sofa. "Myra has helped me change. She's helped me grow in my faith in God."

Right. Everyone around him lately believed in God. The last thing they needed to add to their already rocky relationship was faith differences. "Does that mean we can't be together anymore?"

"You're my husband. God brought us together. And you're the father of my child."

Hope pulsed through him, pumping from his chest and into his belly.

"Yes?" He urged her to keep talking.

"God should be the one to tear us apart." She then nodded. "I promised to love you until death."

She'd wanted a minister to officiate their wedding, and Bryce hadn't minded it as long as they got married. Although he never believed in God for reasons he couldn't even explain, he remembered the till-death part in the vows they'd exchanged.

"I'm sorry I left you." Liberty's words drew him back. "I walked away from you."

"I'm the one who should be apologizing. I didn't protect you." He should have whenever he sided with his mom.

Liberty probably had to sacrifice a lot for their daughter. How did she run a business and take care of Myra? "How long have you had the business?"

"About two years." Her head still on his shoulder, she fingered through a knot in her hair. "Remember the caregiver company Mom was working for? Well, the owner approached her to buy it. But Mom didn't want to run a business, so she asked if I wanted to." Liberty frowned at the tangle as she teased it loose, then pushed the lock of hair back over her shoulder. "Since I was pregnant, I thought running a business would give me the flexibility and financial stability to take care of our baby. So getting approved for a loan was my cue to become a business owner."

"Has it been as easy as you thought?"

She laughed. "Not at all, but thankfully, several employees stayed when the business switched hands. I didn't have to start from scratch."

That still sounded like a lot of work for a single mom. Bryce didn't have anyone to take care of, yet he could never start an investment firm by himself like he dreamed of at times. "How do you do it?"

"My mom helps."

"Didn't you say Rhonda works in your company?"

"She does, but more as backup. She's my main helper with Myra."

What if her mom was sick and couldn't help? She had an uncle who lived in Georgia, not close enough to help out.

Bryce wasn't usually impulsive, but when it came to Liberty, he was a different person.

"I know I don't deserve a second chance." Since she wasn't looking at him, it was a bit easier to talk while tracing slow circles over her thumb. "I can't move on without you." He'd tried that when she'd broken their engagement.

What did she mean when she said she was his wife? Did she mean he could move in and live with them?

Trying to grasp the meaning of her statement, he made his plea. "Please let me into your life once again."

That was too vague since he had no idea if she would move with him to New York. He didn't expect her to, but he needed to work something out so he could be with his wife and daughter.

Liberty was silent, obviously thinking.

Please, I need you. His whole body tensed with the silent plea.

"I'm scared," she finally admitted, not looking at him as she gave her reasons for wanting stable parents in Myra's life.

He admired and understood her concerns because he hadn't even met the child. But he knew he would do anything for her.

"I could take the risk if it was just me—"

"I'll fight for us... this time." Even as the words slipped out of his mouth, he had no clue what and who he was supposed to fight against. "At least I'll try."

She drew out a breath and lifted her head to look at him, her eyes soft with a familiar gentleness. "Let's take it slow."

Not a confident answer, but assurance enough for him to pull her in his arms. Feeling the urge to attempt the impossible, he squeezed her tight, and she shifted, her hands moving around his waist.

Her breathing escalated, and when she looked up at him, her eyes danced in the firelight, searching. Her lips parted, and he swallowed. It wouldn't take much effort for their lips to touch, but even with his racing heart, something screamed, "Take it slow!"

He was almost trembling when he ignored the warning and lowered his chin to kiss her cheek. "Like this slow?" His hoarse voice rasped his throat before he kissed her again, this time on the nose.

Unable to stop himself, he kissed her neck.

She closed her eyes and murmured, "Oh, Bryce..." So she was as affected by the simple kisses as he was. "I missed you so much."

That sounded like a real kiss would be in the slow category. So he cupped her face between his hands, wove his fingers into her hair at the back of her head, and slanted his mouth. The moment his lips touched hers, her mouth opened up, and his body tingled. He relished the familiar softness and warmth of her lips. Her hands were sliding up to his neck as she tenderly kissed him as if she'd dreamed of this moment.

His mind wandered to that summer they'd fallen in love and he would take her into secluded corners around his childhood home so he could kiss her. He closed his eyes and traced the outline of her cheek, her skin just as smooth as silk, the way he remembered it.

His body felt warm—hot as her fingers raked through his hair. And when he separated his lips from hers, her lush lashes fluttered open, revealing dazed brown eyes.

The thundering of their hearts was louder than the crackling of the fire. They stared at each other before she covered her mouth.

"Was that slow enough?"

She shook her head. Her shy smile almost hid beneath the hand covering her mouth.

Overcome with longing, he stroked the tendrils of hair from her temples. He'd missed his wife, and having her so close made the desire unbearable. But she was right. They had to take things slow while he regained her trust. He blew out a breath and drew her back to his chest. Her hair brushed his chin when she snuggled closer.

"Can we stay here tonight?" In each other's arms.

She nodded.

With the heat from the fireplace, in each other's arms, they could keep each other extra warm. That was one reason he wanted her in his arms. The other reason was he still didn't believe she was here with him. He kissed the top of her head. "I'm afraid, if I go to sleep, I'll wake up, and you'll be gone."

"How would I go past the tree blocking the way?"

"It's just a feeling. I can't take that chance." With all the adrenaline zapping through him, he doubted he'd sleep at all.

His mission tomorrow was to start working on getting the tree out of the way. She needed to get home to Myra come Monday. She was also nervous about getting back to work. With this much snow and dead phone lines, the tree service could be another week.

CHAPTER 8

Liberty fluttered open her groggy eyes, then winced at the bright daylight pouring into the room. Her hand felt warm snuggled in a throw almost as soft as Myra's blanket. With the blanket wrapped around her and tucked up around her feet, she shifted on the couch, eased out of the blanket, and slid her feet to the cold hardwood floor.

The heat from the fireplace warmed the room while beyond the window cool white sunlight sparkled off of glittery snow. She shivered at the cold snow still gripping snow to the trees.

Yawning, she outstretched her arm as memories from last night rushed through her mind. She eyed the cushion he'd been sitting on.

He said he was sorry. And he had meant it. The ache in his voice and the pain in his apology were both unmistakable even in the darkness. He wanted a second chance. So did she. When he sobbed while he watched videos of Myra, regret stabbed her over keeping him in the dark about his daughter.

Deep down, she feared he'd break her heart again, but living in fear wasn't right. She also didn't want Myra not to know her dad like Liberty hadn't known hers. The list could go on, especially since Liberty didn't want to live her life without Bryce. If God called her to be single, then she wouldn't argue, but she liked how she felt when she was with Bryce.

Mom's plans had been put on hold the moment she'd had a summer fling with a tourist who never bothered to call her again or respond when she called to let him know she was carrying his child.

Any thoughts of summer always brought to mind Bryce, the best summer of Liberty's life, and the only man she'd ever loved. He was here, sharing the cabin with her.

He'd held her in his warm and steady arms, and my... She touched her tingling lips.

A shiver rolled down her spine as the kiss she'd shared with her husband zinged through her. The heated kiss was unexpected. She'd wanted to take things slow, but she'd lost all coherent thought when she'd met his fiery gaze.

The problem was she longed for more of his touch, his kisses. Not the best way to start the day.

So she focused on the living room's floor-to-ceiling windows beyond which snow-dipped pine trees shimmered almost like a Christmas card as they stood sentinel throughout the property.

Running a hand over her face, she tried to focus on God, the great artist of any season. She needed His strength to enjoy this day without any doubts. That was her prayer this morning.

She listened for movement in the rest of the house, but only heard the ticking clock and the humming refrigerator.

Bryce had always been a morning person. He was a runner, and he always preferred doing so in the mornings. If it weren't for the snow, she might assume he'd gone running, but she doubted it now.

When she reached for her phone from the table, the time showed seven twenty.

In case she had another chance to be kissed by Bryce again, she went upstairs and brushed her teeth. When she stepped out of the room, there still wasn't any movement even as she tilted her ear to listen down the hall.

Assuming he'd left her on the couch for his bed, she'd make breakfast without him distracting her. In the kitchen, as she swung open the pantry door for breakfast ideas, she stilled at a loud whirring noise outside.

Curiosity drew her to the window. Shading her hand over her eyes, she squinted through the pine trees. She could see something red... someone hunched by the fallen tree.

The forest service had shown up to cut the tree, thank goodness! A lightness lifted her heart. Now if she could get her car out of the snow at some point today, it would speed up her departure when the time came to leave tomorrow. But that would mean leaving Bryce. Uneasy about leaving him, she hugged her arms around herself. Perhaps they'd see each other sooner or later.

With renewed purpose, she returned upstairs, changed into a tank top, slid a wool sweater over it, and then pulled on her jeans.

After putting her hat and socks on, she scurried downstairs to the hallway for her jacket. While Bryce was still running or whatever he was up to, she could check the progress of the tree as she brushed the snow off her car and gave it a start.

She trekked through the snow in the borrowed boots from the cabin. Much better than the tennis shoes she'd worn two days ago. A family of deer traipsed past in the distance, scrounging like snow was their normal way of life. The cold brushed against her cheeks, her only exposed skin since she was bundled up.

As she approached her car, she recognized the man gathering branches and tossing them to the pile on the side. Bryce. Her pulse raced, and her stomach fluttered at the sound of him whistling.

Even with a ski jacket and snow pants, he still looked trim and fit.

Not wanting to startle him, she announced her presence once she was within reach. "You cut trees nowadays?"

Bryce jerked and spun to turn, a grin lifting his flushed cheeks as he brushed his gloved hands on his pants. "I doubt the tree service will show up today." His low voice rumbled, and her skin registered its familiar vibration with captivating tingles of awareness. He then tilted his head to the side. "You need to get home to Myra and work."

Her heart constricted, and her gaze tracked the steam billowing from his mouth. There was no place she'd rather be than standing here looking at him. If anything, her attraction for him had grown stronger, more intense overnight, and it made her a little nervous in his presence.

"You're so sweet." Steam fogged around her face with her whisper.

"I'll go for sweet anytime, not sour." Humor lit his eyes. She needed it if she was going to get through the day with him being so nice.

"I'll help you."

"I got this." He snugged his knit hat down to his ears. "You have a baby to take care of when you get home, but I don't."

Right, they still had to figure out what their second chance meant and how to plug him into his new role as a dad.

Although not much progress was made to the tree, which was mostly buried under deep snow, the little Bryce did, impressed her. "How did you learn to cut trees?"

He shrugged. "I'm learning now and realizing it's harder than I thought."

"Starting with a snow-encased tree is not the best way to learn." She bent and picked up one of the loose branches, then tossed it to the stacked pile. "I'm pretty sure we're going to ruin the chain saw."

"I'll replace it if that happens."

She walked closer and bent to the chain saw at his feet. "Would you like me to take a turn?"

He reached for her hand and eased her up to stand. Her feet felt weak when she peered into those gray eyes.

His gaze was penetrating, a searing stare that left the air crackling between them and her holding her breath. His chest rose and fell before he exhaled. "I'll manage."

Her tongue could barely move to form a response. He must have noticed because he continued. "I want to take care of you, starting now." He leaned in and planted cool lips on her cheek, a soft kiss that warmed her insides and left her wanting more.

As if he didn't notice, he let go of her hand and stepped back, crouching for the machine. Its grating whir churned up a stark contrast after the thrumming of her heart.

While Bryce cut the branches, Liberty composed herself and started gathering the branches. They worked in silence with the wailing chain saw slicing through the tree and quiet on the property.

It made sense that he wasn't tampering with the tree trunk until he could get a clear approach.

"Let's take a break." He set the saw on the snowy ground several minutes later.

"Go on ahead. I'll meet you at the house." She dug out the keys from her jacket pocket. "I need to warm up my engine."

When she walked to the car, she could feel Bryce following her. "I'll help."

She yanked open the door, but it wouldn't budge. She pulled harder and fell backward, only to land in his strong arms.

"I got you." Warmth from his mouth teased her neck, and a shiver ran through her body. It didn't help when he wrapped his arms around her waist and spun her around. She had to tug her boot out of the soft snow.

"Let's go have breakfast." The loving affection in the softness of his eyes radiated through her breathlessness. "I'll come back and dig out your car. I can start it then."

This was Bryce, a man she'd known for a long time, her husband, yet she was having a hard time using her words. She nodded, blaming the coldness for her tongue's sudden immobility.

She found her normalcy when they cooked breakfast together on a camp stove they unearthed from the garage. With two burners, he cooked Cream of Wheat, and she scrambled eggs. They were a whisper apart, relaxed as they made plans for their day.

"When was the last time you went snowshoeing?" he asked, mixing the steamy creamy porridge.

"Our first winter together." Well, their first winter in their marriage.

"Oh."

She bumped him with her hip while she scraped the wooden spoon into the eggs. "What do you mean, oh? I've been busy."

"I know." His voice turned serious, and she didn't want him to dwell on the past they'd already discussed. So she redirected their conversation.

"Let's go snowshoeing after breakfast." The car could wait. "As long as there's shoes my size." She'd seen plenty of sizes in the storage shed.

"If there aren't, I'll carry you on my back." He cast her a playful glance before he turned off the burner.

While they ate, they reminisced about the vivid memories of their past. "Each moment I spent with you is vivid," she said. It was like her life with Bryce were scrapbooks pasted in her head. "What about you? Anything in particular?"

He was silent, perhaps taking in her response before he said, "Taylor Swift's 'Blank Space.'" He fixed his gaze on the window as if taken back into the memory itself. "We played that song over and over on our drive to White River National Forest."

"We carved our names on an aspen tree," she whispered, the memory still clear from when he'd completed his first year at NYU.

Bryce nodded. "And we... um—"

"I remember." Just like every moment she'd spent with him. It was their third summer together. They'd been so deep in love. She chuckled at the memory. "We were supposed to elope."

His face fell. "But you broke up with me."

"Your mom found out...."

His lips pressed into a tight line, and he moved his spoon in his porridge. "I guess I thought it was a good idea to tell her our plans."

They were having a good time, and Liberty didn't want to get into that now. Bryce hadn't known better than to blurt their plans out during an argument with his mom. Wendy had pretended to be happy for them just like she acted sorry about their argument. She'd then had Bryce invite Liberty for dinner to celebrate their nuptial plans. The next day, the police showed up at Liberty's house with Wendy claiming Liberty stole her gold necklace.

Liberty cringed over what had been the most humiliating moment of her life—the police raiding their house and Wendy asking for Liberty's purse. Sure enough, the necklace was there in its fancy velvety pouch.

Her chest still hurt whenever memories of that day assaulted her. She'd spent twenty-four hours in jail. Bryce had bailed her out after calling his dad, who vouched for Liberty's innocence.

"I'm sorry Mom did that to you." He reached for her hand and clasped it with his. He'd used the same words then, but in her humiliation, she hadn't wanted to see him again if it meant Wendy would always be in their lives.

Mom had begged Liberty not to date Bryce anymore and risk Wendy playing more dirty tricks. "You're young and beautiful," Mom had said. "You'll fall in love with someone else."

The reality of falling for anyone besides Bryce had felt like a blow to Liberty's stomach, and she'd sobbed more for breaking up with him than she had over the humiliation.

Wendy had been the town's new mayor at the time after all. Leaving her son alone only made sense. Plus, she'd been blaming Liberty for Bryce's career change.

Liberty never told Bryce that, after they reconciled a year later, Wendy showed up at her house and offered to pay her if she would never speak to Bryce again. "He spends most of his time in New York, and you're here. He'll dump you anyway."

Liberty had slammed the door in her face. She'd had insecurities about their long-distance relationship, but Bryce had leaped through hoops to visit her in Pleasant View. He could be the perfect man she desired if it weren't for his mom.

She fought the tears now threatening to blur her vision and turned to Bryce with a pasted-on smile. "Can we not talk about that right now?"

He cleared his throat, his regret clear in his frown. "I understand."

If they were trying to move forward, bringing Wendy up would only hinder their progress. They continued eating in silence, but she only ate out of necessity, her appetite having vanished.

Two hours later, she was grateful she'd forced herself to eat since she needed the strength to trek the steep hill using the adjustable poles to help her balance and traction. She and Bryce walked along a wooded route that sheltered them from unlikely winds.

With hiking trails buried deep beneath the snow, they explored while creating their own paths. Despite the atmosphere, she warmed the more they climbed, and with each step forward, she found the exercise more exerting. No doubt, she was shaving off some of those pounds that still lingered after she had Myra. Breastfeeding had helped her get back to her normal weight, but some of her jeans still fit snugger than they used to.

She'd forgotten how complicated the activity was in comparison to hiking.

Snowshoeing was for enthusiasts like Bryce, who was speaking with ease. On the other hand, she was gasping in between her responses to his questions. "The one thing we never did together was camping." She paused to catch her breath. "You were freaked out that there were no bathrooms and the abundance of bugs—"

A chuckle escaped him as he swung one of his sticks while planting the other in the soft snow. "That's not true."

"Really?" Liberty wagged her head, pondering his exact words when she suggested the trip six months into their marriage. "If I remember correctly, you said you didn't want to deal with bug bites."

His lips danced with a smile, crinkling up his ruddy cheeks, and she resumed their climb so they could get done and out of the cold.

"I'll be happy to camp with you this summer." His words were certain, a promise hanging in them.

She found herself stopping and giving him a sideways glance. "Myra would love it." They'd have to take her along, and no doubt, she would enjoy the outdoors.

"It's a deal." He winked.

Liberty twisted her neck back toward where they'd started. Their footprints were clear in the snow. "If we get stuck, at least someone will find us easily."

"Stuck, huh?" When she looked at him, his brow lifted into a challenge. "Is that your indirect way of putting an end to our hike?"

The truth was she was tired of walking. After all, she'd come up to play in the snow. "Did you just call me lazy?" Her cheeks bunched up into a grin, an idea forming in her mind.

"How could I say that?"

Glancing at her feet and the deep snow, she dropped her sticks, and no doubt, he didn't register what she was up to when she bent and pushed her gloved fingers into the soft snow. She scooped a heap in her hand.

"Uh-oh." Bryce jerked sideways, laughing, but by the time he tossed his sticks down, she was hurling a snowball in his face.

"You did not just..."

Oh no! The challenge on his face indicated war, and she altered her stride to run, but who was she kidding? He was better at using his snowshoes than she was.

She squealed, her voice echoing through the mountain property as she leaped a step or two before his arm hooked around her waist and she gasped when he hoisted her right off her feet.

"You want war?" His spark of mischief warmed her even more.

"Yes," she spoke breathlessly, suddenly lighthearted.

He tried to put her down, but he must have lost balance because she found herself screaming with laughter as they splayed on the ground. With his arm as a protective anchor around her waist, she'd fallen on top of him.

She stopped laughing when Bryce wasn't laughing anymore. He was staring at her, their breath forming clouds around them.

He didn't say anything, just moved his hand over her back to her neck and dragged her down toward his lips and kissed her with such intensity and passion. All rational thought fled, and she kissed him with all she had. She trailed her hands down to his face. The scruff on his jaw snagged her soft gloves.

She loved him so much, and oh, how she'd missed him.

Just as her body trembled and weakened, Bryce drew his face away from her, panting. "About that challenge."

Hmm? Still dazed, she had no idea what challenge he was talking about when his other hand, which she hadn't been paying attention to, rose in her face, shocking her with something cold square on her face.

She sputtered, trying to wipe the snow from her face while using her other hand to swing at him. He was chuckling when he rolled her to the snow and stood, drawing her up with him and setting her down.

When he leaned in to press a kiss on her cheek, she playfully shoved him. But he was too strong, and her push didn't even make him stumble.

"Bryce Solace, you are the meanest person I've ever met."

"And yet you married me." Laughter carried in his voice as he took her hand in his. "What were you and the girls planning to do when you got here?"

She frowned at his sudden question, so he rephrased. "On your girls' weekend, did you intend to do anything?"

"Talk." For sure. "Sled, soak in the hot tub, ski—"

"With the tree blocking the road, skiing wouldn't have been an option."

Good point, so she asked what the guys had planned to do.

"Ski and ride snowmobiles." He shrugged. "Let's talk tonight."

"Isn't that what we've been doing?"

His brow arched, and she knew what he meant. They hadn't dug deeper on why she'd put a pause on their marriage. "Sounds good."

After all, with the power off, there wasn't much else to do but talk.

THE AFTERNOON WENT fast while they both worked on digging her car out of the snow, but there was no sense in that while they couldn't drive it forward. Bryce had backed it out, to the side of the path. He'd also cut more branches off the tree, but every time he tried to attack the icy trunk, the chain saw kicked backward and the chain unraveled, forcing him to stop and realign it.

The power had returned by the time they settled into the cabin. Even if Liberty had done odd jobs before, digging her car out of snow drained her and made her muscles ache.

They'd eaten dinner early with her intending to get to bed right after. But Bryce suggested she take a nap rather than call it a day at six.

Liberty had been laying down for the last hour staring at the exposed beams on the ceiling while she contemplated her fate with

Bryce. He wanted to talk about their past after dinner, and as much as she knew, the past had to be dealt with before moving on. Still, dread haunted her.

Turning to face the window, she peered through the open-slatted blinds where moonlight cast sweeping tree shadows across pristine snow. If Bryce hadn't asked for her phone to look at videos of Myra, she'd be playing music to lull her to sleep.

Laying down was not going to fix their marriage. So she hopped off the bed and walked to the bathroom to wash her face. The long-sleeved top and sweats she was wearing were comfortable. She needed comfort if she was going to trudge through memories.

When she made it downstairs, Bryce's deep voice rumbled from the living room. "Had a good nap?"

"Yeah." Not really.

He stood and ambled toward her, her phone in hand. She took him in, dressed in blue swim trunks and a white T-shirt that encased his broad shoulders while he handed her the phone. "We made a very beautiful baby."

Her neck heated, but how else was he supposed to say it? "Yes."

"Thanks for letting me use your phone."

That was the least she could do. "Anytime."

"I got the hot tub ready for us."

Ah, his attire now made sense. Sweet anticipation and panic alternately warmed and chilled her blood.

He shrugged, arching a brow. "We're going to talk?"

Right. Talk. "Okay."

Unlike her racked nerves, he seemed relaxed as he pointed toward the living room sliding door. "You want to meet me outside?"

He must have remembered the hot tub when he'd asked what she'd planned to do with the girls. She nodded, and seriously, why was her heart racing? He'd seen her without any layers of clothing before. So why did she feel cautious about being in a swimsuit, a modest one-piece?

Her fears vanished when she slid on her floral swimsuit and draped on one of the robes from the closet. She then pulled her hair up and tied it in a ponytail. After all, it was dark outside as long as Bryce didn't turn on the porch light. Okay, she had stretch marks she wasn't ready to expose.

She hugged the robe tight and flitted down the cool hardwood stairs, her bare feet chilling on the wood. Then she opened the sliding door and stilled as a blast of cold air struck her and the LED candles lining the edge of the Jacuzzi caught her off guard. Steam curled from the hot water, the intimate light flickering across its rippling surface. Her fingers tightened around the door handle, and her feet froze in place as the romantic setting beckoned—a romantic setting she hadn't expected.

Somehow, she loosened her grip, slid the door closed, and stepped into the frigid air, all while shivering for another reason. Her back to him, she slid off her robe and hung it on the metal hook stand.

"Hey." Low and soft, Bryce's voice seemed to drift on the steam.

Keeping her head ducked, she tucked wisps of hair behind her ears as the humid air enveloped her and she lowered herself into the hot tub, immersing her wobbly legs in the water.

"It's hot." She winced at the shock of such contrasting temperatures.

Bryce waved her over to sit by him.

"I think I'll stay right here." She eyed the candles. "When did you get the time to do this?"

Leaning back against the side of the tub, he stretched his arms out on either side of him along the edge, nudging a couple of candles backward. "All I've had is time, being up here." His voice was husky. "Of course, it went too fast."

"Yes. It did." She sank deeper and eased her hands into the water, clasping them on her lap.

"When I'm not with you, I fall apart." His voice drew her gaze to him. His eyes were intent on her. "I don't want us to ever split up."

"Me too." She twisted her clasped hands tighter together. One of the Jacuzzi jets kneaded her back.

"I need to know what to do, to make sure you don't walk away."

Again. It was a question and prayer she had to present to God. One thing was certain, though—she'd never stay at his parents' cottage again. Drawing a slow breath, she moved her fingers to the nearest jet, letting the powerful stream of bubbles repel them like the thought repelled her. "You do know I can't ever stay at their cottage again—right?"

At his silence, she moved her gaze to his.

"I now understand." His sincerity made it easy to believe him. He then chuckled. "The day you walked away... you were the angriest I'd seen you."

Oh! She covered her face with hot, wet hands, ashamed of having lost control. She'd had the architect's plan on her phone. Bryce had emailed the plans to Wendy, who printed hers out and showed up wanting to discuss her suggestions. Then Wendy started pointing out how she wanted an additional room for the library and another bedroom designated for her whenever she visited.

"We're neighbors, Wendy. I'm sure you'll be walking in and out of our house," Liberty had blurted, struggling to keep the hurt out of her voice. "You don't need a bedroom here."

"It's not a big deal to add a bedroom for Mom, I guess." Bryce gave a gentle roll of his shoulder.

And that—that act as if none of it mattered, as if she should always give in to Wendy—had undone Liberty. Heat raged through her body. They'd agreed not to involve his mom in their plans, but he'd sent her the house plans. And now... her husband betrayed her once again.

She'd hurled her phone over Bryce's head, intending to put sense into him, but he ducked. Her phone smashed the lamp by the window, then bounced back on the tile floor and shattered to pieces. His mom's jaw hung open.

Liberty had then gone to the bedroom, sobbing and packing whatever of her belongings she could manage. As Liberty walked out of the door, Wendy was still holding the paper and haranguing at Bryce, who looked frazzled and torn between pleasing his mom or his wife.

Liberty yanked the paper out of Wendy's hand and ripped it to pieces in front of her face.

"I was young then." And without the fear of God for her to rely on Him to fight her battles. "I could've hurt you if you didn't know how to duck."

His laughter came out more carefree than angry. "I can laugh about it now, but I thought it was funny how you hurled your luggage at me."

When he'd tried to chase after her while she headed to her car, she'd shouted, "If you come anywhere near me, I'll hurt you badly!"

"I'm alive to tell the story now." His tone was light before he got serious. "If we make house plans again, my mom wouldn't have to know, and we don't have to build on her property."

She liked his optimism to move things ahead, and he should if she was letting him in. But... "It's not your mom who worries me the most."

"No?"

"I don't want to keep you from your mom, but I also need you to stand up for me." Cool air nipped Liberty's neck, and she sank further to a lower step so she could immerse more of her body in the hot water. "When you take your mom's side, I feel like an intruder."

"You're the best thing that happened to me." His voice cracked. "I would never think of you as an intruder."

And yet, he'd made her feel like one so many times. She reminded him of the times they discussed their plans and he told his mom. "I respect your mom." She was his mom after all. "But if we're together, I'm not going to expect her to show up unannounced whenever she pleases."

"That shouldn't be an issue if we don't live in her cottage."

She didn't have to like Wendy, but whether Liberty wanted to be or not, she was a part of Bryce's mom's life, bound by blood now that Myra was in the picture and Liberty was still in love with Bryce.

"You said something about counseling," he said, really trying, and even if she wanted the reunion to be hard, she didn't have it in her to take things slow. "Do you have somewhere in mind?"

She pressed her lips tight, not sure if she should speak up. Then she exhaled. "I can't think of anywhere else but through the church, but with you not believing in God, I'll be flexible if it means someone who has wise counsel to help mend our marriage."

"Church will be fine." He ran a hand over the scruffy jaw he hadn't shaved since he arrived—maybe he hadn't brought a razor since he'd planned a weekend with just the guys. For a while, they spoke about things they could work on to improve their marriage.

Bryce thought she needed to be more communicative where his mom was concerned, and she would be as long as he believed her whenever his mom made up an accusation. But...

"I won't share anything that might risk your relationship with your mom." She raised her chin, then held up her hand in a cautionary gesture. "The last thing I want is you cutting your mom out of your life. My mom means a lot to me—*every* child needs a good relationship with their mother."

Tenderness glowed in his eyes as he snagged her hand, leaned across the hot tub, and brought her fingers to his lips. He kissed them one after another, his gray gaze intense while he whispered, "You *are* an exceptional woman, Liberty Solace."

Shivering at his gesture, but glad they'd covered all that and feeling at ease accepting him back into her life, she slid her hand free. Every bit of her relaxed even as her thumb traced where his lips had touched and her heart warmed. "So... how long are you in town? We need to figure out how your career and time in New York will work out for us to be together."

"If I'd known I'd run into you, I'd have worked out those details."

Fair enough. "Perhaps I'll need to work out some details to accommodate your schedule too. No matter what, we'll figure something out."

"Thank you." He peered at her, his gray eyes so sincere.

Thank You, God, for his willingness to talk and his desire to mend our marriage! Please be with us each step.

"Remember the first time you broke up with me and we reconciled?"

She flicked her fingers along the water's surface, nostalgia sweeping through her. She remembered everything where Bryce was concerned. "Yes."

"You came up with the idea for us to close our eyes and meditate on the good times we had together so—"

"So we could be reminded of what we mean to each other?" she finished for him. She hadn't wanted to think of Wendy's schemes or any arguments. And it had helped when they reflected on what they meant to each other.

"Let's try that again." He reached across the water, holding out his hands, his face glowing in the lights. "This time, let's picture what our future together looks like."

"Okay." Taking his hands, it was easy to close her eyes while her body relaxed into the hot water and soothing jets.

"I'll go first." Bryce squeezed her hands. "We're on our front porch, watching the colors of the sky in different shades of vivid pink and..." He continued describing the sunset, and Liberty smiled, picturing herself clasping Bryce's hand then. "Our hands are calloused, and our hair is mixed with gray...." he continued as if tapping into her mind. "Myra is getting married, and I'm walking her down the aisle."

That had Liberty jump a little. She hadn't grasped Myra starting kindergarten yet, let alone getting married.

"We're surrounded by friends and family...."

At the word *family*, Wendy's contemptuous face assaulted her, and Liberty started shaking.

"What do you see?" Bryce's voice pulled her back, and she tried to refocus on the happy future she wanted with Bryce. But she slid her hands free because all she could see was Wendy's expression as she stormed into their house. Wendy—spending her whole life finding all the wrongs Liberty did so she could take Myra away from her. Bryce—content with his mom raising Myra even if Liberty wasn't part of their lives.

"Dimples, what's wrong?" Bryce's voice was almost at her ear, and then his side brushed hers before his hand clasped hers. "What do you see?"

"I'm scared." Saving him the details was better.

"Don't be." His fingers unclasped hers, then moved to her back, pulling her into the warmth of his chest—oh how familiar his skin felt! He pressed his lips near her ear, and she relaxed as he whispered, "I've got you."

Just as she was about to question how, he nudged her, tucking his chin against the top of her head. "Remember the summer after we reunited from our first breakup? How we went to Hawaii with the Stone family, and Logan dared us to jump off a cliff?"

A shiver went through her, even as she laughed. "That was such a terrifying dare."

"Yet, when you told me you were scared and I took your hand..."

Her fear had vanished, and she'd jumped. It had been the most thrilling experience and far better when they kissed in the water, not caring that Logan and his siblings were above watching and clapping while they screamed at them.

Much later, after they'd turned off the LED candles, they walked together upstairs. Before they veered their separate ways along the hallway, she turned to say good night, and he took her wrist and edged her toward him. "I love you so much."

The vibration in his voice made her tremble. Her lips parted to say the same words, but he lowered his mouth to hers, and when he kissed her, she lost herself in the wilderness of new sensations, warm and wonderful and exciting.

"It's our last night here." His lips murmured over hers between his heated kisses. "Stay with me in the room where we had our wedding night."

Right now, taking it slow was far from her priorities. She nodded, and when he began to loosen her hair and remove the hair tie, she could scarcely breathe since she was trembling.

He was taking all the control. She wanted to start over, and they'd both stayed faithful.

Combing his fingers into her hair, he tilted her head back. She saw the longing in his eyes, just the way she felt. "I promise to do my best, to love you the way you deserve."

If she had any doubts about starting over today, they vanished with his bold confession. And as he scooped her in his arms and toward the familiar hallway to their bridal suite, everything faded—Wendy and all the past mistakes and regrets. It was just Liberty and Bryce. The man she'd fallen for above all other men.

CHAPTER 9

At half past one, Bryce steered the Wrangler down the road with Liberty in the passenger seat. His heart felt light, and his cheeks almost hurt from grinning as he and Liberty belted out the words to Taylor Swift's "ME!" while it played from his playlist. Even as they both practiced their best seated dance moves, Bryce kept his focus on the bumpy snowy road. It was just the perfect song to remind each other they were each unique. Only one Liberty and only one Bryce.

As the song ended, they both sang louder than the diva as they shouted the last line, promising each other no one would love the other like they would.

Before the next song started, Liberty tapped his phone, and the music stopped. "Whoo-hoo!" she said, breathless.

"Why did you turn off the music?" Bryce spoke between breaths. Nothing could contain his smile.

"I don't want you to get distracted when you're driving."

She was distracting enough without the music. Since he'd told her how she'd been on his mind when he played that song, as soon as they got into the Jeep, Liberty wanted to play "ME!" right away. "I'll let this go since you have to enter your number in my phone anyway."

"I almost forgot," she said, and from the corner of his eye, he saw her punching numbers in his phone. She also gave him a breakdown of her schedule that week.

"I'll tell Mom about us as soon as I get to her house." She set the phone in the console. "I'll text you tomorrow about which day you should come over."

To meet his daughter. "I'll be waiting," he breathed out the words like a lifeline before taking one hand off the steering wheel and reaching to touch her. She entwined her warm fingers in his.

Tomorrow was too far away, but he had no choice but to wait. At least she'd texted him some of Myra's videos and photos. They would be a great consolation and comfort as he waited for her text.

Last night, they'd discussed when he should move in, and they'd agreed to give it a few days while they talked to their families—mostly her mom. Bryce had no clue how he would talk to his mom.

"Maybe I'll text you tonight." She squeezed his hand as if reading his inner struggle.

The sun was peeking through the clouds as he descended the hill. The lower he drove down the mountain, the shallower the snow became.

Even though he'd driven her Impreza out of the path, he hadn't succeeded in getting the tree cut. The maintenance man had shown up that morning, but he'd had to park on the other side of the fallen tree before trekking the remaining way to the cabin. He'd told them the forest tree service would get the job done on Wednesday. Too far away for Liberty and Bryce too.

The backup plan was to test the Jeep's ability to drive over the tree trunk, and it had been easy after he had trimmed off the branches.

Now, as he neared the bend in the road, he unhooked his hand from hers. His heart ached as a community of mountain homes came into view. Their time together was almost over. Gone was the lazy morning they'd shared after the breakfast he'd made and served her in bed.

He drove further and past the road leading to his house.

"Did Logan respond yet?" he asked, his mind working on plans for the evening, plans that didn't involve him rushing back to his childhood home.

Liberty reached for his phone and tapped her finger. "He's already waiting in the parking lot."

Good. Bryce needed someone to unload the last seventy-two hours with. Who could be better than his best friend and the partial instigator of his and Liberty's reunion?

"I don't mind taking Uber."

He glanced at her. The glow on her face made him want to forget all the rules and the things they needed to work out so he could take his wife and child with him to New York, where no one would interfere with their lives.

"I can't leave you without a car." He had plenty of cars at home. "I'll have your Impreza delivered as soon as they cut the tree." Or he'd bring it whenever he showed up.

"I'm not on your insurance and—"

"Insurance should be the least of your worries, Dimples." He could afford another car if it came down to her crashing his Jeep. "I'm just glad you're back in my life."

She was more important than any material assets he ever desired, so why hadn't he invested himself in the fight to keep her?

As he turned to I-85, snow splashed, and an engine roared from the snowplow driving past them in the opposite lane. With her instructions, he made a right turn to another unplowed road. After driving past a gas station and random square buildings, he turned into a small shopping center and easily spotted the silver Audi, the only car in the lot.

"That must be Logan."

He nodded to the already shoveled, but empty lot. The snowstorm must have kept people at home. "Looks like all the offices are closed today."

"My employees don't need to report to the office, if it's not necessary." Liberty pushed back her hair. "They log in as soon as they arrive at the client's home."

He pulled in and parked two spaces away from the Audi. A glance through the Audi's tinted window made it hard to see the driver. So he studied Liberty, noticing her silence as she peered at the building while bouncing her knee. A nervous gesture they both used at times.

She was the same beautiful woman he'd fallen in love with all those years ago. Overwhelmed by her presence, he leaned toward her and touched her soft cheek. "I'll miss you."

Her cheek rounded with her soft smile, but no dimples appeared as she turned to him, her eyes serious, her pulse thrumming at the V-neck of her olive-green sweater. "I'm glad Iris and Logan set us up."

The feeling was mutual.

"I'd give you a tour of my office today, but I don't want to keep your friend waiting."

Entering a building with just the two of them, yeah, Bryce might forget everything but the beautiful woman with him. "Which one is your office?" The banner on the building in front of them was a beauty shop.

"Two doors down."

His gaze followed her finger. "Second from the left?"

When she nodded, he tried to squint to read the sign, but couldn't discern the words in the dusky light. She then turned to him, her warm fingers trailing his cheek. "This is it."

It wasn't it. It was just the beginning. In response, he leaned in and kissed her lips. In case she didn't think he was serious with what he'd said yesterday, he spoke again over her lips. "I'm happy when I'm with you."

If she took her sweet time getting back to him, he'd be falling apart.

"Me too." Cupping her hands to each side of his face, she kissed him back before easing away.

When he stepped out, cool air seeped through the arms of his long-sleeved shirt, but his vest kept his core plenty warm.

He went around the front to the passenger side to open her door. He then went to the back for his luggage. Before Liberty got into the driver's side, Bryce gave her a fleeting kiss to say goodbye.

"Tell Logan I said hello."

He raised an eyebrow. "You don't want to say hello yourself?"

Her shy smile sent a rush of warmth through him over the events of their time together. "I'm sure he will have lots of questions. I'd rather save my answers for Iris."

He understood. He waved to her and watched until she drove off.

The moment the Jeep vanished from the parking lot, Bryce heard a beep and spun to the Audi where the driver's door swung open.

"Man." Without stepping out of the car, Logan clapped his hands, a knowing grin spreading out his lips.

"Stalker," Bryce mumbled under his breath while walking to the back of the car, opened the trunk, and tossed in his duffle bag. He then moved to sit in the front passenger seat.

"How'd it go?" Logan closed his door, then scratched his long stubble. "Should I even bother to ask?"

Bryce buckled his seatbelt, unsure how to thank Logan rather than scold his friend for the unexpected reunion. The heated leather seat and warm air through the vent made the car feel a lot hotter when his mind flashed images of Liberty in his arms. Blood rushed through his body, and his cheeks burned. Barely able to look his friend in the eye, he fixed his gaze on the shop Logan had parked in front of. The posters of musical instruments plastering the glass door provided a much better diversion for his brain.

"Honestly." At Logan's voice, Bryce almost laughed when Logan lifted his hand to stop him from answering. "Spare me the R-rated details." He put the car in reverse and backed out of the parking lot.

"I need to get Liberty's car from the cabin." Bryce settled back in his seat, already missing her. If he took her car to her as soon as they got the tree out of the road, he'd have a good excuse to see her sooner.

"You're buying me dinner." Logan started toward the bumpy road.

Dinner might not be a bad idea. Bryce wasn't ready to go home. "Let's do it."

Logan's brown eyes widened when he gave Bryce a fleeting glance before returning his focus to the road. "Now?"

Instead of answering, Bryce blurted the first thing that came to mind. "She's changed a lot." In a good way. He sensed a certainty and confidence in her newfound faith. "She uses words like blessings and grace—"

"Christianity is what you mean." Logan cut him off with a response that summed it up. Bryce's friend and his family practiced their faith.

Several things crowded his mind, but Bryce felt pressed to utter what required a resolution the most. "I have a child!"

The car skidded, and he jerked when Logan slammed on the brakes, his brown eyes wide. "What did you just say?"

Bryce checked the rearview mirror to ensure they weren't blocking cars. Logan had stopped in the middle of the road. Thankfully, there were no cars. "Let's drive out of the road."

So Logan didn't know about the secret. Since Logan's sister was Liberty's best friend, Bryce had wondered if Logan kept that from him. "I take it Iris didn't tell you?"

"How could she keep something that big from me?" Logan creased his brows, shaking his head as he navigated the steering wheel with a tight hold.

"You weren't supposed to know." Bryce ran a hand through his own hair. "If she told you, then you would've told me."

Logan nodded before his nostrils flared. "I don't get it. Why didn't Liberty tell you about your child until now?"

Although grateful for his friend's concern, Bryce didn't want Logan to judge Liberty. "It's my fault." He shrugged, knowing it was the truth. "You know how my mom made some decisions in our marriage."

Logan snorted. "No kidding. Your mom ran your marriage."

Silence passed as Logan focused on the road. A Ram truck drove past them, and Bryce surveyed the world beyond the window—snowcapped mountains and snow-dressed trees.

"How old is the baby?"

Logan's question drew him back. "Myra. She's a year and a half." Bryce reached for his phone from his vest and scrolled through it to find Liberty's text. He stopped short of showing Myra's photo to Logan when he approached the main road.

"I'll show you some pictures at the restaurant."

"On second thought..." Logan drew his brows together. "You don't owe me any dinner."

Bryce wasn't ready to deal with his mom. His dad had probably returned by now, but even so, Bryce needed more time to talk things over with someone who understood. "I insist. Your pick."

Logan came to a stop at a red light. "Then I know just the place."

Bryce glanced back at the phone, his cheeks warming while he studied the photo of Myra embracing Liberty. Her love for their daughter was evident through her smile and affection. Liberty had said Rhonda snapped the picture three weeks ago during their visit to her house.

His heart squeezed, and his panic gave way to fear as doubts crept in. Could he make his family happy? Could he be the father and husband they could depend on?

"You okay, bro?"

Bryce nodded, but he was far from okay. He shook his head since there was no need to lie. "I have no idea what being a good father is like." He let out his breath as Logan steered them into town. "I haven't even grasped what a good husband is supposed to be, let alone a dad."

Bryce's dad was wonderful, but he'd always traveled a lot and had rarely been at home during Bryce's childhood. "I don't want to be away from my wife or my daughter." Like his dad had been away from him. Like Bryce had been away from Liberty during their marriage. Deflated, he leaned back and rested his head on the headrest. "I really don't know."

"You're asking the wrong guy here." Logan slowed as he turned on Main Street. The solar-powered lanterns hanging on leafless trees on Main and the sparkling lights interwoven across the street were a reminder that Christmas was a week away.

"Let's call Eric," Logan continued.

Yes. Why hadn't Bryce thought of that right away? Logan's big brother was Bryce's best hope, his only friend with children.

Once Logan parallel parked in front of an A-frame building, he patted his coat's pocket and pulled out something. "Before I forget, Iris wanted me to give you this."

Bryce took a small Ziploc bag from his friend. A ring rolled inside it. Pulling it out, he ran his thumb over the double heart diamonds in the center. The engraving on her ring was slightly different from his. Hers had Liberty on one side and Bryce on the other side with I love you engraved inside the ring.

"I heard Liberty fell apart when she thought she'd lost her ring," Logan said.

"Thanks." Bryce slid the ring back into the bag as last night's time with Liberty came to mind.

He'd seen the ring mark, and when he touched her finger, she talked about her panic on Friday before she arrived at the cabin. The most encouraging thing was that they both still loved each other.

CHAPTER 10

Sitting in the car in Mom's driveway didn't seem to help while Liberty's mind was spinning from encountering Bryce at the cabin. Their time together all seemed surreal. She turned off the engine and patted her warm cheeks, needing to wake up from her daze.

In a few hours, daylight would disappear since the sun that had peaked in the sky earlier was no longer in sight. Now, she closed her eyes to say a prayer of thanks to God for a safe trip. Then a prayer that Mom would understand why Liberty agreed to have Bryce back in their lives.

She reached for her purse from the back seat. She'd transferred Myra's car seat base into Bryce's Jeep, and although driving such an elevated vehicle seemed strange, everything felt right with Bryce's familiar scent dominating the Jeep.

Besides the photos she saw of her dad, Myra would now get a whiff of him in the car on their drive back home. Not that an eighteen-month-old would understand, but smells were powerful sometimes.

Sucking in a deep breath, Liberty stepped out of the Jeep. She walked toward the garage, careful not to slip on the icy snow. She'd better shovel before she left.

Besides the two lit reindeers in Mom's yard, the Christmas wreath dominating half of the front door offered the only other decoration Mom put outside each year. It was still better than what Liberty had on her house.

Going in through the garage, she punched in the code to let herself into the house.

As soon as she hugged Myra and filled Mom in, she'd be back to shovel and deice the driveway so Mom didn't slip.

Myra's babbling had Liberty's feet speed her stride, and she swung open the door to the kitchen. Her heart galloped in anticipation.

"Hello." She set her purse on the kitchen counter.

"I think Mommy is here." Mom's voice sounded from behind the wall separating the kitchen from the living room.

"Mama!" Myra's tiny voice rang out as Liberty struggled to yank the safety lock from the baby gate. When Myra saw Liberty, she took off in the cutest run-waddle—slipping a few times on the linoleum floors—until she plowed right into the gate.

"Slow down, baby." Mom followed from behind, smiling at her grandbaby.

"Mama!" Myra jumped up and down, fussing. Her purple onesie was tucked into pink leggings. Liberty was trying hard to yank the safety latch.

"I'm here, Starlight." The silly lock wouldn't open.

The urge to swoop up her daughter intensified, so Liberty swung one leg over the gate, then another, as Mom laughed while moving Myra out of the way. Finally, Liberty knelt on the floor and scooped Myra up. "Mmm."

Myra slobbered her face with a wet kiss, and Liberty squeezed her tight. She cooed, swinging her side to side. "Were you good for Grandma?"

Myra's soft hair rubbed against Liberty's neck when she pressed her head to Liberty's chest.

"She was good." Mom yawned. Her rumpled dark hair with gray streaks would look better in a ponytail at times like this.

"How are you doing, Mom?"

Mom spread her arms out, and Liberty extended her other hand to pull her mom into a hug.

"I had a good time with my granddaughter."

Liberty cast a glance at Mom's living room littered with blocks and colorful toys. She'd have to clean that before she left. "Did she sleep for you?"

"It was as if she knew you were coming back today." Mom brushed a stray strand of hair from Myra's forehead. "She didn't sleep well last night and didn't take a nap today."

Myra's little fingers felt grimy around her neck as she moved them around.

"I'll just put her down early tonight." After Liberty's loving on Myra, hugging and kissing her, the little one grew restless in her arms and started to wiggle out.

Liberty put her down, and Myra wandered off to the toys on the floor. Then Liberty hugged Mom again. "Thank you for watching her."

Mom kissed her cheek. "You should stop thanking me whenever I watch her." She then ushered Liberty to the brown sofa in the living room. "Now that she doesn't need to be breastfed, you should go out more often."

There went Mom again, worried Liberty would end up alone.

"You should sign up for the spring singles retreat." Mom sank onto the couch, and Liberty settled for the floor on the tan rug with sprigs of brown while Mom folded her hands in her lap. "I know you're still bent on Bryce coming back and—"

"About Bryce." Liberty braved meeting Mom's gaze, but Myra chose that moment to hand her a rattle. Liberty thanked her daughter before she waddled back to the toy bin in the corner.

Head cocked to one side, lips pressed flat, Mom seemed to be waiting for Liberty to finish her sentence, so she did. "I saw him this weekend."

Mom's mouth opened, then closed, and opened again.

"Didn't you go—"

"At the cabin, it was just the two of us."

While Mom's eyes widened, Liberty rocked a bit, ducking her head as she gave a summary of Iris and Logan's matchmaking efforts. She told her all she could remember but left out last night's details.

"How did he react?" Mom leaned over and placed her hands on Liberty's cheeks, tipping her face up to meet her eyes.

The worry in her dark eyes made sense since Mom had feared Bryce wouldn't be ready to be a dad while he was a busy entrepreneur.

"He was so mad because I didn't tell him." Liberty accepted another toy from Myra, but this time, she kept her gaze on Mom as she shared their reconciliation.

Mom's hands fell away, and she slid from the couch to sit next to Liberty, draping an arm around her shoulder while Liberty talked.

Tears burned the back of her throat as she remembered his reaction when he saw Myra's photos and videos. "He cried."

Silent now, Mom took in Liberty's words, a finger tapping her chin.

"Go ahead and say it."

"All right." Mom tipped her head and swept her with a critical gaze. "You look rested. Happy."

Liberty gave her eyes a gentle roll. "I'm always happy."

"Do you know I've been praying for Bryce to come back to you?"

Wait a minute. Liberty's head jerked up, and her mouth slid open. Hadn't Mom just been pushing her to go to the singles retreat? "Why didn't you tell me? A few minutes ago, you encouraged me to—"

"You were so determined to never call Bryce." Mom pointed a finger at her. "Ever since you ran off with the hippie guy, I learned to let you make your own decisions."

Liberty had almost not graduated when she dated a hippie who wanted to travel from one city to another while they played music.

After only three days of camping with the guy's family, Liberty had known they were comfortable skipping showers for an entire week. "Okay, that was the best lesson for me too."

She suppressed a shudder. That experience kept her from dating, terrified to make another wrong decision until she met Bryce.

"You've always learned by experience rather than me telling you what you should and shouldn't do."

She pressed her lips tight, holding back. Where was Mom going with this?

"I thought, if I push you to go to the retreat, you would call Bryce." Mom tugged at Liberty's sleeve to straighten out her V-neck sweater like Liberty was a little girl. "Don't forget all the times Bryce called my cell that first year after you left him and how you told me to ignore his calls."

Liberty batted Mom's hand away, shrugging her shirt back into place. "I was young, Mom."

Was? She still had a lot to learn, but she wanted to stay and grow in her marriage.

"Bryce isn't who I'm worried about though." Mom slumped back against the front of the couch, one arm on the cushioned corduroy seat behind her, and Liberty didn't have to ask. Myra returned with her fuzzy blanket and plopped on Liberty's lap. "Where does Wendy fit into the equation?"

"I told Bryce we should hold off on telling her about Myra."

Mom's brows squeezed together as if fighting the same questions Liberty had. "And you think he will keep this secret from his mom?"

"He will." He'd meant what he said. "And... well, a part of me wants to believe maybe Wendy has changed." By now, she shouldn't do insane things like taking Myra away from her or using threats to keep her son from marrying whomever he saw fit.

The conversation shifted to work, and Mom filled her in on the basics and scheduling conflicts for Sunday and that day, being snow days. "It ended up working out, though."

Liberty drew out a breath. So things had worked out in her absence. She needed to recruit more people as soon as the year ended. If she had fifteen employees and somehow two or three couldn't show up on a whim, it wouldn't leave her hanging. Liberty then patted her daughter's hair as the little one snuggled into her chest. "I'm also thinking of having Bryce come and see Myra tomorrow." He only had until the twenty-sixth before he left town.

"Just remember Wendy will always be the mother of your husband and now a grandma to your child." Mom's warning words carried no judgment, but rather a caution to tread carefully. "Wendy can't ever take your place in Bryce's life, and the sooner she learns that the better it will be for all of us."

Liberty cuddled her daughter, breathing in the sweet baby scent of her and hoping Mom's prayers for their reunion would get them through the tough days ahead. "I still can't believe you prayed about Bryce."

Mom tilted her head to the side. "Just because you have a challenging mother-in-law, doesn't mean God wants you to walk away from your marriage."

Liberty was still an infant in her faith with some of these things.

As Mom touched her arm, she added, "You need to keep praying for Bryce, that he can learn to stand up for himself against his mom, to stand up for you."

"And to know Jesus."

"That's true." Mom patted Liberty. "And Wendy too."

May God help Liberty to get the strength to pray for Wendy.

Mom had always been so wise, and even in the days when Liberty ignored her advice, deep down, she'd known she had the best mom in the world. "Thank you, Mom." Liberty squeezed Myra instead, kissing her, wanting to be the kind of mother her mom had been. Strong and loving, sacrificial for everything… and she told her so.

Mom's chest rose as she sat straighter. "I had no idea what I was doing when I was raising you."

Liberty shrugged. "Besides me being a little rebellious, I turned out decent." After a few life lessons, of course.

Mom nodded as her cheeks lifted. "I'm so glad you didn't end up marrying that band guy."

The worst mistake Liberty could've ever made. Although she'd continued to date the hippie after she resigned from traveling with him, it hadn't been hard for her to break up with him three months later.

"I'm glad too."

It was time for Mom to find her happily ever after as well. "We should invite Abe over for dinner sometime."

A shy smile curved Mom's lips when she crisscrossed her legs. "I'm too old for romance."

"I'm sure Abe isn't much older than you."

"I'm not interested."

Liberty had taken interest in the widower's appearance on Sundays whenever he and Mom talked in the lobby after church.

"But Abe is." Two Sundays ago, Mom had fidgeted and patted her hair when Abe walked toward them. "He usually has an extra ticket to a play or movie, one of these days you should go."

Mom shook her head, covering her mouth with her hands.

Myra was getting cozy against Liberty's chest, and she didn't want her to fall asleep. "I need to get her home." She then kissed Myra's head, soft baby shampoo wafting from her little one's hair. Pushing up from the comfy rug, Liberty told Mom to keep an eye on Myra while Liberty shoveled.

Mom's face folded in a frown, struggling as usual when Liberty shoveled.

"I don't have back problems, Mom." Liberty had to remind her often why she didn't mind shoveling. Unlike Mom, Liberty didn't have to worry about shoveling since her landlord paid for such services.

WITH MYRA STILL WIDE-eyed after her bath, several hours later, Liberty could only assume her daughter was excited about a bedtime story rather than her tiredness growing into restlessness.

Already in her Tinker Bell footie pajamas, Myra cuddled into Liberty's arms as she carried her to her room and turned on the lamp next to the white rocker and book display shelf.

Knowing the routine, Myra pulled out her book for story time while Liberty sank onto the rocking chair.

Depending on a given day, Liberty usually read two to three books for Myra's bedtime.

Myra picked out *Goodnight Moon*, and the small picture book Liberty had compiled with photos of Myra's family members.

As Liberty opened the photo book with the picture on the first page, Myra, as usual, blurted out, "Dada."

She tapped her little finger on the picture.

"Yes. It's Dada."

Even before Liberty had expected to see Bryce, she'd wanted her daughter to know she had a dad somewhere. Her heart squeezed as a longing for Bryce tightened in her chest.

"Mama, Dada." The little voice pulled her back.

"Yes, baby." Liberty touched the photo, her hand lingering on Bryce's cheek. Would it be so awkward to call him tonight? A video call so he could at least see his daughter?

She lost the reason for Myra's routine, and the book dropped to the carpet when she stood with Myra and hoisted her to her hip. "Let's go call Dada."

"Dada?"

It had to be close to seven. Beyond the split curtain in Myra's window, darkness had fallen outside.

When they made it to the living room, Liberty found her purse on the couch and dug out her phone. She scrolled for Bryce's number, pressed the camera icon next to his name, and tapped the call button.

As she sat on the couch with Myra on her lap, Liberty's hand trembled, and the phone rang. This was a terrible idea. She was about to turn off the phone when Myra yanked it out of her hand, just about the same time Bryce answered.

"Oh, hi there?" His voice was gentle, and when Liberty glanced at the phone in Myra's hand, Bryce's picture displayed on the screen.

"Dada!" Myra burst into laughter, glancing at Liberty, then the screen. Her little shoulders shook, and Liberty shifted Myra on her lap, then centered the phone between her and Myra.

The dim light behind Bryce lit his toothy grin. Music and people talking through his background made Liberty doubt her impulsiveness to call.

Where was he?

"I'll be right back," she heard Bryce's voice over the noise. There was probably a party at his house, and—Oh no, what if Wendy eavesdropped on his conversation? "Sorry to bother you."

"You're not bothering me." His voice trembled, and the screen went blank, silent.

A frown replaced Myra's smile as she stared at the blank screen. Then the background noise vanished too.

"I had to get back to the car." Bryce's face reappeared again, and Myra bounced on Liberty's lap.

"Is your mom—?"

"I'm not home yet," Bryce cut off Liberty's question. "Logan—"

"Dada!" Myra kept screeching, laughter burbling in her voice, and she snatched the phone from Liberty.

"My–ra?" Bryce's voice lilted, catching and roughening. "She knows me?"

She had to have recognized him. He still looked the same. "We look at your photos every day. It's part of her story time."

Myra jabbed the screen with her finger, her eyes squinting. The poor girl was probably confused why the person who looked like a photo in a book was talking.

"Can I..." Bryce shuddered as his voice tremored. "I'm your daddy."

Liberty touched his face on the phone, aching and furious for having kept Myra away from a dad who loved her. "Yes. You are... her daddy," she whispered, struggling to find her voice.

"My... my..." Bryce said.

Myra was punching on the phone nonstop, then tugging Liberty's hand so she could take control, and it was getting hard to talk with her babbling out her excitement.

"I wanted you to say good night." Liberty's voice rose over her daughter's nonsensical words. "I'll see you soon—"

The words died when Myra turned off the phone. She then slid off Liberty's lap and darted for her toy kitchen next to the TV cabinet. Thankfully, Liberty had bought an enclosed cabinet to keep Myra from ramming herself into it.

After another two hours of her playing with the toy kitchen and stacking blocks, drinking milk, and having another bath and story time, Myra fell asleep.

Given the long day, Liberty was surprised Myra woke up twice in the night. Too spent to go back and forth to Myra's room, Liberty gave in to bringing the baby into her room in the portable bed she kept there.

It was a blessing when Myra slept in that morning while Liberty read her Bible, prayed, and worked on making the employees' Christmas week schedule. Whether she would have people sign up for the shifts even with bonus pay was another thing entirely.

By the time she looked at her phone, she had a few text messages. One from Iris, a group text to Tessa and Liberty. She wanted to meet sometime tomorrow for lunch or tea and added for Liberty to bring Starlight along.

Liberty needed this meeting with her friends to talk about everything.

Another text came from Bryce: I loved meeting Myra last night.
She responded.
Liberty: She liked meeting you too.
Bryce: I didn't sleep.
That was probably her fault.
Liberty: I shouldn't have called you. I'm sorry.
Bryce: Glad you did. Is today too soon?
Today was perfect, but she needed to figure out her schedule first. At nine, she should know whether she needed to go to work or not. By then, people usually messaged to cancel their shifts. So she typed.
Liberty: I'll text you later. I miss you.
Bryce: Counting down the minutes till I see you both.
Adrenaline spiked, leaving her wishing she could cancel everything to keep her day available for Bryce. With renewed strength, she was determined to get things done as fast as possible.

CHAPTER 11

Bryce walked from one room to another, his shoes clicking on the tiles while he checked and listened for any beeping on his phone. He'd just concluded a ten o'clock virtual meeting with Harold and Jeff, two of his business partners, as they met with Javir. He was pitching his new invention—a smart watch with a built-in voice sensor to assist the blind when they went shopping. They already had apps that could read labels on the shelf, but Javir's idea of a watch with no need to upload apps was a sleek idea.

Bryce was sold on the idea, but his partners had been polite and listened to the client, then suggested Javir seek out Angel Investors who were always looking for new businesses. Any new invention could be a risky investment, no doubt. But wasn't any risk worth it, if such inventions could also take off and improve people's lives—the main thing about investing that appealed to Bryce since earning money was no longer his primary goal. However, his partners insisted Javir's product didn't contain enough new benefits to distinguish it from the apps and other assistance devices already available.

As a venture capital firm, they played it safe by investing in solid, well-established companies. Bryce's passion didn't help on days like today when he had a good feeling about Javir's idea. If investors hadn't taken a risk in supporting their tech company during its early stages, Bryce and his partners wouldn't be where they were.

Perhaps he could go in alone and give Javir's idea the chance to take off. Sure, the startup may never become an industry leader, but anything could happen in business.

Close to noon, thirty minutes after the meeting ended, he received Liberty's text. She'd had to fill in for one of her employees, but she texted her address and suggested he stop by her house at five.

Even if Liberty didn't ask for his help, he wanted to help take care of Myra, but he had no idea what to do with a toddler. While he couldn't help babysit, there had to be other ways to help.

As he settled in the back room with panoramic windows, the room where he'd first fallen in love with Liberty, Bryce sat on the couch with his laptop. In the search, he typed "how to run a caregiver business." He needed an idea of how that business worked, so he could understand how to help her.

As he read the things required to run a smooth operation, one stood out the most—hiring a scheduler. If she had a scheduler, perhaps things would be easier for her.

Hoping he wasn't overstepping, he called the number of a small local company. If Liberty thought he was out of line, he'd call it his Christmas gift. Thank goodness for Christmas.

The call went to voicemail, so he left a message requesting someone call him back.

After answering some work emails, he headed to the kitchen and slugged down a protein shake. He wasn't hungry enough for a meal—not when he was a mix of nerves and excitement to see his daughter—so he dodged Rita's requests to make him something more substantial, then rinsed his cup in the sink.

Thankfully, Mom was out and about handling vendors or whatever she did while planning Christmas parties. Bryce didn't intend to tell her where he was going tonight. He'd dried his hands and headed to the garage when Dad emerged from upstairs.

"Glad I caught you, son." Dad clamped a hand on Bryce's shoulder. "I was hoping we could go to the country club and play racquetball. It's been a while since we had any one-on-one." Releasing his grip, he raised a gray brow, one side of his mouth quirking into a smile, which Bryce easily returned.

"Since I rarely see you, sir, that's not an offer I can turn down. I'll drive us." Bryce jiggled the keys already in his hand. Maybe he'd have the chance to talk Dad into taking a shopping trip after their game.

As he backed his Land Rover out of the garage into the gray-sky day, Bryce winked at his dad. "Not surprised you picked racquetball. You know I'm terrible at it."

"You mean to say all the lessons I gave you were wasted?" Dad laughed, the motion shaking the shaggy gray-streaked brown hair he always had cut at a uniform three inches long, with no shape whatsoever, and kept combed back from his forehead.

"I probably needed more than three lessons." The moment the words came out, Bryce winced and took his gaze off the driveway to glance at Dad. Dad had given him those lessons and been patient with them too. Now, he fisted his knuckles on his sports pants as he stared at the snow-covered grounds. Oops. Bryce better smooth that thoughtless remark over. "I mean, I guess racquetball has never been my thing."

"It's not too late to learn." Dad kept his face averted, his voice a whisper as he adjusted the collar of his white polo.

Perhaps a different subject would be best.

Although Bryce hadn't been too close to Dad while growing up, they'd bonded after Bryce left home. Dad visited him twice a month at Harvard. Even when Bryce switched to NYU for business school, Dad initiated visits that didn't coincide with Mom's stay in the Hamptons.

"Liberty is giving me another chance." No better subject could clear the awkwardness than Bryce's love life. "I'm meeting with her tonight."

Shifting in his seat, Dad patted Bryce's knee. "That's wonderful, son."

His response wasn't a surprise. Dad was never against Bryce's relationship with Liberty.

Bryce steered around the bend from their twenty-acre property and to the unpaved road.

"You think it is?" He needed more family support and assurance this would work out.

"How are you planning to tell your mother?"

Right, Dad would know Bryce hadn't talked to Mom yet. Bryce twisted his grip on the steering wheel. "You think she will give me a pat on the back?"

As Dad cleared his throat, Bryce kept his focus on his approach to I-85.

"Liberty always made you happy."

If only Dad had chimed in whenever Mom bashed Liberty. Well, maybe even that wouldn't have given Bryce the confidence to stand up for his wife. After all, no one stood up to Mom in their family.

"Why do you let Mom walk all over you?" Whoa. He hadn't intended to blurt that out, not after so many years of keeping things to himself. Bryce opened his mouth to take back the question, but as he stopped at a red light, he glanced at Dad, who sat there clenching his jaw.

It was probably best not to ask any more questions. Maybe he would just turn on the radio. He'd almost reached for the dial when Dad spoke.

"If you and Liberty ever have a child, you'll understand. Sometimes you have to play the fool."

I already have a child.

Wait a minute. Was Dad saying his distance from home and putting up with Mom's insults had everything to do with him protecting Bryce? He could've divorced Mom a long time ago.

Bryce let his foot off the gas when the light turned green. But if they were having a heart-to-heart, he had to know one more thing. "Do you and Mom love each other?"

Dad choked out a mirthless laugh, his gaze focusing through the passenger window. "Once upon a time, your mom was my world." Pain grated against the rough edges of his voice. "She's your mother."

That still didn't answer whether he still loved Mom.

Engraved in limestone, the words *Pleasant View Country Club* came into view, and Bryce drove toward the wide-open black double gate.

"Why are you together if you don't love each other anymore?"

"Sometimes you have to weigh the consequences, the aftermath, before you make a decision." Dad's answer only confirmed what he knew.

Bryce's heart ached as he snuck a peek at his father. Dad's burdens weighed heavily on his slumped shoulders. If Mom overwhelmed Bryce at times, what had she done to Dad, who was married to her?

"I'm sorry." The words slipping off his tongue encompassed so many sorries. Sorry for thinking his dad was avoiding him during his childhood. Sorry for taking Mom's side in arguments. Sorry for not being able to help his father build a better life. Dad worked so hard to provide Bryce and Mom with a luxurious lifestyle and deserved so much more from them, from life. "I want you to be happy."

"Divorcing your mother wouldn't be a picnic." Dad's voice was low, his words distant as he rubbed his chin, lost in thought.

Bryce now understood the strength in Dad's silence. He was in the relationship for the sake of keeping their family together. As if sensing Bryce's internal assumptions, Dad added, "My job keeps me busy enough. Don't worry about me."

With his mind spinning, Bryce drove below the building into the heated underground garage. Without Dad knowing it, he'd just taught Bryce the value of family, endurance, and patience. If Dad could put up with Mom, even without his wife's affection, how could Bryce ever not fight to make things work with Liberty?

HOURS LATER, THE GARAGE lights lit a path for Bryce to Liberty's front door. With his heart pounding and his hands shaking, surely the small gift bag he carried would slip and fall at any moment. He pulled the hoodie of his plaid flannel from his head, despite the snow-covered ground. Even as shaken up as he was, his body was heating up. Meeting his daughter thrilled and terrified him, bringing sweats and chills in waves.

Would she accept him, would she giggle like she'd done on the phone, or would she cry when she saw a strange man?

After playing racquetball, he'd showered at the gym and changed into Levi's and a cream flannel shirt. He'd then dropped off Dad and avoided going back into the house.

Since he'd had less time to shop, he drove to Main Street and stopped at one of the toy stores. Although Liberty had told him Myra loved stuffed animals, she must have a few of those by now.

Overwhelmed by the choices, he'd called Eric for toy ideas and was told to buy anything that made noise. Being a bike lover, Bryce bought an indoor tricycle, but the box was so big he left it in the car for now. Maybe he wouldn't give it to her. These cookie-cutter single-family homes built so close to each other didn't appear to offer much floor space. Liberty may not want the baby cruising in the house with it.

He switched the bag to his other hand, staring at the red door, and took a slow breath, then another. Closing his eyes, he rubbed the back of his neck, frighteningly light-headed. Man, it felt as if waiting for Judgment Day by an eighteen-month-old—the same judgment he'd passed on to his dad all those years.

He reopened his eyes, facing the white sign hanging from the door. Above an artsy outline of poinsettias, the word *Rejoice* arched like a promise in red font to match the door.

He eyed the house next door, then the next, taking in the area. Christmas lights sparkled as if offering hope to his doubtful heart. Liberty's house was one of the few without lights. She was always into Christmas, but now, when would she have time to decorate?

Time to knock. He could do this. Taking a deep breath, he sensed a glimmer of something for the first time, as if there could be a higher power—God.

The day he'd driven to the cabin, he'd wondered if there was a God of miracles, who could bring Liberty back into his life.

Is that You, God? What did God look like, anyway? *Again, if You are there, let tonight be successful as I meet my daughter.*

Bryce's heart thundered as a child's laugh compelled him to lift his hand and press the square button on the doorframe.

Muffled footsteps approached, and he squared his shoulders, composing himself. When the door swung open, the air nearly left his lungs at the sight of his two precious girls.

"Welcome." Liberty's brown eyes sparkled beneath the light streaming around her in the front room. Her hair cascaded over her shoulders onto a V-necked red dress—a dress matching the child's hoisted on her hip.

Bryce gazed at his daughter. Her big eyes gleamed under the porch light as she scrutinized him as if wondering where she'd seen him. Although afraid to frighten her, he couldn't help but ruffle his daughter's curls. They whispered against his palm, as soft as spun silk. "Hello, Myra."

"Dada?" She tapped at Liberty's chest, then pivoted back at Bryce.

"It's Da...da." Bryce spoke over a sudden lump, his heart melting.

"It's cold. Come in." Liberty ushered him in, and the warm air heated him. Or maybe it was more than just the air. Maybe it was the feeling of welcome, of coming home. The smell of cinnamon and pine hung in the air. The dull tree in the corner of her living room must be fresh.

"When did you get the tree?"

Ducking her head, Liberty smiled shyly. "I got it today. Can you tell?"

Besides the toys scattered underneath it, the tree didn't have a single decoration.

"Myra will yank off all the ornaments. But I still want us to decorate the tree with you."

"I'd–I'd love that." When he looked at Myra again, she'd tucked her head against Liberty's chest, but her gaze remained intent on him.

He walked closer to narrow the gap between them, then kissed Liberty on the lips before burying his nose in Myra's soft curls and savoring her sweet scent, slightly soapy from a recent bath. Liberty's vanilla-scented hair mixed with Myra's baby smell felt like home.

Little fingers crept on his neck. "Dada?" Then the baby wiggled, and her weight was leaning into him.

"You want to go to Dada?" Liberty smiled between them.

Bryce dropped the bag in his hand to the hardwood floor so he could hold the baby—his baby. Joy lifted his chest. He hadn't expected his daughter's acceptance right away.

"I'm Dada." His voice shook as he closed his eyes and squeezed Myra tight. "I can't believe she's letting me hold her."

At the sniffling, he opened his eyes and caught Liberty swiping at her tears. "She knows who you are."

Almost half the battle was won.

"Let's go have a seat." She led the way to the seating area, her familiar curves swaying beneath the sweater-like dress. The moment he
sat with Myra on the lime-green faux-leather couch, he remembered
the bag he'd dropped at the doorway and told Liberty it was hers.

While she left to fetch it, Myra touched Bryce's buttons on his
flannel, then his clean-shaven jaw. She was the most beautiful toddler
he'd ever seen. He didn't understand what Liberty meant when she'd
said at the cabin about Myra having his eyes, but it was hard to tell
the toddler's eye color with the dull fluorescent light. He guessed
them to be brown like her mom's. He couldn't help but squeeze her
tiny frame in a hug, then kiss her head. Could all this be real, or was
he dreaming?

"Oudi." Myra pointed to the kitchen and wiggled on his lap.
"Oudi."

"What does she mean?" he asked Liberty as she reappeared at
their side.

"She wants her water." Liberty started toward the kitchen.

But Bryce stilled her with a hand on her arm. "Is it okay if I go
with her to get it?"

"It's in the fridge."

Myra was already sliding from his lap, so he followed her. Her little wobble and unsteady footsteps were so fascinating to watch, and
he couldn't stop grinning.

A roadblock of a white gate blocked the kitchen entryway, so he
had to call Liberty to help him out. She twisted something, and the
gate flew open. She then left him and Myra to fend for themselves.

The front of the fridge was full with nicely decorated frames of
Myra's photos. No doubt, Liberty had decorated the frames.

As soon as he opened the fridge, Myra snatched up a pink sippy
cup with a cartoon character.

Bryce's chest puffed in anticipation of getting her gift as they
walked back to the living room. Although not spacious, the unclut-

tered house offered enough room for Myra to scoot around on her toy.

Liberty was on the couch, pulling out the black velvet box from the bag.

Since Myra was more interested in emptying the toy basket, Bryce approached his wife. "We have such a beautiful baby."

"Yes, we do."

He knelt on the creamy rug and took the box from her, setting it on the table. "I'm so proud of you." How she'd managed on her own to take care of their daughter.

"I wouldn't have made it without God's help. And Mom."

He'd never felt more compelled to know about God than he did now, but that could wait. He slid the ring from his shirt pocket and retrieved it from the Ziploc bag. "I'm honored to deliver this."

Liberty gasped, her lips dancing with a smile as she held out her unsteady left hand.

"Liberty Solace, I don't deserve you—"

"I don't deserve you either, but—"

"—we have one thing in common—"

"Love." Her eyes locked with his, and something deep, warm, and tender swelled through him. Small diamonds danced beneath the light as he slid the ring on his wife's finger. He then leaned in, cupped her face between his hands, burrowed his fingers into the back of her head, and slanted his mouth over hers. Soft and tender, this kiss was a reopening and a start to a new beginning.

"Oh, Bryce." With her hands against his chest after the brief kiss, her eyes were dreamy, the way she'd always looked at him. And his chest swelled beneath her palms as relief overtook him. She still held the same sweet familiar affection for him.

He reached for the box on the table. "May I?"

The glittering trifle sparkled, slinking across his fingers as he unhooked the necklace from its velvet case and released its clasp.

Liberty slid to the coffee table with her back to him and gathered her hair off to one side. "I still have the one you got me last time."

"It's time you get another."

"It's beautiful."

He threaded the necklace around her throat, unable to resist tracing a finger along her delicate skin. "Not as beautiful as you." He then kissed her neck and thrilled when she shivered. "I brought something for Myra too."

Liberty laughed, spinning toward him with a little clap when he told her what it was. Honestly, she looked more excited about the simple toy for their daughter than she had the expensive designer necklace. "She'll love it."

He chuckled. "I got her a tricycle, but I'm afraid I haven't brought your vehicle over. I haven't heard anything yet about when they can unearth it."

"Thank you for letting me borrow your Jeep."

"It's *our* Jeep." He stood and walked toward the door for Myra's gift.

Although big, the box wasn't heavy when he carried it back to the house, but if he'd known how many straps and ties were attached to the toy, he'd have had the store reps open it before he left.

Impatient little fingers kept yanking the toy out of his hand. Liberty did her best to hold Myra back while Bryce equally did his best not to toss the tricycle into the wall. By the time he'd freed the toy, he was as breathless as if he'd just biked the steepest mountain.

He sank onto the cream carpet, hugging his knees. Joy lifted his chest when Myra's eyes lit up as she pressed one noisy button after another.

Blinking signal lights, honking horns, and music of all sorts provided a cacophony new to his world. "Looks like someone knows what to do with this."

Myra scooted the toy toward the door, then back to the living room.

They spent the next several minutes watching Myra play before Liberty served him chicken parmigiana and asparagus—Bryce's favorite meal of hers. She'd cooked it earlier and kept it warm in the Crock-Pot.

While they ate around the kitchen table, Bryce was torn between staring at his wife or Myra strapped in the high chair. Her little fingers grasped the chopped pieces of peas and pinwheel-shaped pasta. The way she chewed was incredible.

"How many teeth does she have?"

He'd only seen a few front teeth.

"Four on the bottom and four on top."

Wanting to know everything about their toddler, he asked a handful of questions as they ate. Liberty was patient when she explained to the best of her knowledge.

Bryce enjoyed the dinner, but he'd already known Liberty was an incredible cook.

When he complimented her, she waved her spoon at him. "I only know how to cook your favorite food."

How did he get so lucky? "I'm so lucky."

She squished her face, then frowned, and focused on feeding Myra. "How did you get away from your mom?"

Her sudden question made him reach for his water. He took a sip and set it back on the table. "She's planning a Christmas party, so I haven't seen her much today. But I had an amazing time with Dad...."

Her shoulders fell when he shared what he'd learned about those extended work trips that broke his heart as a child. "I always knew your dad used work as an escape."

A part of Bryce had known as well, but another part of him had wondered if he'd been the cause.

Liberty wiped Myra's pudgy cheeks, then reached across the table, and grasped his hands. "I'll be praying for him." She squeezed his fingers. "And your mom too."

She didn't have to pray for his mom, but that had been one of the things he liked about Liberty—she'd always done her best to stay optimistic in any given circumstance, to do her best by those around her.

As if hearing his thoughts, she freed her hands and patted his before wagging a finger at him, her dimples flashing. "That doesn't mean I'll be friends with her, though."

"I understand, Dimples." And he did.

Myra started fussing and putting the peas and pasta in her hair.

"Bath time." Liberty scooped her from her high chair. And as soon as Bryce helped clean the dishes, he followed Liberty and Myra to the bathroom.

He didn't want to miss anything. So he held the towel Liberty offered him and squatted a few feet away as Liberty poured a dollop of baby soap into her palm and lathered it on Myra's back. She then washed the baby's hair.

Myra clapped, splashing water on herself and her mom.

"I'm surprised she doesn't cry."

"She loves to swim." Liberty took the towel and wrapped it around Myra, cuddling the hood to her hair. "She thinks the bath is a pool."

Minutes later, Myra lay on what Liberty called a changing table in her bedroom while Liberty diapered her and then slid her into footie pajamas. Then Liberty announced bedtime story, and Myra toddled across the plush cream carpet to the display shelf and handed Liberty two books.

Bryce's chest constricted. This little bundle of cuteness understood what was going on around her! Fascinated, he grinned at Liberty.

She grinned back. "Would you like to read her bedtime story?"

He'd never done it before. He palmed the back of his neck, rubbing at the sudden tension as if he were about to do a presentation before an investor group. "Um, sure."

Liberty nodded to the white wooden rocker next to the lamp, so he sank into it.

While Liberty sat on a colorful ABC rug, she lowered her face to her daughter. "Myra, take the books to Dada."

Myra did as asked and then waved her chubby little hands up to Bryce. Dimples flashed on her knuckles as she opened and closed her fingers.

"She sits on your lap when you read."

Ah, that made sense. Bryce scooped Myra to his lap, warmth bubbling in his heart.

Opening and closing her hand in a gripping motion, Myra pointed to the crib several feet away. "Banki."

Liberty stood, left for the white crib, and returned with a pink blanket where a fleecy printed teddy bear cuddled into the flannel.

While Bryce read *Where the Wild Things Are*, Myra's little body shook against his chest, chortling whenever he pointed at the strange-looking creatures. Her laughter inspired him to add animation to his voice. He had no clue he could fake voices.

Now and then, he sneaked a glance at Liberty, and she flashed a thumbs-up.

The next book squeezed his heart. A photo book with family members. When he opened to his picture on the first page, Myra squealed, "Dada!" At the next photo, she called out, "Mama!"

"Nana." Her little finger tapped Rhonda's photo. The next two pages had him blinking—Mom and Dad's photos.

Myra called them by Nana, Papa.

Family. Like Dad, Liberty valued family. She put up with his mom for the sake of keeping the family together.

When Liberty carried Myra to the crib, Bryce imitated Liberty when giving their daughter a good night kiss. She then asked a speaker to play "Silent Night." As she switched off the lamp, a snowflake-shaped light plugged into a wall sent dim light into the room before they walked out, closing the door quietly.

"She likes to sleep with the light on?" he asked as they walked through a dark hallway back to the living room.

"My fault for not teaching her to sleep in the dark."

"She also likes to sleep with the music?"

"I only use it on days when she's restless. She had a sleepless night before I returned from the cabin, so she's still a bit off-schedule."

He wanted to help in any way, but everything with fatherhood was foreign to him. "I don't know what I'm supposed to do, Dimples." He raised both hands, empty and helpless, when they were back in the living room, then flopped on the sofa, the faux-leather cushion cold beneath him. "I want to be a good dad. I want to be a good husband."

"You're off to a great start." She tucked a knee beneath herself as she sat beside him and squeezed his hand. "You did great with Myra."

A strange catch lurched his heartbeat. "You think?"

She nodded, and warmth cascaded through him over how she'd made him a part of Myra's bedtime routine. He hadn't had enough of his daughter. His wife too, but he'd never watched a baby sleep before. "If I go and watch her sleep, will she wake up?"

"Let's give her a few minutes to unwind. Then you can go back in."

In the meantime, he got reacquainted with his wife and asked about her workday. Questions he'd wondered about since she'd texted him earlier that day.

"What do you do with Myra if your mom is scheduled to work?"

"I take her with me sometimes. Like today."

He inched closer, savoring her vanilla scent while she spoke of the clients who loved the companionship and appreciated her bringing Myra along. "We don't stay longer than two hours, so she doesn't break their china cabinets."

She brought up some of the most fascinating things about her job, and he laughed as she recounted some unusual incidents. As she spoke about certain clients by name, her flashing eyes and peek-a-boo dimples said she found her job rewarding.

Bryce avoided talking about his uncertain plans. He still had no idea how to leave New York for Pleasant View full time.

He couldn't pluck Liberty and Myra from their established lives here, but he wanted to be rooted in their lives.

Later in the night, he sat in the rocking chair as he watched his daughter's chest rise and fall. The night-light cast a glow over her sweet little face as she snuggled her blanket to her chest. His eyelids felt heavy, and the chair's spindly spokes cut into his spine. But there was no better place he'd rather be than in this cozy house with his wife and daughter.

CHAPTER 12

Having four garages had its advantages on days like today when Bryce had had to park the Land Rover and discreetly take an immediate hallway. The perfect detour led the way to his room with little chance of running into his mom.

Last night, he'd forgotten his phone in the car when he walked into Liberty's house. Good thing he'd left it there since he'd found several missed calls and messages from Mom when he checked the phone this morning:

"Call me, please."

"Bryce, you're ignoring me—why? What have I done to deserve this?"

"Please, darling, call."

The last message came in at eight a.m. "Where did you stay last night? If I don't hear from you, I'm going to file a missing person report."

Give me a break! Surely, the police had more to do than to leap at Mom's demands. He was an adult for crying out loud.

The final message was from Dad, a text saying Bryce better join him and Mom for lunch at noon before she went ballistic.

So, Bryce found himself walking to the dining room for an unplanned meal. He wasn't hungry after the fruit and oatmeal he'd shared with his wife and daughter that morning. He'd fallen asleep in Myra's room and woken up that morning with a blanket draped over his chest and feet. He'd then walked to the living room to find Liberty curled on the couch. Overwhelmed by love for his wife and moved by her vulnerability, he'd knelt there and touched her sweet face, eventually startling her awake.

As he approached the dining room now, light streamed through the south-facing window where Mom and Dad sat, both in their own thoughts.

Mom's dark blazer complemented her trim waist and even darker frown as she assessed her manicured nails. Dressed in a blue-striped button-down shirt, Dad hunched over his phone.

The moment Mom saw Bryce, she let out a dramatic gasp. "Oh, darling!"

The ebony chair scraped the marble floor when she pushed it to stand and hurried around the glass table to throw her arms around him. "I was so worried about you."

His muscles stiffened, his embrace not as genuine for his mom, but he wasn't ready to get into it. "I'm a grown man."

He eased out of their brief hug and kissed her cheek. He loved and respected her, which would make the next minutes intense if he brought up Liberty. But he couldn't keep his wife a secret when he intended to be with her from now on.

He moved to sit next to Dad in case he needed to kick his foot under the table for backup—which wouldn't be very discreet with the glass tabletop. He then reached for the water glass from the placemat next to his mom, assuming that had been his planned place setting.

Servers brought food, a big bowl of arugula salad with diced chicken, tomatoes, and other delectable toppings. Another server brought the serving plates and silverware, while someone set bowls of savory soup before them.

Mom's voice came out tight. "Thank you, Karian."

"Thanks," Bryce and Dad added simultaneously.

"Heather"—Mom's voice grated—"tuck your shirt in properly."

"Yes, ma'am." Cheeks flaring red, the young woman ducked her head and pushed in the corners of her shirt.

Poor girl. The employees were diligent in their work, yet Mom could fire them today or tomorrow, leaving a blot on their work record as well as depriving them of income.

As the smell of garlic and grilled chicken permeated the room, his stomach growled. He might be hungry, after all.

Dad scooped the salad using tongs and added it to his plate. He then unfolded the white cloth napkin to retrieve the silverware.

Mom was gnawing her bottom lip, smearing her peachy lipstick, her shoulders tense. Maybe this one time she'd keep thoughts to herself so they could have a normal conversation.

Yawning, Bryce reached for his water to take a sip. He was starting to feel the effects of sleeping in the rocker.

"Where did you stay last night?" Mom folded her hands on the table. She'd have made a great prosecutor if she hadn't set her mind to be a politician, something she'd claimed as a hobby after not making money when she wasn't reappointed as mayor for a second term.

Well, this was it. With her gaze still focused on him, he had no need to lie, and this time, he didn't care about hurting her feelings as long as he was honest. So he cleared his throat. "I've asked Liberty to give me another chance."

Mom gasped and put her hand on her mouth.

As a thick silence passed, Dad winked at Bryce before forking his salad. He didn't even pretend to be surprised.

The plates rattled when Mom slapped the table. "How can you have an appetite?" She scowled at Dad. "Did you hear what your son just said?"

Dad chewed his salad, then nodded.

Mom's jaw twitched before she leveled her glare on Bryce. "And what do you mean *you* asked for another chance?" Her voice rose as he tried to ignore her while he spooned the salad from the serving bowl to his plate.

"Isn't *she* the one who walked away from *you*?"

Good woman, leave me alone. He clamped down the words when she jabbed a finger toward him. Good thing she was across the table. Otherwise, the finger could be used as a weapon against him.

"Did you forget she crushed your heart?"

Because he'd sided with his mom far too many times. "I'm fully responsible for her leaving."

"You're not going to date that woman again." Mom huffed, and her fiery gaze seared Dad. "Tell him. Tell your son how foolish this is."

Dad dabbed a napkin to his mouth, obviously used to tuning her out. But when he glanced in Bryce's direction, those eyes the same gray as Bryce's held a mischief Bryce hadn't seen before. "What your mom is trying to say is that she's not ready for you to become a man."

Bryce covered his hand over his mouth to stifle a chuckle. Dad had a sense of humor after all.

"This is ridiculous." Mom's nostrils flared.

In case she'd forgotten, Bryce lifted his ring finger. "She's my wife."

Wife or not, he *did* need to date her again during their second-honeymoon phase.

Apparently not caring if she ruined her perfectly coiffed hair, Mom dropped both hands on her head as if agonized. "Oh no... Oh no." She shook her head. "Now everything makes sense. You were with her at the cabin. You *lied* to me. That's why you turned off the phone so I didn't call you." She railed on about how Liberty always brought out the worst in Bryce, how she'd messed up his future when she talked him into switching careers, and how he'd always lied to her whenever he snuck out of the house to see Liberty.

"Mom, stop!" Bryce snapped, not meaning to, but he wasn't going to put up with her insulting Liberty to his face. He tossed the napkin on the table and pushed back the chair to stand. "It doesn't matter what you think. Liberty is my wife and will always be."

He started to leave, but Mom yelled, "Don't you dare leave this table, Bryce Ree Solace!"

Whenever Mom called his full name, he would listen and do as told, but his chest was burning as he stormed out of the room.

He could hear Mom still calling. Then came Dad's deep voice. "Let him be."

It must have taken a lot out of Dad to say something of that sort.

The next turn Bryce took after passing the living room was the hallway to the gym. There, he commanded the smart speaker to play rock music loud enough to block everything out while he punched the bag, once, twice, harder and more times until his knuckles hurt.

He then hit the treadmill, sweat dampening his forehead. The shorts he was wearing weren't designed for a workout, but he'd had no time to think of his attire when he went to the gym.

His anger subsided, and he was on his way to his room when Mom cornered him at his door.

Her face fell when she saw him, and she worried her lower lip through her teeth again, smearing them with peach lipstick. "Your dad thought I overreacted."

That was an understatement. He might as well get everything out of the way so they didn't have a repeat tomorrow. "I'm going back to see Liberty tonight."

Mom inhaled sharply, obviously trying to contain her disappointment. "I can't have you gone every night you're here." She touched his shoulder. "You're leaving as soon as Christmas is over, and we need to have some family time."

Why wasn't she pestering her husband for family time? Bryce had his own family now.

"Liberty is not welcome here." He folded his arms across his chest, knowing Mom didn't care for her. "I love you, Mom. But she's my wife, and I need to spend time with her and—" He stopped himself before he blurted out Myra.

Mom tipped her head up at him, her eyes tear bright. "Why don't you invite her to the Christmas party on Friday?"

What on earth? "You just said—"

"This is my way of trying to respect your decisions."

No way would Liberty come, and who could blame her? He didn't even want to ask. Was Mom genuine about this, or was she plotting something? What had made her change her tone? Liberty would know. So he just gave a curt nod, not committing.

But all those questions lingered as he showered. With his brain too crowded, he found himself calling Liberty on his way into town to shop for Christmas decorations.

She answered on the second ring, her voice crisp and cheery—until he confided his argument with Mom. He palmed the back of his neck, rubbing the prickly hair at its base while keeping his right hand on the steering wheel as he navigated Pleasant View's well-groomed roads. "She's also extended an invitation for you to the Christmas party."

"You know she'll never accept me."

Cringing, he had to agree. At this point, it was hard to tell if his mom was so cold she could disrespect the woman he loved. Why couldn't Mom see how sweet and kind Liberty was?

"I wasn't even going to tell you, but I needed to talk to you anyway."

In her silence, he kneaded the back of his neck harder, then returned both hands to the steering wheel to make a turn.

"I don't want to be angry at your mom." Her soft words came through sincere, carefully crafted. "Maybe she's changed. I'll think about it some more."

Not wanting to press her into his mom's invitation, he changed the subject. "Don't cook tonight. I'm bringing dinner."

"You're not cooking it?" Laughter lightened her tone once again, and he pictured her dimples flashing.

"I'm cooking, Dimples," he teased. "In a commercial kitchen."

She chuckled through the phone, warming the dark recesses inside his heart. He couldn't wait to see her. "Where are you and Myra now?"

"We're getting ready to leave the office to meet Iris and Tessa for lunch."

"Lunch this late?" It was almost two. "Be sure to save room for dinner."

"You can count on that."

"Well, let me know if I can pick up anything besides the Christmas tree lights."

"Myra and I just need you home in one piece."

The words wrapped around him like one of Liberty's hugs or Myra's fuzzy blankets, making him feel safe and secure. As he ended the call, her excitement to see him strengthened him to stand by his family—even if it meant standing against his mom.

But surely, Mom wouldn't make it come to that, would she?

LIBERTY MET WITH HER friends, Iris and Tessa, at one of the less crowded diners in town. Whiffs of garlic and butter drifted in the open space. They'd already eaten, and some of their used dishes were cleared from the table. Although her friends ate full meals, Liberty had settled for soup.

"This is nice." Iris, an architect engineer in Boston, feathered through her short brown hair, and the blonde highlights fluttered past her shimmery blue-painted fingernails as her brown eyes flashed. "We haven't gotten together in so long. I'm glad we didn't miss the chance while I'm home for the holidays."

"I do miss our get-togethers." Tessa, a physical therapist starting her own business as a personal trainer, scooted to the end of the country-style booth, her hoop earrings jiggling against skin a darker shade of brown than Liberty's.

Myra, strapped in a high chair at the head of their booth, babbled to her audience, her cheery voice overplaying the Christmas instrumentals.

"And this little one is growing so fast! Yes, you, Starlight." Babbling baby talk back, Tessa straddled the wooden corner of her booth to add strawberries to Myra's plate. As she sliced the berries, she told them about the Christmas packages she'd sent to the soldiers earlier that month.

"Girls, I have a confession to make." She wiped her strawberry-coated fingers on a paper napkin, then leaned forward, whispering as if she didn't want the two other customers in the diner to hear. "Is it odd that I'm falling for a soldier I've never met?"

"He wrote to you again?" Liberty squeezed the lemon into her water and set the rind on the edge of the saucer.

Tessa's black hair bounced in a loose ponytail with her nod. Passionate about the soldier ministry at church, she collected donations throughout the year and bought items to send to soldiers at different bases around the world.

Iris shoved her half-eaten pizza slice to the side and tapped those aquamarine-blue nails on the walnut table. "Tell us everything."

A sheepish smile stretched out Tessa's lips. "It's really nothing."

Liberty added a couple of animal crackers to Myra's high chair tray as Tessa gave a summary of her soldier. "Our conversations sometimes get deep on things like faith and family, and his plans for what he wants to do when he gets out of the army. He has a great sense of humor."

Her eyes dreamy, Iris threw back her head and clasped her hands together as if praying. "That would be *so* romantic if you two fell in love. The perfect story for a movie."

A long-distance love story with a soldier *would* make a perfect movie. Still, Liberty frowned. Nurturing a long-distance relationship wasn't easy, especially if you had a mother-in-law like Wendy. "Has he talked about his mom yet?"

Iris waved her water straw. "Who cares about the monster-in-law when love trumps everything?"

At times, it did, but it took more dedication for Bryce and Liberty to find their way back to each other each time they broke up. Her chest tightening, Liberty held her tongue and peered out the large window beside them. Framed by the frosty scene etched onto the glass, cars bustled toward Main Street while the mountains rose beyond the town.

"I understand your concern." Tessa leaned back in the booth, flattening her palms on the tabletop. "But, like I said, we've only been writing to each other, getting to know you basics."

Liberty knew about the snail mail letters Tessa and the soldier had exchanged. "Have you progressed to email communication yet?"

"Wait a minute." Iris's eyes widened, and she jabbed a finger against the table. "He sends you *written* letters?"

"Yep."

At Tessa's response, Iris scooted over, nudged Liberty beside her further down the bench so she could face Tessa more fully, then asked questions. Apparently, Tessa had received almost ten letters in the last three months and a handful of emails.

Iris shrieked, which caused Myra to imitate her screech. "Do you have any emails or letters to show us?"

"Piz! Piz!" Myra pointed at the half-eaten pizza on Iris's plate, so Iris reached for the plate to hand it over.

But Liberty snatched it away. "She'll choke on this."

"Not when her mother is a nurse," Iris said, speaking over Myra's fussiness for not getting what she wanted.

With the three of them giving her extra attention, she calmed down, especially when Liberty handed her a kid-safe beaded necklace she always loved chewing on.

"You haven't told us anything about your time at the cabin." Tessa waggled her brows, perhaps not wanting to be probed about her soldier any further.

"The forced proximity." Iris's hair flopped to the side when she shifted back to face Liberty. Knowing glinted in her eyes. "What *exactly* did you two do?"

Liberty felt her cheeks blushing, and as her body temperature kicked up a notch, she fanned herself. Then she diverted her gaze to the couple seated in the far corner booth.

"Waiting." Tessa waved a hand in Liberty's face as if to make sure she was paying attention.

"We've decided to try again."

"That part I knew. I sent the ring with Logan." Iris stared down at Liberty's ring finger, and so did Tessa. The diamonds shimmered in the sunlight streaming through the big window beside them.

With so much Liberty wanted to tell her friends, she sank back against the padding on the booth and started with bits and pieces—showing up at the cabin, discovering Bryce there, trying to flee, and getting her car stuck.... Her chest warmed over how sweet Bryce had been carrying her back inside and fixing her a sandwich, and she kept going, sharing all the things leading to their final night together. "He stayed at my house last night."

Her eyes sparkling, Iris clapped and jumped in her seat. Her shoulder knocked into Liberty's. "Finally!"

"Not like that." Liberty held up a hand, although eager to have her husband back full time. He seemed more interested in his daughter, which was understandable since he was meeting her for the first time. "He stayed in Myra's room."

"Oh!" Tessa touched one of Myra's dangling pigtails.

"He's coming over tonight to decorate the tree with us."

Iris twisted the aquamarine stud earring on her ear, her lips curving. "I accomplished something this year."

As Iris kept her gaze on Liberty, Liberty mouthed a "thank you" to her friend. But she also had to be transparent about her fears. "If you can, please pray for me about Wendy."

"It's not like you're ever going to be friends." Tessa reached for her water. "As long as you stay away from her, you shouldn't worry."

Liberty had told the girls about her phone conversation with Bryce. "What about their Christmas party?"

Iris tapped her soft-blue fingernails on the table. "Since you're the godly example in this, you should be forthcoming about Myra." Iris, being a part of a blended family, obviously spoke from her point of view. "If Wendy hasn't changed, seeing her granddaughter could help her do things differently."

Shivers prickled Liberty's arms with her fears of losing her daughter. But perhaps Iris was right, and Wendy would be more thrilled about her own flesh and blood than she was with Liberty. In their years apart, Bryce hadn't moved on with a woman Wendy approved of, so maybe Wendy would be more accepting of Liberty.

"She'll find out about Myra since Bryce is back in your life." Tessa tucked her index finger into Myra's gooey grip and jostled the little one's hand, her voice dropping into baby talk. "You're too bright a light to keep hidden, aren't you, Starlight?"

Liberty held her hands out to her friends, squeezing them once they grasped them. Her chest tightened, and tears prickled her eyelids. God was so good to send her such wonderful friends. "You guys are so wonderful."

When they released her grip, they talked about the Christmas Eve service. Iris planned to attend services with her family at their home church. Tessa planned to be there with her family.

By the time Liberty parted from her friends, her mind was fuller from strategy possibilities than her tummy was from the cheddar broccoli soup.

She got home two hours before Bryce would show up, so she hadn't expected to see his Land Rover already parked in her driveway and him sitting on the snowy roof. A staple gun spit into the neighborhood's wintry silence.

CHAPTER 13

Upon seeing the Jeep, Bryce climbed down the ladder. Bruno, the man he'd hired from the labor agency, said he could finish putting up the final string of lights. Daylight would soon disappear, and the chill air nipped at his exposed neck and ears. But Bryce was content to have been a part of the labor. Paying someone else to do certain things wasn't as rewarding as doing it for someone you loved.

"What are you doing up there?" Liberty shifted Myra to her other hip.

"We need our house to match the rest of the neighborhood." He sauntered toward the Jeep she'd parked behind his Land Rover.

"Dada... Dada!" Myra wiggled, lunging forward as she lifted her hands toward Bryce. Gray eyes the same color as his brightened.

She wants me? After sliding off his work gloves, he tossed them on the Jeep's hood, then leaned in to kiss Liberty.

Myra dove for him and gripped his jacket. A tug pulled at Bryce's heart as he scooped her into his arms. Her amber cheeks glowed red from the cold.

"My jacket is probably cold." He held her a bit away from himself, worried about getting his daughter cold.

Liberty grinned, then leaned in and snugged the red hat with an Elmo cartoon down to Myra's ears. "I think she can survive the cold."

They walked toward the house like a normal family while he asked about her day and her time with her friends.

"It's always good to see the girls." She adjusted the diaper bag strap on her shoulder. "How was your day?"

Myra's little fingers tickled his neck as she cuddled in on his shoulders. Their time spent together that morning before he left was paying off. While Liberty spent an hour making scheduling calls, he had played with Myra. She was a busy little thing, too curious for her own good as she rode the tricycle. She then emptied the toy basket, filling it and starting over by emptying it again. He'd loved reading and building blocks with her.

"After that lunch with my parents, I went shopping for outdoor lights." Liberty had only requested lights for their tree, but he'd had no idea if she had any outdoor lights or not. "I wanted to surprise you when you got home, but—"

"It's a special surprise. Thank you." She squeezed his shoulder.

Inside the house, she started microwaving hot cocoa. Then the doorbell rang, so Bryce headed to answer it, assuming it was Bruno.

Sure enough, the husky man was done. Bryce had to make sure the lights worked before Bruno left, so he returned inside and hoisted Myra to his hip. He then called Liberty to join him outside. It wasn't too dark, but dusky enough to see the neighbors' twinkling lights.

"We'll probably need you to turn on the switch," he said to Liberty, hoping the outside plug worked. Assuring him that it did, she headed inside. Shortly later, the darkness vanished as radiant sparkly Christmas lights shimmered along her roof and twined around the two posts beside her door.

"Ook." Myra's hands tapped Bryce's cheek, her eyes shining in the Christmas lights.

"It worked!" Liberty returned, and her smile was worth any amount of time he'd spent working with Bruno.

Manual work shouldn't make him feel this happy, but when it was for his wife, it fulfilled him. His chest tightened as something primal, protective, and prideful roared to life. He outstretched his other hand, and Liberty walked into the embrace.

She wrapped her arms around his waist, stepping on tiptoes, and her warm lips brushed his cheek. "Thank you, sweetheart."

As her joyful voice rendered him breathless, they stayed there while Myra babbled nonsensical words, probably still fascinated by the lights. He didn't want this moment to end, never wanted to lose this happiness now erupting in his chest.

"Ahem."

At the man's voice, Liberty stepped from their embrace.

"I'll meet you in the house." Bryce handed Myra to Liberty before he reached for his wallet from his pants pocket. The agency had pointed out it was a cash-only pay, so he'd made a stop at the ATM.

Seeing the good job Bruno had done and Liberty's broad smile, Bryce gave the man three one-hundred-dollar bills as opposed to the one hundred dollars he'd mentioned before he'd hired him.

"Merry Christmas!" Bryce said. He'd used those words often, although he didn't think much about them until now when he was involved in the Christmas preparations.

Bruno lifted the money into the light. Then, as he registered the amount, his brows creased, and he turned his gaze back to Bryce.

"I have no change." He spoke in a thick Latin accent.

"Keep the change."

The man's toothy grin warmed Bryce. He needed to do things like this more often. He mostly interacted with people through his business connections. Making a local person smile on his account was different, something missing from his life.

The house was as warm as his heart when he walked back inside and eased out of his jacket. He hung it up on the coat hook by the front door.

The rest of the night passed in a surreal glow as Christmas music played while they chose ornaments from the box and hung them on the tree. Most of them Liberty had handmade while she was pregnant with Myra. Myra's photo of her first Christmas highlighted one of the small decorative frames.

The ornaments reminded him of Liberty's craft hobby. Obviously, she'd been busy with no time for nurturing her hobby lately.

He breathed in deeply when he picked up another ornament from the box—a framed photo of him with Liberty at NYU. One of the times she'd come to visit him. He glanced at her to comment, but she was trying to convince Myra a tiara was better than the glass angel ornament clutched in her pudgy grip.

She gave up when Myra snuggled the angel closer to her chest. As Liberty reached for another ornament from the box and stood, he snuck behind her and kissed her neck. She shivered, and he took her hand with the ornament of their photo. She smiled when she registered his motive, and they hung the ornament on the tree together.

Myra loved tossing out the ornaments from the box and to the floor, then yanking them off the tree. She was too adorable with pink ribbons in her pigtails, and Bryce had to pick her up, squeezing her tight and swinging her side to side. How he loved his daughter and his wife!

"Do you think we're hanging up toys for you?" He kissed her soft cheek.

Myra tried to wiggle out of his hold, and he tickled her neck. Her little shoulders shook when she broke out in giggles, and his heart nearly exploded with happiness.

When they finished decorating the tree, they sipped hot chocolate until the food from their favorite Thai restaurant arrived.

Myra ate sweet potatoes and peas Liberty microwaved for her. Left to him, he'd have fed their daughter Thai noodles and steak.

"Simply Thai, I remember this." Liberty raved about the dinner, and Bryce's chest puffed at her praise, glad he'd ordered food from one of their favorite restaurants.

Unlike yesterday, when he'd watched Liberty bathe Myra, today his wife asked if he wanted to give Myra a bath.

How could he say no when he wanted to be the best husband and father for his family?

The adventure began when Myra splashed water in his face and Liberty watched. Her head fell back as she laughed, happy to see him drenched. He fought the urge to splash water on her, but that could create a bigger mess for them to clean. He was already too spent to add more chores to his list.

Bathing his daughter wasn't a chore since she cooed while splashing water and clutching one of her bath toys—a yellow duck. Okay, it was slightly a chore. He had no idea what he was doing, and his wife continued to watch him while he washed Myra's hair.

By the time he finished, his drenched shirt clung to his body. He fished the slippery child from the water. "Unfortunately, I don't have any spare clothes."

"I still have one of your T-shirts—the one I was wearing when I left." Laughter still carried in Liberty's voice. Their fingers brushed when she took Myra from him and wrapped her in a towel. "I might have sweats that fit you."

He'd intended to stay when he showed up today, but he'd forgotten to pack clothes.

Much later, after he'd showered and changed into his old T-shirt that smelled like rainwater as fresh as Liberty, he read Myra a story and put her to bed without Liberty's supervision.

Liberty wasn't spoon-feeding him. She'd just left him with Myra in the baby's room, saying, "You can figure it out."

"You have no mercy," he'd teased, and Liberty teased back—or had she been serious when she'd said he'd understand no mercy soon because it was his turn to change a stinky diaper next time Myra went potty?

With Myra in bed, Bryce was toasted and flopped on the couch, resting his head on Liberty's lap. He couldn't ask for a better pillow while she raked her fingers in his hair. "You were incredible today."

Man, she had to do this every day, taking care of their mischievous girl, and he thanked her for doing so.

"She's worth it." Her fingers stilled in his hair, one strand still in their grip. "I'll go to the Christmas party. Myra will come too."

Whoa. His breath caught in his chest. "Are you sure?"

She breathed shakily as if she were releasing the breath *he* was holding. "Yes."

He tilted his head up so he could see her face to make sure she wasn't guilted into this. "You know I understand if you don't want to go."

Her fingers resumed stroking through his hair, and Bryce closed his eyes, relaxing. He'd always loved the feel of her fingers in his hair.

"Maybe if she knows she has a granddaughter, she might act differently."

Did she intend to tell Mom about Myra? That was a question he'd better not clarify. If he hadn't heard her right, he didn't want her thinking he was pushing her into anything.

Still, the ease by which Liberty was willing to venture into his mom's presence astounded him. He opened his eyes. Hers were unreadable. "Why are you doing this?"

"God would want me to forgive." She tipped a shoulder in a half-shrug. "Plus, we all need second chances." She then went on about how everyone was a sinner and all needed to seek God's forgiveness daily.

Her words sliced like a sharp sword to his heart. Suddenly uneasy, he turned to the side and focused on the cabinet that secured the TV. "How do you know God exists?"

"I've never doubted God's existence." She continued to run a hand through his hair, fingers massaging his scalp. "I always believed He created the universe, but I had a rebellious spirit in me."

"I know." His lips quirked. When they'd just started dating, Liberty had told him all sorts of mischief, including her running away with a hippie boyfriend to tour the world as they played music.

"Your excitement for life." The mischievous gleam in her eyes when he'd seen her in her early teens had always intrigued him, but that summer, it drew him in, igniting something in him too. "It had a lot to do with me falling for you." Plus her confidence.

Her fingers stilled again. "Having Myra and seeing the different stages of her development on the ultrasound was the most fascinating reminder that only a higher power, *God*, could breathe life into something as strange as a bean and turn it into a human being."

He had to agree. After he'd looked at the 3D ultrasound images yesterday morning, several questions spun through his mind on things like how a human being could breathe or how a tiny embryo became a human being.

How *did* life get breathed into a person? That seemed more surreal, a question that needed deep research.

"What other proof do you have?" He always needed proof, perhaps the lawyer in him, but it helped him pick wise investments too. And believing in God seemed like something that should be approached as an investment—the biggest investment one could make in the future, if eternity were real.

"For me, I sense and feel my belief in God is true. I don't need proof." Her voice was gentle. "But for those who need proof, the Bible confirms God's existence."

No way would he ever read the Bible.

"Let's look at the Christmas story...." She talked about the birth of Jesus who was supposedly God, sent to earth in the form of man so humans could relate to Him. She then went on about prophecies and their fulfillment, Old and New Testament things all foreign to Bryce.

"It all comes down to believing in what we can't see." Her gaze flitted to the closed cabinet. "Believing in God or not, it's a leap of faith."

She then used an example that resonated.

"Let's say you wear a helmet in hopes that, if you fall, you won't get hurt as much. It doesn't guarantee your survival. But there's a hope wearing it will protect you. It's the same way with faith in God. If there's even a small chance God is real, wouldn't you want to know?"

He nodded as he tried to grasp how faith played out. If there was evidence, then he was interested in reading it at some point.

She raised a hand and waved it at herself before resting it back on his head. "I'm not intelligent enough to know all these things."

She was very smart. Both on the street and in books. But when he told her so, she just chuckled.

He didn't want to tell her he'd think about it, but he intended to look through the facts now that she'd pointed out a starting place. He turned again to look at her beautiful face. She was wearing a blue pajama shirt. He was grateful she still wanted him in her life, even if they had different beliefs. That alone compelled him to want to believe in her God, Eric Stone's God, the God Eric attributed with healing him from chronic disease.

Liberty had stopped moving her hand in his hair, and he already missed it. Her lips curled, and her dimples deepened. "What's going on in your mind?"

He reached out to touch her cheek, her skin so smooth. "I love you, Dimples."

What other truth was better than that?

Her fingers resumed their job on his head. "Are you going home tonight?"

He thought he was home, but she probably meant his childhood home. "Do you want me to?"

Her response was immediate. "No."

There was no place he'd rather be. "I'm all yours, Mrs. Solace."

"In that case—welcome home." At that, she breathed in deeply, then bent down until her mouth claimed his.

CHAPTER 14

Liberty's muscles jerked with rising tension as Bryce parked the Land Rover in the garage of his childhood home. Myra hummed happily during most of their thirty-minute drive. That and her babbling had helped Liberty not overthink her decision.

"Ready?" Bryce shut off the ignition, and the vehicle's interior lights illuminated his nicely combed hair.

Her stomach tightened in knots, but she pasted on a smile as she brushed a hair from his blue button-down shirt. "I can't wait to see Charles." She could count on his dad's friendly face besides the workers who had to smile to earn their stay.

Bryce faced her, his hand touching her cheek. His thumb slid into the spot where one of her dimples often appeared, and he whispered, "I'll be right beside you, Dimples."

Hmm. It had been so long since he'd done that. But did he mean it? So many times, she'd thought she'd have his support only to find him unable to stand beside her. But today, Wendy would be too busy entertaining her guests to waste time harassing Liberty—right? "I'll be okay."

As much as she tried to convince herself, she knew this wouldn't be a normal party. Not once Wendy discovered Myra.

Bryce stepped out and went around the front to open the door for her. She reached for her utility handbag. Stylish enough to be a purse, it came in handy to carry Myra's extra clothes, food, and diapers—a perfect diaper bag.

The time on the dashboard showed 5:13. Way earlier than she'd wanted to arrive, but Wendy requested they show up early so they could catch up before her company came.

Taking Bryce's offered hand, Liberty stepped out of the car.

"I'll get Myra." He kissed her cheek, and his relaxing eucalyptus scent almost made her forget where they were.

The Land Rover was the only one in the two-car garage, but Bryce had always had his own garage at the house. If she wasn't still driving his Jeep, it would be in the other space here.

As if Wendy had been watching them through the camera, the moment they stepped out of the garage and into the front room, heels clicked on the tile, and they both headed to the kitchen area.

Liberty's hand gripped the purse straps on her shoulder as Wendy stalked toward them, immaculate in her black wrap dress with a golden necklace sparkling at her throat under the recessed lighting.

"There's my dashing... son." Her words trailed when her gaze narrowed on Bryce's hip. Her brows drew together before she foisted off a smile. She touched the golden bow on the waist of Myra's red dress. "Who do we have here?"

"This is Myra." Bryce kissed Myra's head. Liberty had styled her hair in two pigtails and tied them up with beaded golden ties.

"Twee!" Myra pointed at the Christmas tree dominating the corner by the kitchen. She wiggled, determined to get down. She would, no doubt, love to tinker with the shiny ornaments. Thankfully, Bryce shifted her on his shoulder.

As if Wendy just realized Liberty was there, her lips curled into a deceptively sweet smile. "Liberty, dear"—the familiar fakeness Liberty knew so well shivered over her spine—"I didn't know you had a child."

"Yes. You have a grandchild." Now might be a better time to get it over with.

Bryce turned to look at Liberty, blinking. He then winked, a secret assurance that she did the right thing.

"She's not Bryce's child, I hope." Wendy let out a forced chuckle and stepped back. Her cheeks flared almost as red as her lipstick. "You've been separated for ages."

While Liberty thought she knew Wendy well enough, she hadn't prepared for this. She stood straight, determined not to feel bothered by Wendy's remark. Before she could articulate her response, her husband spoke.

"Mom." Bryce shifted Myra to his hip, then kissed the top of her head. "This is my daughter."

"Did I hear I have a granddaughter?" Charles came down the L-shaped stairs, adjusting his navy tie.

"When did this happen? Did you know and not tell us?" Wendy's voice rose dangerously toward a shriek as she planted herself between Liberty and Bryce. "Do you have proof she's your daughter? Did you even bother to investigate if she dated other men?"

Proof. Right. Why hadn't Liberty thought of getting a paternity test for Bryce? He'd believed her right off. Or did he not?

"Merry Christmas, Liberty." Charles spread out his arms, oblivious to his wife's questions.

Regardless of Liberty's racing heart, she managed to turn and keep her back to Wendy as she stepped into Charles's arms for a warm hug.

"So good to see you again."

"Good to see you too, Charles." His gentleness was always a calming presence. She stepped out of the embrace, wishing she'd seen him on a different day. More gray scattered through his shaggy brown hair, but he looked classy in his crisp white shirt tucked into dark dress pants. Although he'd always traveled for work and spent a lot of time away from his family, he was the kind of dad she would've liked to have had.

"What's my granddaughter's name?" he asked, and Bryce side-stepped his mom to get to his dad.

"Myra."

"Like her great-grandma." Charles touched one of Myra's piggy tails, his face radiating warmth. "Can I hold you, Myra?"

Myra tucked her head in Bryce's neck, her fingers clinging to Bryce's collar.

"You want to say hello to Grandpa?" Bryce lowered his chin, peering at Myra. "She has gray eyes. Just like me and you."

"I need to get ready for the party." Wendy's disinterested voice caused everyone to give her attention. "I'm glad to have a grand-daughter." She sucked in a breath, then stood taller. "But I don't do well with surprises, and it was unfair to only tell us now."

She then mumbled under her breath. "Make yourself at home, Liberty."

Gripping her purse tightly, Liberty intended to make herself at home by making sure the purse stayed with her at all times. The last thing she needed was Wendy sneaking something in her handbag again, then suing her for it.

Her chest rose and fell as she finally dared to breathe when Wendy vanished and the clicking of her heels became muffled the further she went.

Her gaze drifted to her family. Yes, she was proud to call Charles family, Wendy not so much. Charles was making car noises, and Myra thought it was the funniest thing. Her giggles cleared the tension from Liberty's shoulders.

Charles's trick worked, and soon Myra was leaping for him. His smile spread wide as he took his granddaughter in his arms. After minutes of squeezing and loving on Myra, Charles eyed Liberty, looking her up and down in her navy dress. "I love the snowflakes on your dress."

Liberty warmed to his compliment and fiddled with the vertical bar on the necklace Bryce had given her. "Thank you."

She'd bought the long-sleeved dress last year for her employee Christmas party. No doubt she was underdressed for Wendy's guests, but she wasn't here to make an impression. As long as she was married to Bryce, she'd always be Wendy's enemy.

A young man showed up to ask if they wanted something to drink, but they all didn't need anything.

Since Myra kept pointing to the Christmas tree, the four of them walked toward it, and as they neared, Charles lifted her high where she plucked off a red ornament.

"I don't want to cause any trouble if she breaks it."

"She can break as many as she wants." Charles kissed Myra's cheek. "Grandpa will buy an entire box if he has to."

After a while, Myra squirmed, so he set her down.

The doorbell rang, and soon voices followed in the main entrance hallway. A middle-aged couple emerged as the maid directed them to where they were supposed to go.

Charles greeted them by their names, introducing them to Liberty as family friends. Their warmth was a contrast to Wendy's barbed personality.

Bryce and Liberty left Charles to walk with his guests to the banquet room where the party was taking place.

"I need to change her diaper," Liberty said, noticing a bulge beneath Myra's gold tights.

Bryce shuddered. He'd changed Myra's poopy diaper, and although he'd been brave about it, he'd insisted on wearing a mask the next time he changed a poopy diaper.

"It's just wet," Liberty assured him, surprised he wasn't aware that if it was nasty it would be reeking.

Using the bathroom toward the front entrance, Bryce offered to change Myra. He laid her on the bathroom sofa. And as Liberty had guessed, it was just wet.

"I want to take Myra on a tour of where I met her mom." Bryce eyed Liberty with a glow that rushed back all the memories of that summer.

"She would like that." Liberty held the bathroom door for him and Myra to walk through.

The three of them passed the front room to the hallway leading toward the back room's open French doors.

Bryce flipped on the switch, and light filled the spacious room.

Liberty set her handbag on the table before the sofa.

Besides the now peacock-blue wall and matching-toned sofas, drapes, and area rug, the towering built-in bookshelves anchored the place in the familiar. The bouquet of mixed flowers by the sliding door wafted a fresh aroma in the room while, through that door and the massive windows, she could imagine the breathtaking scenic views.

Despite how Liberty felt about Wendy, she had to give the woman credit for always keeping the house up to date and modern. There always were fresh flowers in the main rooms delivered every other day.

Liberty glanced at the floor-to-ceiling windows. It was dark, but she didn't need to peer past the back porch light to remember the mountain backdrop and immaculate flower gardens, now fully dressed with snow.

"Mama!" Myra's chirrup drew Liberty from her thoughts, and her daughter's dress twirled as she spun in circles in the center of the room.

Bryce knelt on the rug with his phone in hand, probably recording a video.

Only after Myra fell, did she stop spinning.

"Oh no!" Bryce tossed his phone on the plush rug and crouched to Myra. "Are you okay?"

"She's okay," Liberty promised. It wasn't the first time Myra spun. "The rug is soft." She then lowered herself next to Bryce, who was running his fingers on Myra's cheek.

Myra's gaze flitted between her dada and mama, her lips twisting before she erupted into sweet laughter as she flapped her hands.

"You silly girl." Bryce scooped her up, but she squirmed out of his hold.

"With such an empty room, she thinks it's a playground."

And just like that, Myra was off to the bookshelf, opening the lower—and apparently empty—cabinets. She crawled into one and squealed nonsensical words Liberty assumed meant house. At least, she was out of reach from the decorative vase in one of the cubes and the books.

Bryce interlaced his warm and firm fingers with Liberty's, leading her to the nearby sofa across the room.

"I'm glad you told Mom about Myra." He sat and pulled her down on his lap. "I was nervous she'd find out before we told her."

But Wendy didn't seem to believe Myra was Bryce's daughter. Well, that was Wendy's problem and not Liberty's. "Your dad took the news well."

Bryce moved her to face him and cupped her chin. She was too big to be on his lap, but she loved how he treated her with such affection, affection she'd missed during their years apart.

When he leaned in and pressed his lips to hers, she kissed him back. But the cabinets slammed, and they tore apart.

Myra started dashing toward them, a smile bunching up her face when she stopped by the coffee table. "Aik." She pointed to the handbag. "Aik."

"What language are you teaching our daughter?" Bryce laughed.

So Liberty kept up with the teasing, wagging a finger at him. "Your fault for not taking gibberish lessons."

"Dada... aik."

At Myra's continued persistence, Liberty eased off Bryce's lap and stood to retrieve Myra's sippy cup. She all but snatched it out of Liberty's hand and tilted her head to drink. "Someone was thirsty."

Myra then yanked her blanket from the bag and ran back to the bookshelf with her cup and blanket in hand.

"Aik is milk?" Bryce asked, shaking his head.

"You better sign up for Myra's gibberish classes, you know."

"Is that so?" He pinned her with his dark gray eyes, then stood and moved behind her, wrapping his arms around her waist. "You look beautiful tonight."

Her skin tingled at the warm rumble close to her ear. Just as he planted a kiss on her neck that squeezed her knees to jelly, a haughty voice polluted the air.

"I believe you came here for a party."

Liberty jumped, tearing apart from Bryce.

"Oh," she said, forcing herself to find her composure.

Wendy gave Liberty an unreadable cursory glance before looking at Bryce, who was already reaching for the handbag from the table. "People are already here. Ashley is looking for you, darling."

Ashley? That name was familiar. When she looked at Bryce for a hint, his face had gone hard, and it matched his response to his mom.

"I'm here for Dimples and Myra."

Liberty didn't miss how he used Dimples to his mom. Rarely did he use that when it wasn't just her and him.

Wendy flitted her gaze to Liberty and gave a half-smile before sashaying toward the bookshelf and speaking over her shoulder. "You have to greet people, don't you?"

Forgetting what she was supposed to do, Liberty turned for the door, then to Bryce who ushered his chin toward the banging cabinet doors that were opening and closing. She needed to get their daughter, but Wendy was right next to Myra.

"Myra, darling." Wendy put her hand out for Myra. "Come on."

Myra eyed Wendy, then toddled a step backward and looked around as if needing an escape.

"Come here, sweetie," Wendy urged.

Liberty strode past Wendy, thankful she'd worn her silver flats, and scooped her daughter up.

Bryce placed his hand on Liberty's shoulder, and they walked out of the room, leaving Wendy behind.

THE BANQUET ROOM WHERE Wendy hosted the party had taken on a cozy wintry glow. With the regular lighting off, ribbons of twinkle lights entwined around gossamer maroon and gold fabric strung across the high ceiling while candles flickered from the tables and strings of "White Christmas" strummed from the piano before the tree. A pianist in a white shirt, black tie, and suit moved his head, clearly attuned to his music.

Charles beamed and beckoned Bryce and Liberty as they wove past the tables and people occupying them. Maroon cloth napkins wrapped the silverware in a perfect complement to the white linens draping the round tables. Matching maroon candles glowed in vases surrounded by the beribboned centerpieces—fresh cedar and pine boughs adorned with cranberry sprigs, pine cones, and shiny apples.

Myra shifted on Liberty's hip and pointed at the white Christmas tree decorated with maroon, green, and gold ornaments and swaddled in massive golden ribbons and delicate cranberry strings.

Charles waved them over to his table. Only one person, a man who didn't look much older than Charles, occupied one of the six chairs.

Liberty's stomach coiled. Charles was making them sit at Wendy's table?

Before they reached him, people who knew Bryce greeted them from one table after another. He had to introduce her each time, which made Liberty feel as if she was new to his world. Yet since these people were in his mom's circle, Bryce hadn't had the opportunity to introduce them to Liberty earlier in their relationship.

Another woman with lips redder than Wendy's gave Liberty a critical eye after Bryce introduced Liberty as his wife and Myra as his daughter. She then looked at Bryce. "Your mother said you're divorced."

"You must have misunderstood." Bryce tapped the woman's shoulder, leaving no room for questions. "Good to see you again." He reached for Liberty's hand, clasping it in his as he led them to his father's table.

Servers in maroon vests passed along appetizer trays and set fluted champagne glasses on most tables. Beyond a side door, another table stood as a makeshift bar. People chatted in line, while others walked away with red or amber drinks.

"Willy." Charles spoke as Bryce pulled out a chair for Liberty. "This is my daughter-in-law, Liberty."

Liberty reached out to shake Willy's offered hand. "Nice to meet you."

Willy's smile glowed in his eyes. "And who's the beautiful young lady?"

"My granddaughter," Charles said before Liberty could respond, pride and affection raising his voice and chest, "Myra."

Food was served buffet-style. A server approached their table and told them they would be the first to make their way to the buffet table set on the opposite wall from the drinks. Not taking any chances, Liberty took her bag with her while Charles hoisted Myra to his hip.

Myra's head was tilted the entire time as she took in the array of lights strung across the room.

Liberty's stomach growled when they reached the food table where servers were standing guard and ready to serve them. Tall vases lifted maroon candles well above the serving dishes, and steam carried the enticing promise of meat, garlic, sage, and other spices. Liberty offered to carry a plate for Charles, asking what he wanted to eat.

"As long as I get a filet mignon, I'll let you decide the rest," he said.

Bryce carried a plate for himself and one for Myra. "Is there anything here she can eat?"

Liberty scanned the long table, with fancy meats, then a few banners down where she had no idea what was offered. "I'll let you know when we get our sides." She'd packed a squeezable applesauce and two other squeezables for Myra in case there was no food Myra could eat.

Liberty went for salmon piccata and broccoli with mashed potatoes. The server curved a filet mignon onto Charles's plate, and Liberty added broccoli and garlic-roasted potatoes. Bryce got the prime rib, penne pasta, and broccoli. Pasta was perfect for Myra.

As soon as they sat, they were interrupted by a blonde with long hair falling to the side of her peach dress. It had the longest slit Liberty had ever seen.

"Bryce!"

Bryce's smile turned uneasy. "Hey."

Liberty shifted her gaze to Myra who sat on the empty chair between her and Charles. He was holding Myra's hand and keeping her from yanking the candles nestled in the wreath centerpiece.

"Myra." Liberty shook her head to indicate no with her face serious. "We're not messing around with the candles." Liberty slid the candles further away, off-centering the piece.

Myra's lips folded. Then the lower one quivered.

"No, Starlight. Not now."

"What happened?" Charles touched Myra's shoulder, and Liberty assured him she would be fine. She still sped up chopping Myra's noodles into small pieces and set the plate in front of her.

Liberty pretended to feed Myra as she eavesdropped on Ashley's conversation with Bryce. "I've been divorced for three years."

That could explain why Wendy invited Ashley.

Despite Ashley's striking beauty making Liberty a bit insecure, she consoled herself that Bryce loved her. He was barely responding to Ashley, so that was a good thing.

Charles's silverware clanked when he cut through his meat, among the chatter of voices in the room. Liberty's mind spun as she finally remembered Ashley was Bryce's ex, back before he'd spent the summer with Liberty. If he hadn't pursued Ashley all those years, then he wasn't going to start now.

When his warm hand slid around her waist, Liberty managed a glance at the blonde just as Bryce said, "This is my wife, Liberty, and our daughter, Myra."

Ashley's eyes widened. Then she smiled, her lips thinning. "Your mom said you're not married."

Bryce frowned. "When did she say that?"

"Two days ago?"

Wendy had probably wanted to make Liberty jealous. Feeling her shoulders tightening, she took her gaze off Ashley—letting Bryce deal with his ex.

His strong arm moved to Liberty's shoulder. "Well, she lied to you. You should ask her why."

Liberty's stomach churned. Maybe she shouldn't have come. She'd been naïve thinking Wendy had changed.

"Have Yourself a Merry Little Christmas" started as the pianist hit all the right notes, and Liberty's mind didn't register the rest of Ashley's conversation until she left their table. She might have said "nice to meet you," but if she did, Liberty didn't remember since she was gobbling her salmon. It wasn't as flavorful as she'd thought. She doubted any food would taste good in this house.

"Are you okay, sweetheart?" Bryce whispered as Charles's silverware clanked against his porcelain plate.

"I'm just hungry."

He tried to explain about Ashley from his past, so Liberty told him she remembered their conversation about her. Then she nodded to his plate and squeezed his thigh so he wouldn't worry about her. "You should eat your dinner before it gets cold."

Even though she liked the idea of not having Wendy at their table, Liberty was surprised her mother-in-law sat at a different table from her husband.

Whenever Liberty scanned the room to locate Wendy, she'd move to another table. Perhaps she had to interact with her guests. But like Liberty, Wendy seemed to be keeping an eye on her too. Each time Liberty discovered her at a different table, the woman had her gaze on her. If looks could kill...

Creepy. Liberty hadn't asked Bryce how long they were supposed to stay, but she didn't mind leaving soon. Even with Charles's kindness, she could only handle so many of Wendy's daggers.

With Myra scattering most of the noodles on the table and fidgeting in the chair, Liberty told Bryce she was taking her for a walk.

"I got her," he said, tossing his napkin to the table.

"You're still eating."

"I'm done. I'll get her," Charles offered.

Liberty reached into her bag to find wipes to clean Myra, but the bag looked emptier. Myra's blanket. She'd carried it to the bookshelf with her sippy cup.

Liberty needed to get those items. If they forgot the milk, it would spoil and reek up the room before anyone realized it was in the bookshelf's cabinets. After wiping Myra, she told Bryce where she was headed.

He reached for his napkin and wiped his hands. "I'll come with you."

"Finish your dinner. I'll be fine." She grabbed her bag and then scanned for Wendy. She was still at the same table. This time, thankfully, she seemed to be listening to whoever was talking at the table of five. "I won't be long."

Liberty still had to cling to the bag, in case Wendy was up to no good.

When Liberty made it to the back room, the double doors were still open, and she switched on the light. She sped to the bookshelf. The blanket was still in the cabinet, so she shoved it in the bag. It took her a few minutes of crawling alongside the bookshelf to find the pink sippy cup half full with milk.

At the clicking of the door locks, she jumped to stand, and the cup slid out of her hand and thudded on the floor. With her heart in her throat, Liberty spun and caught Wendy's back to her as she closed the doors. She was a stalker—that much Liberty knew.

Wendy played dirty tricks like a stereotypical politician, but Liberty doubted she was capable of hurting her physically or worse. When Wendy spun around, she swept her auburn hair from her shoulder and sneered. "Liberty."

What did this woman want? "You scared me." Liberty summoned all her self-possession as she stooped to pick up the cup.

Wendy laughed, then brushed her hand in dismissal, and took a couple of steps toward her. "You have Charles and my son all wrapped around your fingers, but you won't fool me." Brown eyes icily pierced Liberty.

Wendy was a bully, but Liberty was no victim. Except, when she forced herself to stand straighter, her fingers tightened around the sippy cup. "What's that supposed to mean?"

Wendy planted a hand on her hip. "You thought, if you named your child after my mom, you could trick my son into believing she's his daughter."

Liberty's stomach dropped at the woman's cold words, and she pointed the sippy cup at her. If she was within reach, Liberty might be tempted to shove the cup in the woman's face. Despite her emotions coiling, she spoke weakly. "My mistake for thinking you've changed."

Wendy's penciled brows lifted. "Don't pretend to be innocent." She wagged a manicured finger at Liberty. "You messed up my son's career, ruined his hopes of ever finding a reasonable wife, and are now tricking him into parenting another man's child."

That was going too far. Her chest was burning, her temperature rising as she contemplated the most hurtful thing she could say. Now might be a good time to remind her to tend to her husband instead of interfering with her son.

Calm down. Liberty closed her eyes, took a breath, then opened them. She bit the inside of her cheeks, too angry to shed a tear.

"If money is what you want—"

"Don't think because you use your husband's money." Liberty lifted her hand, ready to throw rapid-fire words at her. Maybe if she stated the facts, this woman would stop showing off. "Charles's money doesn't give you a ticket to abuse people."

"Stay away from my son!"

It was Liberty's turn to try a mirthless laugh. Somehow, though, the sound stuck in her throat. Did Wendy think they were still in high school? She took a few steps toward Wendy. "I need to go."

The woman had major issues, and Liberty didn't want to waste any more time arguing. So she sidestepped her to get to the door.

Wendy shoved her shoulder and stepped in front of Liberty, blocking her way. "Did you hear what I just said?"

Oh no, she didn't just do that. Anger burned through Liberty until she could feel it erupting from her stomach and rising to her chest. She lifted Wendy's hand from her shoulder. "Bryce is an adult."

Wendy had no idea how she'd messed Bryce up in so many ways, moments when Bryce felt inadequate to run a company on his own, when he doubted he was good enough, when he struggled to make his own decisions. "You need to stop using excuses, saying he's your only son—"

"You'll never measure up!" Narrowing her eyes to a glare, Wendy raised her chin. Liberty would've done the Christlike thing and walked away, but Wendy's next words rolled off her spiteful tongue. "You will always be a failure like your mom, raising another fatherless child."

She'd had enough. Losing control was an understatement. That instant, Liberty felt the urge to grab Wendy's shoulders and shake her or even slap her. But as she tightened her fingers around the sippy cup to gain her calm, Liberty didn't think twice. She twisted open the cup and dumped the milk in Wendy's face.

"My mom is twice the woman you are!"

Wendy gasped and scrambled as the milk flowed over her chest onto her black sequined dress. She swiped at her face. "You're crazy!"

She was the crazy one.

Now that Liberty had avenged her mom, why was she trembling, and why didn't she feel good about it? She put the lid back on the cup as Wendy called her all sorts of names.

The right thing to do was to apologize. But right now, Liberty wouldn't mean it, and Wendy wouldn't accept her apology, anyway. Liberty stood there, still conflicted between apologizing and walking away, when the double doors swung open and Bryce walked in.

She let out a shaky breath, relieved he was here.

It took him a second to assess the situation when he looked at Wendy, frowning and mumbling while swiping at her dress, then looked at Liberty, still shaking and wrapping her arms around herself.

She could run to Bryce, but what if he was upset with her for dumping milk on his mom?

A muscle ticked in his jaw before he stepped between them, keeping his gaze on Liberty's attacker. "Mom? What did you do?"

"Me? *I'm* the one drenched in stench." Wendy grimaced, then touched the white mess on her chest. "It's your wife you should be yelling at."

Liberty's tongue was frozen, her limbs unwilling to move.

Wendy swallowed, standing taller, and her stance changed. "Liberty's determined to ruin my relationship with you."

"Are you kidding me, Mom?" Bryce shifted his back fully to Liberty, his voice rising. "All she's ever done was to love me, and if you gave her the chance to..."

Liberty's heart was racing. Bryce now arguing with his mom was her fault. She shoved the cup in the bag, entertaining the idea of bolting to get Myra, but she didn't want to leave without Bryce, especially now that he was standing up for her.

"You're blinded whenever you're with her!" Wendy threw her hands up before storming out of the door.

Bryce spun to face Liberty. His gaze darkened, and he tugged at his hair, frazzled, before he pulled her into his arms. Liberty let out a shuddered breath and threw her arms around him. She fought the tears burning in her eyes. If she broke down in Wendy's house, Liberty would be crediting her for being the Queen of Mean. Her lips quivered against Bryce's chest. "Can we go... home, please?"

"What happened?"

She didn't trust herself to talk, afraid she'd have a nervous breakdown. Plus, she didn't want to give him another reason to fight with his mom. So she chose to remain silent.

"I'm so sorry." Bryce ran his hand over her back to comfort her. "I'll go get Myra, okay?"

Liberty nodded. She would've wanted to say goodbye to Charles, but she needed a fast escape from this cold house.

He walked with her to the garage before he went for Myra.

Her mind spun, almost exploding with Wendy's voice and insults screaming in her head. She needed to pray, but she was far too worked up. She didn't even have the strength to call her friends. Mom would be the right person to call, but she hadn't told her she was coming to Wendy's house. Everything to reunite with Bryce had happened too fast, and now Liberty was facing the consequences.

CHAPTER 15

Tension radiated through Bryce while Myra cried half of their drive back home—Liberty's home and now Bryce's, even if it was a temporary residence for them since she house-sat and paid minimal rent.

When Myra stopped crying, Bryce attempted to ask Liberty what Mom had said. Her refusal to answer left him uneasy. The uneasiness made him downright queasy when they walked into the house and she kissed Myra on the cheek before asking him to put Myra to bed, saying she needed time to herself.

Liberty *was* capable of throwing things when she was upset, but she'd only done that to him, not to anyone else—and especially not to Mom. Mom must've said or done something huge to compel Liberty to dump milk on her fancy dress.

As he changed Myra's diaper and dressed her in a jumpsuit, he wasn't concerned about getting the job done perfectly. Myra wasn't complaining. She was rubbing at her eyes, seeming tired.

Poor kid. They hadn't gotten home until almost nine, way past her bedtime.

Thankfully, she knew how to pick her favorite stories. Otherwise, the water running from the bathroom, which was next to Myra's room, would've distracted him. No doubt Liberty was upset. She'd always loved taking long showers to subdue her anger.

He read the going-to-bed book while Myra snuggled to his chest and a thickness clogged his throat. He cleared it away as he read about the sun setting and everyone taking a bath.

Terror seized him over tonight's uncertain outcome. When Liberty felt like talking, was she going to kick him out of her life, and Myra's too?

He'd never growled at his mom on Liberty's behalf, but walking in and seeing Liberty's ashen face had twisted something in him. A surge of protection for her had all but taken over. If their years apart had taught him anything, it was that he never wanted to get back to that place again, a place without Liberty in his life. He'd been busy enough, but a deep hole had hollowed out his heart where his wife was supposed to be. And at the edges of his mind, there'd been that ache of always knowing he couldn't talk to the love of his life whenever he wanted to. Not again. He'd do anything to keep from losing Liberty again, even if it meant never talking to his mom again.

By the time he read the final page of the day being done and saying good night, Myra's breathing had grown steady. When he glanced down at his daughter, she had her eyes closed. His chest hurt even more. Was this the last time he'd read her a story? No!

Even if they didn't get to reopen the photo book Myra had chosen for story time, Bryce had to flip open the pages. It wasn't a good idea, though, because he saw a photo of his mom.

His body jerked, tightening. *Thanks, Mom, for ruining my life once again.*

He argued with her, but he'd never been as furious as he'd gotten today, as he still was now.

After putting Myra down in her crib, he edged the door closed. This unease inside him deepened as he walked toward the closed bathroom door. The shower was still running. He crossed to their bedroom and flicked on the light.

Everything was clean and simple. From the mahogany queen bed that was nicely tucked in with a floral-print yellow comforter, to the two black wall plaques.

He stripped off his shirt and tossed it in the laundry basket beyond the night table. While he slid off his shoes, he paused to read the plaques across from the bed. He'd read them the first night he'd stayed, but he couldn't remember them now. Perhaps by the time he was done reading, Liberty would emerge from the bathroom.

Delicate white scrollwork embellished the first plaque, swirling around the words—*I can do all things through Christ (Philippians 4:13).*

It didn't make sense at all. So he eyed the one next to it—*With God all things are possible (Matthew 19:26).*

For some reason, that resonated as he remembered the day he drove to the cabin. He'd wondered if there was a God of miracles to bring Liberty back to him. He'd doubted it, but then Liberty showed up at the cabin that evening....

Bryce shivered. Goose bumps scattered on his arms as the surreal moment resurfaced.

There's a God of miracles, his inner consciousness whispered. Suddenly cold, he rubbed at his bumpy arms. The undershirt and undershorts he was wearing weren't warm enough.

With God all things are possible. He wasn't looking at the plaque anymore, but the words replayed in his mind.

With water still running, he stepped out of the bedroom and twisted open the knob on the bathroom door.

Liberty's sobs were louder than the streaming water.

His gaze skittered to the glass on the shower where she was standing. Still in her dress, she had her head tilted back while cascading water poured over her face.

His heart hammered against his ribs so hard he was amazed he could come up with the idea of sliding open the glass door and turning off the water.

"Oh, Dimples." His voice cracked, and he stepped into the one-person shower behind her. He then slid his arms around her waist.

His T-shirt instantly dampened from her wet dress while he struggled to speak over her stiffened back. "Please don't cry."

The muscles on her back released a slight tension when she let out a shallow breath. If only he could erase what Mom had said. He'd do anything to make her happy, but right now, he had no idea how to start. All he could do was kiss her neck, then her cheek, and hold her. He stayed silent, absorbing the tension radiating off her while he moved his hand around her back, erasing the tightness from her muscles.

She then spun and wrapped her arms around him, burrowing her head against his chest. She was shaking, and her hair was dripping. He never wanted to let her go from his arms. But he pressed his lips against her wet hair and whispered, "I'll get a towel, okay?"

Her gasped breath was the answer, and he eased out of her arms to grab one of the towels folded on the metal stand.

After helping her out of her wet dress and wiping her hair, he held the dryer to her hair, then carried her to their bedroom.

Minutes later, they'd changed, and Liberty almost seemed back to normal when he lay down beside her, tucking stray strands of hair from her face. The lamp on the table wasn't blinding, but shone enough light for him to look into her beautiful face. Her eyes were still red. He could give her time if she wanted to talk. It didn't seem like she was kicking him out of her life, so he'd wait until tomorrow—or if she never wanted to say anything at all, he'd have to be fine with that too.

She snuggled closer, and he savored her body heat as it seeped through her silk pajamas.

"Do you have doubts about Myra being your daughter?" Her sweet breath tickled his neck.

"No." He'd never had any doubt. Plus, Myra had his eyes, and her skin color was a perfect combination of his and Liberty's. "She's my daughter." Myra even knew that.

Liberty's hands tinkered at the edge of his V-neck nightshirt, brushing against the hair at the top of his chest.

"You usually like evidence. How come you didn't ask for a paternity test?"

"I believe you." He kissed the top of her head. Liberty had never given him a reason to doubt her love for him. If the many chances she'd given him weren't enough, his mom had made sure to let him know whenever she saw Liberty talking to or walking with any guy in town.

How Mom had won even one term as mayor still boggled him. Back then, Bryce never questioned her on how she knew Liberty's whereabouts.

"My mom will never know what you mean to me." He moved his hand to curl around her neck and kissed her lips. "She and Dad don't have what we have."

Poor Dad!

She touched his cheek, her eyes searching his. "Let's get a paternity test."

"We don't need one."

"Your mom does."

"You don't have to waste your kindness on my mom anymore." She'd tried, and Bryce was almost to the edge of not wanting to cross paths with his mom either. He was done, for now at least.

"I don't plan on going anywhere near her." She sighed out the soft words. "You'll deliver the tests once we get them, but I'll steer away from her for a long time."

"I understand." He gave his wife a fleeting kiss, grateful she was trying to prove it to his mom, even if she didn't need to. "I'm so proud of you."

Her determination to get tested got Bryce thinking. Whatever Mom had against Liberty had everything to do with Mom's insecurities and nothing to do with her concern for his happiness.

"I don't think God is happy with how I handled things tonight." Her brows pinched close, and regret trailed her words. "I'm sorry."

"God understands." Mom had it coming. "Next time, Mom will think twice before she corners you."

Liberty laughed a little, and he felt lighter. She didn't need Mom's approval when she already had a mom, and he told her so. Curious to know what Mom said to make Liberty lose her cool, he asked.

She raked her hand through his hair. "It's best I don't tell you."

He cupped her chin. "Why's that?"

"I don't want you getting angry at your mom."

That kind of selflessness made him fall more in love with her. The kind that tightened his chest and made him want to pursue the God she believed in.

She moved her hand from his hair, her fingers trailing along his cheek. His throat burned with tears as he looked into her sincere eyes.

"I love you, Bryce," she whispered.

He could barely speak through the emotion tightening his chest, but oh, how he loved her so! He didn't know how to express it in a way she could understand.

So he drew her closer and smothered her lips with his, losing himself in her warm embrace. Even if she didn't want him to hate his mom, he disliked Mom for doing this to her, to them.

DURING THE DAYS LEADING to Christmas Eve, Bryce loved waking up with Liberty next to him. Even if she woke up early to pray and read her Bible, he woke up much earlier to make her coffee and breakfast—if toast and store-bought muffins counted. He wanted her to eat before Myra woke and before Liberty made her morning work calls.

Besides that, out of habit, he checked the stock market daily. It was always good to know the value of his stock investments, especially in the newer companies he'd backed. He'd also heard from the scheduler company and had hired one. She would start on the twenty-seventh, the day after he left town.

He'd let Liberty know about it tomorrow when they opened their Christmas gifts. It would be the easiest way for her to accept his help. Still, he was tempted to tell her tonight whenever they got back from the Christmas Eve service he was already anxious about.

At least Dad was coming too, so there'd be two of them unfamiliar with church stuff. Yesterday, Bryce spent the entire day with his daughter while Liberty went to work. When Dad called, Bryce and Myra had met him for an early lunch at the country club. Dad seemed as eager to spend time with Myra as Bryce was. When Bryce told him about their plans for Christmas Eve, Dad had asked if he could join them since Mom had decided to take a last-minute trip to a resort in Vail with a couple of her friends.

Something clattered on the living room floor, and Bryce paused with the purple cartoony cup in his hand to glance at his daughter. She was fine, just making her usual noise of banging and throwing loud toys around her play area by the toy kitchen.

She looked adorable tonight in her lacy white dress with a big red bow on her chubby waist. Bryce nodded, pride surging through him for choosing a perfect dress. He then resumed filling the cup with water like he was supposed to before his daydreaming.

As he returned to put Myra's water in the bag, shoes clicked through the hallway, and his wife emerged.

His jaw hung as he took her in. She was always stunning, but tonight was—wow! Her dress was another one he'd bought when he bought Myra's.

"You look wonderful," she said as she stared at the button-down gray shirt he'd worn over black pants. He'd worn a coat to keep him warm given the wintertime and all.

Bryce cleared his throat and shook his head, then went to plant a kiss on her cheek. "You look stunning."

Liberty scooted away from him, giving a little swish that sent her maroon skirt swinging just above her knees. The sash dividing the skirt from the dress's black top emphasized her slender waist.

"All thanks to you." She touched the diamond drop necklace and peered at Myra, who was getting busy taking down the ornaments in her reach. At least, she knew how to put them back sometimes.

"Ready to go?" Bryce asked, not wanting his dad to get there and wait in an unfamiliar place.

"I'll just grab my Bible, and we'll be ready."

Good thing they'd left when they did. They'd arrived in the church lobby long enough to bask in pine and cinnamon from the baked goods before Dad called, letting Bryce know his driver was turning into the church parking lot.

Bryce told him to have his driver drop him off at the front. That made it easy to spot him when he emerged in his dark suit, white shirt, and red tie.

They walked over to meet him just as the same woman who welcomed them at the door shook Dad's hand. Her kind face aglow, she asked if it was Dad's first time to visit. Then, just like she'd told Bryce, she sent Dad to stop by the cookie and hot chocolate booth.

Myra tugged at Bryce's coat and pointed at the table where people were gathered to have their cookies. Bryce ignored her, not ready to be covered in cookie crumbs if she ate one while he was holding her.

Three or four Christmas trees positioned in the lobby lent a festive feel while soft music, similar to Myra's lullaby songs, played through the speakers as people stood, talking and greeting each other.

"Merry Christmas, Charles." At Liberty's warm smile, Dad spread out his hands, and she walked in for an embrace.

"Merry Christmas, Liberty." He kissed her cheek.

"Thanks for coming."

"Thanks for inviting me to your Christmas party." He then surveyed the lobby and the families, couples, and random people walking in. "You said Rhonda is coming too?"

"She'll meet us in church." Liberty tucked a wisp of hair behind her ear. "She probably had last-minute preparations before we go to her house."

Dad nodded, so Liberty asked if they were ready to walk into the sanctuary, then led them through the doors and down an aisle.

Although Bryce remained slightly tense in the unfamiliar environment, the people greeted Liberty by name, and her introductions of him and his father and their warm responses soon had him relaxing.

Having Dad here without Mom felt a bit awkward. But again, Bryce shouldn't feel sorry for her since she'd taken off with her friends and left her husband behind.

Ever since the party, Bryce had been too angry to answer Mom's calls. She was almost toxic—or maybe she *was* toxic. Whenever he was with Liberty, he felt alive and happy—until his mom said something about his wife. And after Liberty's tears on Friday, Bryce was still wounded by Mom's actions. He'd have to face her when the paternity results showed up on Wednesday. The same day he was leaving for New York. He'd stopped worrying about what Mom had said since Liberty had moved on and hadn't brought Mom up in any of their conversations.

As they sat down, he absorbed the beauty in the stained glass windows surrounding them. An older man was passing out baskets of candles, and he handed Myra a glow stick.

Soon a male voice sounded through the speakers, and everyone faced the stage. The speaker introduced himself as the associate pastor.

Two men and two women appeared on the stage as he walked off.

The worship leader asked everyone to stand and join in singing "Joy to the World" as the words were displayed on the screen that was above the stage.

Standing to his right side, Liberty sang the words in a soft lullaby voice. To his left, Myra hummed the tune, nestled comfortably on Dad's chest. Meanwhile, he and Dad stood there like robots, mutely staring at the screen.

Rhonda arrived as the song ended and another one started. When she leaned in to greet Dad, Myra leaped from Dad to her. Although Bryce hadn't seen Rhonda since his reunion with Liberty, they'd talked on the phone one night when she called Liberty.

"Hi, Bryce," Rhonda whispered, and he matched her hushed tone through the music. She then went to sit on the empty chair Liberty had reserved on her other side.

When they sang the next song, Bryce read the words, not attempting to sing for fear of scaring people in the nearby seats with his croaky voice:

"For Unto Us a Child Is Born
Unto Us a Son Is Given
Unto Us a Son Is Given
And His Name Shall Be Called
Wonderful Counselor

The Mighty God..."

If the song said "His name *shall* be called," did that mean the child wasn't born yet?

> "The Prince of Peace
> The Everlasting Father..."

As the song continued, Bryce's gaze flitted to the guitarist. His eyes were closed, but he wasn't missing a single note as he strummed and shook his head, clearly attuned to the song. By the time the song ended, Bryce's mind was buzzing with questions about the unborn child.

When the pastor announced what to read, pages rustled, and phones lit as people looked for whatever reading was required.

Bryce found the man's accent interesting. He even leaned into Liberty when she extended her Bible toward him.

The words were also written on the screen where Dad focused his gaze—*With God all things are possible (Matthew 19:26).*

Bryce blinked at the words from the plaque at home.

The pastor pointed out another section of the book to go along with God's miracles. Bryce squinted, struggling to see the tiny print in Liberty's Bible. He wanted to follow along with the pastor's pace as he read, but he decided to listen instead.

Something about a virgin visited by an angel.

"The Holy Spirit will come on you, and the power of the Most High will overshadow you.... You are to call Him Jesus... Son of the Most High."

This was all confusing. No wonder Liberty said it took faith rather than trying to grasp each detail.

However, he had to know the why and where. He'd blame that on the years in law school. Evidence was a big deal in getting the facts straight.

When the message ended, the tan-skinned man asked the singers to return to the stage. He also said they were going to light candles to celebrate Jesus's birthday.

Jesus was already born? Where was He?

The lights dimmed, and a woman came to light Dad's candle. He was asked to light Bryce's candle, and Bryce did the same for Liberty. Rhonda declined to light her candle since she had Myra who already had her stick glowing.

Liberty reached over past her mom to light the candle for the man on Rhonda's other side. The chain kept going until everyone had their candles lit.

The singers led them in "Silent Night," a familiar lullaby and Myra's favorite. When they sang the part about sleeping in heavenly peace, it felt like a memorial. A rise of goose bumps prickled his skin as he took in the candles that sparked light in the vast room, consuming the darkness.

Even the closing song after they turned on the light seemed to match with everything he'd heard during the service as they sang about the Light of the World who had stepped down into darkness.

Just like the tiny candles had lit the darkened room, little puzzles seemed to piece themselves together in his mind—puzzles about the baby Jesus Who came into the world.

The song continued with the singers asking the Light of the World to open their eyes and let them see.

He wasn't blind, but his heart was closed off to all this religious stuff.

When church was over and they made their way back to the lobby, Liberty introduced him and Dad to the pastor. Streaks of gray highlighted the man's dark hair along the edges. He was probably in his forties.

"Pedro." His handshake was firm and his voice enthused. "I'm so glad you're here.

"Me too."

"How long are you in town?"

While Bryce hadn't told him he was visiting, Liberty had mentioned emailing the pastor to set up a counseling session. "Not for long, but I'll be back." He hadn't even had time to talk to his business partners about his intentions to move back home to his wife.

"You and Liberty should write to me whenever you want to meet." Pedro then pulled out something from the top pocket of his red button-down shirt, then handed over the business card. "Liberty has my number, but in case you need it too."

"Thanks." Bryce pocketed the card and stepped aside for Dad to take his turn. He might need to call if he couldn't find answers to the topics Pedro taught about during church.

A few people hovered behind them, and all likely wanted a turn to ask Pedro questions.

Not far from them, Rhonda shook hands and chatted with people who seemed to be her friends. Their smiles and fondness for Myra hinted they knew his daughter well.

Liberty tugged on his arm. "Let's take our photo in front of one of the Christmas trees."

"Abe." Liberty interrupted the men standing in a loose circle. A tall man with a clean-shaven head stepped out of the circle and smiled at Liberty. "Merry Christmas."

"Merry Christmas to you too." Abe scratched his salt-and-pepper beard, and when his gaze turned behind Liberty, he waved at Bryce.

Liberty twisted her neck, her hair swooshing to one side as she introduced Bryce. "I don't think you've met my husband before."

While Bryce shook Abe's hand, she also introduced Dad. Then she asked Abe to help take their photo.

"It's my pleasure."

While she handed Abe the phone, her gaze swept to the group of women where Rhonda and Myra were. She cupped her mouth. "Mom!" When Rhonda turned, Liberty told her to join them for picture time.

Rhonda scooped Myra from one of the women.

"What tree would you like behind you in your photo?" Abe tugged at his tie.

"They all look spectacular," Dad said, and they all followed him to the nearest Christmas tree since people were taking their photos in front of the other trees.

When Rhonda joined them and greeted Abe, the man's hand shook. It got even worse when he lifted the phone to snap their group photo. Abe could very well have a tremor in his hands, which might make their photo blurry, but Bryce didn't want to make the man uncomfortable by pointing it out in case it was a serious problem for him.

"Can you try to take another one?" Liberty asked, squeezing Bryce's waist. He wanted to whisper into her ear that their photos would no doubt be blurry.

"Thanks, Abe." Liberty scooted forward and rescued her phone. "What are your plans tonight?"

He fidgeted with his tie, and his gaze dragged down to Rhonda, who was busying herself with Myra's lacy hair band. "I was hoping to drive and see some lights."

"You should join us for dinner."

Rhonda stifled a cough and lowered her lips to Myra's head, planting a kiss.

This is interesting.

Liberty continued to talk up Rhonda's roast and all the food they needed to eat.

Abe swallowed and stared at Rhonda. Then finally, Rhonda puffed out a breath and lifted her chin to stare back. Her lips parted.

Something definitely was between them. Bryce steered his gaze back to Abe. The man's chest rose and fell, and his forehead almost appeared to be breaking out in a sweat. They both seemed to forget they had an audience until Liberty spoke.

"I'll text you Mom's address."

Without giving Abe and her mom time to figure out their responses, Liberty walked to her mom and took Myra. She then whispered in her ear, producing a shy smile from her mother.

Clearly embarrassed, Rhonda moved to Dad and touched his arm. "Charles, I hope you can still join us for dinner?"

Dad gave a subtle nod, his lips curling into a smile. "I wouldn't miss the best roast in town."

Bryce winked at his dad. They were going to have a wonderful evening of fun and matchmaking.

CHAPTER 16

Later that night, Liberty curled up on the couch with her sweet husband. Bryce was dressed in red reindeer-print pajamas similar to hers. Myra, now in bed, had the matching pajamas Liberty had bought two days ago as their Christmas Eve presents. They'd opened their gifts as soon as they returned from Mom's house.

Once they put Myra to bed, they'd then called their friends Tessa, Iris, and Logan to wish them a Merry Christmas. Like Bryce, Logan was leaving on the twenty-sixth, while Iris was going on the twenty-ninth.

As soon as they'd showered and changed into their new pajamas, Bryce was eager to ask questions from the message at church. He was now scrolling through a Bible app on his phone. Liberty had referenced the Bible when he'd asked why in the song it seemed like Jesus wasn't born yet in "Silent Night," it seemed like Jesus was dead and in Heaven.

"I found Isaiah 7:14," he said, his brows drawn together, so she leaned in, their heads almost touching as she encouraged him to read the prophecy about Jesus's birth.

"'Therefore, the Lord Himself will give you a sign...'" He paused and glanced at her, then back to the screen. "'The virgin will conceive....'"

He lowered the phone. "This is almost similar to what Pedro read earlier." The lights from the tree next to him sent an extra spark in his eyes. "The virgin—"

"Yes." Liberty wasn't too sure of all her facts. She believed in God because she just *knew* He was God and sovereign. So she shared the few facts she knew, further explaining what the pastor taught about the angel visiting Mary.

Bryce leaned back on the edge of the couch. "How many years is it between the time Isaiah prophesied Jesus, and Jesus's birth?"

Uh-oh. She blew out a breath and whispered a silent prayer. Maybe she should have asked all these questions a long time ago. Right now, she had no idea, but she couldn't just say, "Deal with it and believe like I do." So she tucked the puffiest part of her hair behind her left ear and a foot underneath her on the couch. Then admitted she didn't know all the facts nor have all the answers. "Let's research on the internet and see if we can find something."

His fingers moved on the screen as he typed in his question. "Seven hundred years?" he said seconds later, his eyes widening.

Whoa. Liberty's jaw dropped. She hadn't known the prophecy and its fulfillment were so many years apart. Over the next several minutes, Bryce looked up the prophecies about Jesus's birth, and Liberty admired him for trying to find out more about what he may want to believe.

Having faith was always the best thing to do, but Bryce's curiosity was helping prepare her with answers for people like him in the future—people who needed evidence on why they should believe what she believed.

They read John 1:1–3, a perfect reminder of how it all started with God's word and without Him nothing would be in existence—He was the light that shone into the darkness.

"Like the light from the candles that lit in the dark church." Bryce's brows unfurrowed as his face lit as if a spark within him ignited.

When they stopped and she prayed with him before bed, a verse popped into her mind: *You will seek me and find me when you seek me with all your heart.*

She prayed God would reveal Himself to Bryce as he genuinely sought for God. Then she whispered amen, and Bryce pulled her to his side, embracing her fiercely. She squeezed him, and she felt his racing heart.

"Thank you for not giving up on me."

Guilt pricked her heart. She'd given up on him when she walked out of their marriage. "Thank you for not giving up on me too."

She breathed in his subtle eucalyptus scent. She would miss him when he was gone, but he was only leaving temporarily. He intended to talk to his business partners about the details of his departure from New York. In the meantime, she and Myra could fly every so often to see him. She had plenty of miles saved up from the business card she used.

The night ended up being short when Myra woke up much earlier than usual. Perhaps she also sensed her dada would be leaving them soon.

Liberty and Bryce sat on the creamy carpet in front of the tree where wrapped and unwrapped presents had sprung up overnight.

Myra's eyes lit up when she saw the small stand-up piano eating up the space by the tree. She darted for it and started pounding the keyboard. Liberty turned to her husband, questioning all the extra toys he got for Myra. Liberty had already wrapped presents for their daughter under the tree. "I don't want her to get spoiled."

Bryce squished his face. "Sorry. I just couldn't help myself—and I do have last Christmas to make up for."

Myra noticed a mini chair tucked at the back of the tree. "Tia."

"Merry Christmas, Starlight!" Bryce reached for Myra's hand and drew her toward him, hugging her. "You want to help me get the chair?"

She wriggled herself out of the embrace as her response.

"It's your chair," he said after drawing it away from the tree and pulling open the storage bin underneath it. Liberty had to admit it was a clever purchase. Myra eased into the chair, resting her little hands on the attached desk. "She fits in it perfectly."

Since Myra was happy bouncing between the two toys she had so far, Liberty handed Bryce his present from her. Wrapping it had been tricky, and by his grin, he knew what it was before he yanked off the wrapper.

Myra was at their side, and with her short attention span, she was now interested in throwing the wrapper up in the air.

"Oh my!"

Bryce ripped off the rest of the red wrapper and unzipped the bag, then pulled out the guitar. "I love it." He twanged a couple of strings, beaming, then set it aside and crawled to Liberty and placed a soft kiss on her lips.

"I thought I'd replace the one that got lost," she whispered, not wanting to dwell on the guitar she still assumed his mom had maliciously stolen from under their Christmas tree. She'd shown up when Liberty was wrapping presents and asked why she was giving Bryce a guitar since "He doesn't even play."

Liberty had responded that what she gave Bryce shouldn't concern his mother. Then, two days before Christmas, the guitar went missing. It had bothered her so much that she'd broken down and told him a week after Christmas.

"My turn." He handed her a manila envelope.

What on earth? Raising a brow, she broke the seal and removed the papers. A résumé and contact information for a scheduling company in town, to be precise. She flipped to the next paper, the name of a candidate who would be scheduling her employees. Her heartbeat escalated as her mouth slid open. One just for her?

"I've already paid."

Liberty's mouth froze. Overwhelmed by his thoughtfulness, she couldn't form a response. After moments passed and she thought she could speak, she raised her gaze to his, and her hand flew to her warmed heart. "You got me a scheduler?"

"One less thing for you to juggle." He shrugged as if it were no big deal, but it was a *huge* deal to her.

Scheduling employees and finding replacements was the hardest part of her job. She'd known she needed a scheduler, but she couldn't afford to hire one.

She set the papers down and crawled to his spot, lunged into him and threw her arms around him. He fell back, but thankfully, the squishy faux-leather couch kept him from toppling all the way down.

"It's not a very romantic gift, but—"

"It's perfect." She scrambled off him and back to her spot on the carpet.

Bryce reached for a big box and handed it to her. She smiled when she pulled out the lace-up knee-high winter boots. While stylish, the rubber feet and fuzzy insides would keep her warm and dry. "I love them."

His sheepish smile tugged up one corner of his mouth. "Again, it's not romantic, but practical."

"Who needs romantic things when I have you?" She waved a hand, but even before she could return it to her lap, Bryce slid a tan box tied with a red ribbon onto her lap. She fingered the soft-as-silk ribbon, then untied the box. Her brows inched up when she lifted the lid to a bunch of confetti. He merely grinned and shrugged, so she rooted through the fancy papers for the present until her fingers connected with a thicker paper. She unearthed it and unfolded a notification of a car that would be delivered in a few days.

A gasp slid free before she clamped her hand over her mouth. "An Audi SUV?" He'd spent too much money on her. "I already have a car."

"You need one to sustain you in the winter."

"I don't plan on going back to the cabin, not in the winter."

His knowing look raised her temperature as if he'd submerged her in that hot tub. "I plan to. You'll be coming with me."

Oh my! She returned his sly smile with a coy one of her own.

"Where am I going to park all these cars? And when the house owner shows up in January, he'll need a place to park."

Bryce tinkered with some guitar chords, tuning it. "I'll leave the Jeep at the garage tomorrow when I bring Mom the paternity tests." He paused as if thinking about something better. "Of course, I can just email her the results."

She didn't want him avoiding his mom. It wasn't right. So she clasped his hand and squeezed. "Regardless of some friction I have with her, you should talk to her before you leave."

He tilted his head, frowning. "Some friction?"

She shrugged and winked since she wanted to downplay her relationship with Wendy.

"Some friction is the understatement of the century."

The longer it took, the harder it would be for him to get back to normal with his mom. That had been the case when she'd walked away from Bryce. The longer she took to call him, the more she felt she could manage without him.

It still boggled her that Bryce trusted her about Myra. What if the clinic made mistakes and the results ended up wrong? Panic snuck into her heart, and she tried to shove it away while Myra bounced on Bryce's lap.

He then presented some New Year's Eve plans.

"I asked your mom to watch Myra." He squeezed Myra close to him and kissed her plump cheek. "If it's okay with you, I want you to come to New York on the twenty-ninth until the first."

"Okay." She liked the idea of having a date with her husband, but would Myra be okay with them gone that long? She needed to work out flight details and connect with the new scheduler he'd hired.

"We'll video call your mom any time of day or night to check on Myra."

Liberty smiled at that, but she couldn't make her excitement last without Wendy popping into her mind.

"Are we staying at your Hampton home?" Their family vacation home.

"No." He shook his head too fast. "Not even at my penthouse."

She let out a breath, relieved. Wendy even had a room at his penthouse so she could show up there anytime unannounced. If they weren't staying at the family house in the Hamptons or his penthouse, then... "Where are we staying?"

"It's a surprise."

Anticipation coursed through her as Bryce grinned and handed Myra another one of her presents to open. He then reached for his guitar and settled it on his lap.

"I have this song." He started strumming, and a few measures later, Liberty recognized the tune.

"'The Best Day' by Taylor Swift."

He continued picking with his fingertips. The melody floated through the room, the strains soothing and peaceful.

Bryce was a gifted player, and although Liberty had played the guitar with her boyfriend before Bryce, she had to admit he knew how to hit all the right chords.

Even Myra stopped tinkering with her toys and decided to jump up and down, dancing and humming off tune.

Love shone in his eyes when he gave the final strum that took Liberty back to her twenties and to the man she'd fallen in love with, the man she still loved and would love always.

Taylor Swift had always been her favorite artist, but after Liberty had Myra, she only had time to listen to Bible kid jams and nursery rhymes, and if she was lucky enough to be in the car alone, then maybe, she would turn on K-LOVE for contemporary Christian music.

"Whenever I miss you, I sing that song." Bryce's voice faltered. "The best times of my life have always been with you. Whenever I thought of our earlier days together, it gave me hope we'd be together again."

Her eyes stung at his sincerity.

"Don't cry." Bryce set his guitar down and scooted closer, then snuggled her in his arms.

Sighing, she rested her head on his chest. "They're tears of joy." It bubbled inside like a volcano.

His chest rose and fell beneath her. The protective warmth of his arm around her and the soft kiss he planted atop her head warmed her as he whispered, "I love you."

Liberty realized how they needed this New York trip—a planned trip to focus on them, their relationship and reintroduction to their marriage.

CHAPTER 17

Christmastime in New York was extraordinary with all the unique light shows Bryce had taken Liberty to. She'd been to New York during their brief year or so of marriage, but she hadn't had the chance to be there at Christmas.

Her first days in town felt like a whole week with the whirlwind of nonstop activity Bryce packed into them.

Since she'd arrived late on Saturday, they'd had room service at his hotel, and Sunday morning, they'd gone shopping at Saks Fifth Avenue, a high-end department store Bryce insisted on taking her to. Everything was overpriced, and when she told him she had everything she needed, he argued that it was the first shopping spree he'd had with his wife and he wanted to make it memorable.

Uncomfortable overindulging, she would've been content window-shopping, but she still got a cocktail dress and heels when he mentioned a cruise dinner he'd booked them on.

After shopping, he brought her to Brooklyn Botanic Garden. The magical artistic light displays set along beautifully illuminated paths through the gardens had enchanted her. Then they'd taken the Dyker Heights Christmas Lights tour and ended their day at the ballroom where they'd danced and stayed the night.

Even after she'd changed her mind and wanted to stay at his penthouse, Bryce said he'd already paid for their hotel stay and didn't want to take any chances of his mom showing up and interfering. All it took was him bringing up Wendy's name to convince Liberty to stay at a hotel.

The following day, Monday, was New Year's Eve, so they had taken a nostalgic stroll to the Rockefeller Tree earlier that morning.

Liberty wished Starlight was here to see the abundant lights. But she loved spending time alone with her husband, doing things they'd never done before. Except for dancing—they'd definitely danced in the past.

It was hard to determine her favorite part about the trip, but when they boarded the cruise at six thirty, away from the hustle and bustle, it became the highlight. Having the city at a glance was remarkable as they watched and listened to live piano and a singer in the background.

With a perfect window view, Liberty clasped Bryce's hands from across the table. The LED Christmas lights illuminated his face. Dressed in a crisp white shirt, black tie, and black suit, he looked more handsome than on their wedding day.

Beyond the window, the Manhattan skyline offset another yacht decked out in holiday finery, and Liberty sucked in a quick breath as if she could take the sight and hold onto it forever as it passed by. "This is so beautiful," she barely whispered over the music. How could she thank him for making their time together so special?

A warm smile opened his mouth as he brought her hand to his lips and kissed it. "You are more beautiful."

He told her this more often. Everyone on their lower deck looked happy to be here for the special occasion. Being surrounded by exuberant strangers, all adults, emboldened Liberty to show public affection for her husband.

She unclasped their hands and edged the champagne flutes to the side. They hadn't requested champagne, but every table in the room had a glass next to the water glasses. Bryce's brow crinkled when she stood and leaned in across the table to press a kiss on his lips.

"Mrs. Solace." He cupped her cheek and kissed her back softly. "You are awfully brazen today."

"I can't help it." She slid back into her chair, then winked. "After all, I may not get another chance this year."

Soon the servers passed around the room filling their water glasses and reminding them of the open bar with wine, beer, and cocktails. They both decided to stick with water since they had another celebration to attend after the cruise.

Dinner was an Italian buffet with chicken parmigiana, Bryce's favorite, as well as eggplant rollatini, antipasti, caprese salad, and an abundance of desserts.

"I like your chicken parmigiana better," Bryce said after their dinner. And Liberty laughed, saying she expected him to say that if he wanted her to cook his favorite meal again.

As the festivities continued throughout the yacht, surely everyone on the two floors above them was having as much fun as they did on their floor. They danced to a nice mix of music that included something for everyone.

Liberty had to pinch herself a few times and squeeze her husband tighter. She touched his cheek more times than not, and she couldn't help but kiss him chastely every so often. He even commented that she was scaring him. "I feel like you're saying goodbye to me."

She would say goodbye tomorrow since they'd be apart for a week or two or however long his work required.

"I want to make sure I'm not dreaming," she responded, feeling like she was on cloud nine. How many people had the chance to dance on a yacht while enjoying views of New York?

When the yacht stopped, they went outside. In the crisp night air, Bryce stripped off his coat, then draped it on her shoulders. "I am real," he said, pulling her closer and leading her toward the deck railing. "Our love is real."

She couldn't agree more. The 360-degree views from the water towered around them while reflections from the city lights and tall buildings shimmered on the water. Seeing the Statue of Liberty lit up as close as they did, she had to take a picture. She patted herself but felt Bryce's phone in the pocket of his jacket she was wearing. "My handbag."

"We left it at our table," he said. "I can go and get it."

"I don't need it. I just wanted to take a photo of the scenery. And us."

"How can we not get a photo with the statue behind us?" Bryce said, his tone light. "It's named after you."

Although Mom had freedom on her mind when she'd named her Liberty.

At that, she retrieved the phone.

When she asked Bryce to turn around so they could pose with the Statue of Liberty in the background, a woman standing nearby offered to take their photo. The woman then handed her handbag to the man she was with.

As Liberty thanked their photographer after she took their photo, Bryce offered to take the woman's photo with her husband, and they paused to take the same background view.

The evening went too fast since the cruise fun ended at nine thirty. It was just the perfect time for them to head back to their hotel. As she and Bryce sat in the back of the yellow taxi, driving past Times Square to their hotel became a challenge. With the place lit up from the festivities, traffic backed up as if every person in New York was headed down to catch a bit of the action.

"Would you like to FaceTime now?" Bryce's warm arm brushed against her neck as they sat right next to each other as if the seat belts hadn't done their job separating them. They'd intended to make the call from the hotel, but at this pace, they might reach their hotel at midnight.

"I think you're right." Liberty pulled her phone from her handbag. It was ten fifteen. "It's eight fifteen in Colorado."

"You think Starlight is still awake?" Bryce asked as Liberty punched the video icon on her phone.

"We'll find out soon." Last night, Myra had been in bed by eight since she skipped her nap.

"It's Mama and Dada." Mom's face appeared on the screen, but she had her neck turned, obviously talking to Myra.

"How's everything going, Mom?" Liberty moved the phone between hers and Bryce's face.

Bryce draped his arm on her shoulder, his cheek touching hers. "Hey there, Rhonda."

"I hope you two are having fun, instead of worrying about your daughter." Mom waved a finger between them. "Myra hasn't even missed you for a second."

Things clattered in the background, no doubt Myra busy scattering books and blocks all over Mom's living room. That Myra didn't run to the phone when her grandma told her it was Mama and Dada left Liberty more relaxed about being away with Bryce. Instead of talking about Myra like she would while away from her daughter, Liberty asked Mom if she'd talked to Abe since the Christmas Eve dinner.

Abe had laughed and teased Mom a few times during their dinner. He and Mom even shared some inside jokes. He'd felt comfortable enough to follow Mom to the kitchen and help her slice the pies, which had given him time alone with Mom.

"Don't you two have enough love in your lives? Why should you want to hear about my love life?"

"We do, but we're married." Bryce squeezed Liberty's arm. "So we want reminders of how to feel when you're newly in love."

Mom smiled shyly. "He's taking me out to dinner on Saturday." Then the screen went blurry before Myra's face appeared. Something white dusted her cheeks and forehead.

"Starlight," Bryce whispered with a gentle fondness. A few days before he'd flown to New York, he'd started calling her Starlight. "What happened to your face?"

Myra lifted a toy phone while babbling her nonsensical words. Yep, she was fine without them.

"We tried to make some cookies." Mom explained her attempt to involve Myra in making cookie dough she intended to freeze.

Memories of Bryce's attempt to cook at the cabin rushed into Liberty's mind, and she chuckled. "She cooks like her dada."

"There's nothing wrong with that." Bryce poked her rib cage, and she jumped, feeling ticklish. "I have to cook for you sometimes."

They didn't chat much longer. Mom needed to give Myra a bath and get her to bed.

Just before eleven, they reached the Chatwal Hotel. Happily, they didn't have to leave their hotel to be a part of tonight's festivities. Their suite offered amazing views of the Times Square ball drop, so they'd watch it from their private terrace.

After showering and changing into comfortable clothes, they sat on the cozy sofa by the window. The massive bouquet of mixed flowers on the table in front of them wafted its soft fragrance into the room, the scent of roses reminding her of those first days with Bryce.

It didn't feel like it was just the two of them. With their window slightly open, the noise in the party room downstairs joined them.

Then the butler showed up twice to deliver a tray of decadent appetizers and Pepsi, Liberty's favorite. After the cruise buffet, they weren't hungry. He also served them Sparkling Grape Juice Cocktails to toast in the New Year.

She snuggled her head against her husband's chest, savoring his nearness as he kept a protective arm draped on her shoulder. She didn't want this night to end, but she had to return to Pleasant View tomorrow. Myra needed her, and Liberty had to work too.

As if reading her thoughts, Bryce asked about her plans for the week.

"Thanks to you, I get to enjoy my job even more." Scheduling employees, taking last-minute calls for absentees, and rescheduling the no-shows was going to be someone else's responsibility. She hoped it worked. "I'll try to put away the Christmas tree." She told him of the landlord's visit to Pleasant View in the second week of January.

"I don't want you and Myra staying with some strange guy." Bryce stiffened his chest, so she shifted to look at him.

"He's a harmless old man who moved to a warmer climate after his wife died. He's coming to town to visit a couple of his buddies." Liberty had met him through one of her clients. "He's like Myra's other grandpa."

Bryce's jaw clenched, and he pulled her back to rest her head on his chest. He then kissed her hair. "I'll try to wrap things up here as soon as I can. I want to be home before his visit." He then admitted his fear to transition to a small town, the fear of missing out on regularly interacting with clients. There were still hurdles with the companies where he was a board member, and he was unsure how that would play out with his absence from New York. "I'm still convincing my partners I can handle things remotely."

His heart raced below her cheek as he shared his thoughts on investing in a starter company that could further benefit the blind.

"I know you can do it, even without your partners' help." Her chest swelled, and she let out a contented sigh, proud of his willingness to step forward on his own. Something out of his nature. "That's a leap of faith," she said, remembering their conversation about faith, hoping it would make sense when used in a point of view he could relate to.

"A leap of faith." He nodded, his chin brushing the top of her head. "I like that."

She hadn't entertained the idea of making changes herself. But since he made more money than she did, perhaps she and Myra needed to move to New York. Liberty could focus on raising their daughter from home. Then Bryce wouldn't stress over transitioning and, no doubt, taking a pay cut. She shared her thoughts.

"Myra needs to stay close to Rhonda." His hand moved over her back, the gentle caress of his fingers soothing. "We still need to have our house built in Pleasant View. It's our home."

They talked about plans to schedule counseling sessions for the new year and Bryce's desire to buy land to build a home since they still had their plans from years ago.

"We don't need to build a house." Property had gone way up within the last few years.

"We might have to add a couple of rooms in case Myra gets a little brother or sister someday," he said, seeming deep in thought as he ignored her statement. "I know property is more expensive nowadays, but I have more money than I did back then."

"We never talked about how many kids we wanted to have."

They were busy talking about their dreams and plans for the future, not paying attention to the time, until noise erupted downstairs.

"Six! Five! Four!"

"Three," Bryce said, then slid his arm around her middle to hoist her onto his lap. "Two."

"One!" they shouted simultaneously, matching the noise downstairs.

Fireworks boomed, followed by loud cheers. Beyond the window, neon lights from the fireworks and confetti flew in the air.

"Happy New Year, my lovely wife!" Bryce curled his hand around her neck, and as Liberty wished him a Happy New Year, he cut off her words with a tender and passionate kiss.

Liberty got lost in the kiss while "Auld Lang Syne" sounded from various voices downstairs, the same song she heard every year with nonsensical words. But this moment, this year as it wound down and a new year started with her husband in her arms, she focused on Bryce as the confusing song faded in the background. She had no doubt, once again. Where Bryce was concerned, she'd made the right decision to have him back in hers and Myra's lives.

CHAPTER 18

"I'm so sorry, sweetheart." Liberty sandwiched the phone between her ear and shoulder as she dipped a spoon in the plastic bowl and lifted it to Myra's parted lips. Flapping her arms and laughing, Myra rocked the bowl on her high chair tray while she chewed. The oatmeal smelled terrible today. It wasn't burned, nor was it stale. But it had a smell that made Liberty feel nauseous.

She had been feeding Myra breakfast when Bryce called in a panic about the two companies they'd invested in having declared bankruptcy and his firm losing money. "What's the worst-case scenario?"

He let out a sigh. "That shuts down any chance of convincing the partners about Javir's startup."

Liberty straightened and glanced at the window where morning light pooled into the kitchen sink. Snow still covered the ground, which wasn't unusual in mid-January. "I'm so proud of you for wanting to help his company."

For some reason, he'd been passionate about helping the new entrepreneur produce a smartwatch for the blind. So she'd been praying God would give Bryce wisdom on whether to pursue it as a solo venture or to drop the thought.

"I don't know what I'm going to do." He sounded defeated, and she had no idea how to help him.

"Mo... mo." Myra pressed the tips of her fingers together, one of the few finger signs Liberty had taught her before she started talking. She wanted more oatmeal, but the bowl was almost empty.

Liberty scraped the spoon to gather all the remaining mushy grain just as an idea popped into her mind. "Have you talked to Eric about this?" Besides being a shareholder with Bryce in a couple of companies, Eric was established with several successful investments. He'd also mentored Bryce in his career.

"I can't believe I didn't think about him." Bryce chuckled, his voice picking up more energy. "I should call him with a proposition. I don't know what I'd do without you."

He'd do fine without her, but he did need Someone helping him. So she reminded him who was behind all wisdom and success. "Without God, everything we do is meaningless."

"I'm starting to believe that." He puffed out a breath, and the sound rustled through her phone speakers. "I've been reading about ancient Egypt and Israel and looking into several books to research the validity of the Bible manuscripts and God's existence. It's interesting that the places in the Bible are real."

Liberty reached for the sippy cup from the counter and set it on Myra's high chair tray as Bryce's rising excitement made his words run together. He talked about the Red Sea and the book of Exodus, particularly the story of Moses from his birth through God parting the Red Sea. "If God can create a path in the middle of the sea, then there's a lot I need to learn about Him."

"He's worth your time," Liberty whispered, her chest tightening as her eyes welled up. She'd been so emotional lately and had no idea why. Perhaps they were tears of joy. She whispered a silent plea, a prayer that God could continue to show Himself to Bryce one day at a time.

"Down! Down!" Myra started chanting, kicking her pudgy legs and pushing at the tray as she wiggled.

Bryce laughed. "Sounds like Starlight's done eating. Mind if we switch to FaceTime so I can talk to her?" Since he knew their morning schedule, he'd called instead of video chatting to avoid distracting Myra during her breakfast.

Now they switched mediums. Then after wishing Bryce a wonderful day of business meetings and ending the video chat, Liberty cleaned Myra's face with a wet wipe and hoisted her out of the high chair. "I'm going to let you play for a bit."

She'd better figure out something to eat. She'd gotten so used to Bryce serving her breakfast in bed that she'd almost forgotten what she used to eat before his morning toasts, muffins, and occasional scrambled eggs.

The two weeks since she'd returned from New York had flown by too fast. Things had taken Bryce longer to wrap in New York than he'd expected, but she'd been too busy to do a countdown for his return.

The landlord had left on Sunday, two days ago. During his visit, Bryce had called, worried about the houseguest staying with them. To ease his worry, Liberty had introduced the gentleman to Bryce, and they video chatted. They realized they were both passionate about mountain biking, so they talked about various trails in Pleasant View, some of which Bryce hadn't been to. By the end of their call, they'd become future bike buddies.

Even though Liberty's amazing scheduler made things easier, she still had strategy meetings with employees once a week and visited some of her clients, and Myra alone kept her going nonstop.

As she sat on the couch to eat while keeping an eye on Myra, the first two bites of cereal nearly gagged her. Touching her stomach, she cringed. Maybe she'd better not eat cereal after all. She took the bowl to the kitchen, and not wanting to jump over the baby gate or move it, she stretched over to set the cereal on the counter.

With Myra content putting toy animals in the farmhouse next to her kitchen, Liberty fired off a group text to Iris and Tessa to update her prayer partners on Bryce's research. Seconds after she clicked send, her phone rang, and Tessa's face popped up on the screen, then so did Iris's shortly after.

"Hey." After pressing to answer, Liberty turned her back to the couch. The lime green, usually cheery, seemed too bright this morning, and she couldn't imagine sitting there.

"Let's keep it quick, girls." Iris held up a hand, pink manicure flashing against her blue blazer. "I want to know the details, but I have a meeting in twenty minutes."

With almost nine here, it'd be nearly eleven in Boston.

"What exactly did he say?" Tessa's dark ponytail bounced as she passed rolled-up exercise mats, medium balls, and colorful dumbbell sets. Liberty, having been in Tessa's home studio a few times, easily recognized the room.

"It's not much different from what we said last time." Liberty nudged aside the tricycle as she moved to sit next to Myra and handed her the cow that hadn't made it into the farmhouse yet. "He's been reading the Bible...."

While Liberty relayed what Bryce had shared, Iris fanned herself. "I don't need to start crying before meeting with a client."

Tessa tilted her head to the side, beaming. "Isn't God so wonderful!"

"I know..." Liberty whispered as emotion clogged up her throat.

"No tears. Let's stay focused." Iris blew out a breath.

"Yeah, let's not give Liberty another reason to cry."

Sitting up straighter, Liberty frowned at Tessa. "What do you mean by that?"

"She means you've been emotional ever since Bryce came back into your life," Iris clarified, and when Liberty tried to argue, Iris rolled her eyes. "You cried when telling us about the cruise *and* when you described that silly calf you saw on the farm beside the road."

"But he was so cute!"

"Let's not forget the streamline of *Cheaper by the Dozen* last week." Holding up a hand and arching her brows, Tessa cut Liberty off. They kept Iris in the loop when they watched a movie online together by pausing and chatting during the movie. "That movie is not sad at all."

"It's hilarious," Iris said while Liberty tried to recall the family movie with all those kids. She couldn't remember which scene made her cry.

"I'm a mom," she defended. "Anything with kids makes me cry."

Myra wandered to the other side of the room, leaving a trail of farm animals on the floor before she toddled to her tricycle, climbed on, then scooted around.

Trying to redirect their conversation, Liberty asked for prayers for Bryce, his decision to invest in Javir's company, and his motivation to search for spiritual answers. Then she asked about Tessa's soldier, Chad, but Tessa ignored the question and commented about Myra sounding like she was having fun.

"Put Starlight on the phone," Iris said, probably getting the hint that discussing Chad was out.

Liberty was sauntering toward Myra when the doorbell rang.

"Let me first see who's at the door." Liberty sidestepped the farm animals on her way to the door, then peeked through the peephole. And her stomach dropped.

Wendy stood there in a black blazer and sleek pants that matched her tan blouse. The woman didn't have a job, but she dressed as if she were headed to an office—Liberty was her job, her mission she had to assume.

Liberty tiptoed away from the door, afraid her mother-in-law would hear her say her name when she told her friends about the unwanted guest.

"That's odd that she's at your house." Iris's brows squeezed together, the questions in her expression exactly how Liberty felt.

"Especially this early," Tessa added. "How does she even know where you live?"

Liberty let out a slight snort. "Wendy never has trouble finding me whenever she feels like it."

Myra hummed as she swung her little arms, waddling back to her toy kitchen in the living room.

"I'll call you guys back, okay?"

"Don't hang up. We want to hear everything," Tessa said, but Iris needed to get ready for her meeting.

Toys clanked as Myra fidgeted with the plastic dishes.

Liberty walked toward the door with shaky limbs, and the bell rang again as she touched the doorknob. Her hands trembled when she turned it.

"Liberty." Inclining her head in a regal gesture that showed off her French twist, Wendy offered a deceptive smile.

"Wendy," Liberty said, her voice shakier and less confident than she wanted to appear. Her gaze darted to the driveway as she composed herself. A driver waited behind the wheel of a black Lexus parked there. At least Wendy didn't have police with her today. Liberty gripped the phone tighter in her hand, moisture building up on her palms. "How can I help you?"

"I came to see my granddaughter." Wendy raised a flashy purple gift bag. Her other hand clasped a silver clutch bag. Then she sidestepped Liberty to enter the house. "Can I come in?"

Can I say no?

Wendy's heels clicked on the hardwood floor as she walked toward the kitchen, scanning the main area and living room. Her gaze steadied on Myra absorbed in a loud ABC house learning pad she kept sliding in and out of her kitchen oven.

Liberty cleared her throat. She did owe Wendy an apology, didn't she? "I'm sorry for pouring—"

"Spare me the apologies." Wendy jiggled the flashy bag in Liberty's face, then marched toward Myra. "I'm here to give my granddaughter a present."

"Wow." A distant voice sounded from the phone, reminding Liberty that Tessa was still online.

Liberty ended the video call, even though Tessa did have a point about witnessing whatever Wendy had come to say. With Wendy's back to her, Liberty hit record on her phone so she'd have evidence of some sort should Wendy make up a story about her.

Moving toward Wendy and Myra, Liberty set the phone on the table upside down. "I thought you said she wasn't your granddaughter."

Ignoring Liberty, Wendy ruffled Myra's hair. "Hello, Myra."

Myra lifted her head and frowned as she took Wendy in.

"I got you something, darling."

Instead of taking the offered bag, Myra unfurled her brows and seemed to accept Wendy's smile. She then reached for the green and white ABC pad and handed it to Wendy. "Pa... pa."

Wendy tucked her clutch bag in her armpit and accepted the pad. Her face softened, and her smile seemed warm as she pressed the toy and it erupted with an ABC tune.

"I can tell you are very smart." Wendy's voice rose over the toy noise. "Just like your daddy."

Bryce was intelligent, no doubt. But Liberty tried not to assume the words contained a dig at her while Wendy knelt on the floor, picked up one of the plastic cups, and handed it to Myra. "One of these days, Nana will take you to a high tea."

"Tea." Myra smiled, putting the cup to her mouth. Liberty's heart warmed slightly. She'd come to terms with the fact that Wendy would never accept her, but if Wendy loved her granddaughter, Liberty would let Wendy be part of Myra's life. But having her come here without notice sure was awkward.

When Myra's attention wavered and she waddled to Liberty to be carried, she scooped her up and hoisted her to her hip, then asked Wendy, "How did you find out where I live?"

Wendy stood with a mirthless laugh as she brushed imaginary dust from her hands. "As long as you clawed back into my son's life, it's my business to know where you live."

She then reached for the bag on the floor and pulled out a white box. Liberty strained to see what was on the box. Was that an iPad and the Apple logo? "This is for Myra."

Like Myra needed an iPad. What was the catch? The last thing Liberty needed was to accept the gadget only to be accused of stealing it from her house. She leaned against the TV cupboard to support herself from Myra's weight as she eyed the box like it was about to suck the blood out of her.

"We don't need your gifts. She's not ready for an iPad." The fact that the box wasn't enticing enough for Myra to reach for it should be an indication. Okay, Myra loved tinkering with Liberty's phone, but only when she expected a video chat.

Wendy set the box on the floor, then assessed her manicured fingers, thinking of something before she spoke her mind. "You were smart to send me the paternity results." She looked at Liberty, then Myra. "Thankfully, Myra has Bryce's eyes and calm temperament."

"What's that supposed to mean?" Liberty tightened her arms around Myra, feeling the tension radiate in her body. Even when Myra wiggled to get down, Liberty feared if she let her go Wendy might snatch her away and take off. That could be the only reason she was here.

Wendy's plucked eyebrows lifted as she crossed her arms. "My granddaughter is not going to be raised by someone with such a temper." She pursed the lips she'd loaded with lipstick. Then she traipsed toward the kitchen, her heels clicked, and each step jabbed like a sharp pin piercing through Liberty's heated body. "The house doesn't look safe for my granddaughter."

She kicked one of Myra's toy farm animals aside as she walked to the kitchen and stopped at the gate. Tapping her fingernails on the gate, she scanned one side of the kitchen, then the other.

Thankfully, Liberty was still in her slippers. Otherwise, she would've tripped as she wobbled toward Wendy while struggling to keep Myra tight in her arms.

Wendy moved down the hallway and peeked into Myra's bedroom. "Hmm."

Liberty should be screaming and commanding her to leave. She was trespassing as she assessed the other two rooms and the bathroom before she emerged toward the hall where Liberty had remained standing.

Chilled to the bone, Liberty shivered as her fear resurfaced. *This* was why she'd kept Myra a secret from Bryce. "What do you want, Wendy?"

Wendy stood straight, those too-red lips spreading out. "All the open outlets in the kitchen and your bedroom." She nodded toward the tricycle and the farm animals Myra had scattered on the floor. "So many tripping hazards. You'll be hearing from my lawyer."

Liberty's body heated, and a burning sensation ignited inside. She opened her mouth to call her out on the creep she was, the villain of her story, but then she remembered Wendy's comment about her having a temper. Her body shook, and she needed to collapse on the floor. For Myra's safety, Liberty set her down. That was a pause long enough for her to muster her self-control before she elevated her shoulders and looked at her mother-in-law. "Are you threatening me, Wendy?"

She couldn't afford a lawyer, even if she had a clue where to find one who could win against Wendy. It was Wendy's word against Liberty's.

"Oh, sweetie." Wendy smirked. "I don't make threats. If you'd stayed away from Bryce like you should've, none of this would be happening." She took a step toward her, and Liberty lurched a step backward. While Wendy radiated confidence, Liberty was crumbling and clasping her hands so she didn't show their instability. "I'll make sure that you never get to see Myra again."

Those words lit a match on the gasoline welling up inside her, and as if sparked to life by reality, Liberty's boldness flared from wherever it had lain dormant.

With Wendy, Liberty was way past earning affection. As usual, her only hope was to call her on her manipulation.

"I thought it would be nice for you to be in my daughter's life." Shaking her head, Liberty clenched her fisted hands at her sides, then loosened her grip, and raised her chin. Perhaps Wendy would understand if she appealed to her from the perspective of a mother. So, keeping her voice even, Liberty touched her mother-in-law's hand and whispered, "How would you have felt if someone had threatened to take Bryce away from you? If someone had said you'd never see your son again?"

"That"—Wendy jerked her hand away, her lips flattening and face hardening to a degree Liberty had never seen—"that is what *you* did to *me*."

Feeling as if her heart was in her mouth made it easy to lose control. Shaking again, Liberty pointed a finger at her mother-in-law. "I don't want you in our lives *ever*! Stay away from me and from my daughter!"

"You should've thought about that before you brainwashed my son into marrying you!" Wendy's neck blotched red as she called Liberty all sorts of offensive names, making Liberty dizzy as one after another vile verbal assault pummeled her until her mind started to spin.

"Leave!" Liberty spoke through a lump of threatening tears. Breathless, she bent over so she didn't collapse and have her daughter stolen from the house.

Whatever Wendy was saying, Liberty cut her off again, and she yelled louder, pointing to the door. Tears burned the back of her eyes. If she wasn't afraid she'd pass out, she would've taken a stride and shoved the woman out. "Get out of my house, now!"

Then a thud sounded on the floor, and Myra burst out crying. Liberty staggered to get to her daughter in the living room. Thankfully, it was her phone that fell, not Myra.

Liberty moved to the couch, sinking into the cool faux leather, and held Myra tight. "I'm so sorry, baby," she said, rocking her daughter back and forth, sobbing and kissing Myra's head and cheek. She savored the sweet smell of her child, aching and panicked over what she'd do without Myra in her life. "I'm sorry."

When Myra's wails subsided into soft sobs, her little fingers trailed along Liberty's cheek, and she kissed Liberty. Liberty's heart squeezed, stirring more tears as she wondered if she could protect her daughter from her devious grandma. Would Bryce stand up for them, or would he watch in silence as his mom kept Liberty away from their daughter?

Of course he would stand up for them. He did so at the Christmas party.

The door slammed, declaring Wendy's departure. Sirens sounded not too far from her street, which was rare in her neighborhood. Liberty focused on her daughter until her door burst open again. She jerked as two police officers stormed into her house. *Oh no! What has Wendy done this time?*

CHAPTER 19

"Thank you, Lord!" The prayer flew on Liberty's lips so fluidly when the police weren't at her house to take her daughter away or arrest her. Standing on her front porch, with Myra on her hip, Liberty cuddled her daughter who was pointing to the red and blue lights from the police cruisers parked on the street.

The two men dressed in navy uniforms spoke to Wendy, getting her statement since Liberty had already given hers.

The air seeped through her thin long-sleeved shirt, Myra had a long-sleeved shirt too, but goose bumps scattered on her cheek. That morning couldn't have been more full of surprises.

She'd better get her daughter inside now that she was temporarily done with the police. She'd only expressed her concern over Wendy's threats to take Myra away from her, but she didn't want to press any charges should Wendy promise to leave her alone.

When the police burst into her house, they'd said someone called 911, but all the dispatcher could hear was yelling and screaming in the background. So they'd tracked Liberty's number and hence the sudden rescue. Liberty kissed Myra's soft cheek. "God used you today, my sweetheart."

Of all the buttons Myra could tinker with on the phone, she'd gone for the emergency call button.

Although the police had more important things to do than deal with family battles, having their presence on the day of the intruder brought Liberty some satisfaction. She shouldn't be happy Bryce's mom was or could possibly be in trouble, but having the police here might give Liberty a chance to file a restraining order. They'd know she wasn't overreacting.

Speaking of which, she even had a recording—that was if Myra didn't delete everything whenever she punched all sorts of buttons. "We'd better go inside, baby." Liberty gave one more glance at the police cars.

A familiar blue car pulled up and parked across the street from them. The driver's door swung open. Tessa flew out and slammed the door closed. She adjusted her bright orange sweater over her dark leggings as she looked both ways on the road before sprinting across it.

At the welcome sight, Liberty's heart lifted. How did she know about this? Liberty certainly wasn't expecting her today after they'd spoken on the phone.

"Teta." Myra pointed as Tessa walked past the police and Wendy.

Not stopping to acknowledge the others, Tessa kept her gaze intent on Liberty and Myra. To ease the questions crinkling her friend's face, Liberty smiled to indicate she was all right.

When she met them on the lower step, Tessa wrapped her and Myra in a warm embrace. "Are you guys okay?"

"Teta." Myra lifted her hands for Tessa, who took her, then kissed the top of her head.

"How's my Starlight?" Tessa moved Myra on her hip, and Liberty waved for them to go inside the house.

"Did she call the police on you?" Tessa's voice held a protective edge as she stayed standing close to the front door as if ready to go out and fight. "This is where—"

"Myra called the police, actually. I'd left my phone out, attempting to record Wendy's visit. Then I forgot about it, and Myra found it. She must've been punching all sorts of buttons on it. When Wendy and I screamed at each other, she panicked and dropped it. And then, of course"—Liberty rolled her eyes—"*I* panicked and thought she'd fallen."

"That's my girl." Tessa lifted Myra up in the air, grinning at her, and Myra giggled. "I'm getting you a phone for your birthday, you know."

As they walked to the seating area, Liberty shared Wendy's threats and told Tessa about the present which was still on the floor.

"Oh no!" Tessa set Myra down and reached for the box, then stuffed it in the gift bag. "There's no need for this to come back and bite you. The woman always has a hidden agenda."

Liberty agreed when Tessa suggested she take the bag to Wendy and hand it over while the police were still around. So they walked out with Tessa holding Myra on her hip and Liberty carrying the gift bag.

"Why did you come over?"

"Someone had to keep an eye on you with that woman around."

That meant Tessa had changed her client's appointment. She'd gone above and beyond.

Once again, Liberty warmed, grateful for her wonderful friends. "I lose self-control around Wendy." She knew how to press Liberty's buttons. "Thank you for coming."

They approached Wendy's car, keeping a good distance, and stopped, not wanting to interfere with the police. Liberty waved to the driver, who must be cold sitting in a car that wasn't running all this time. The man waved back with a half-smile.

"I feel for the driver and all Wendy's employees," Tessa whispered, and Liberty had to agree.

"I don't know how to tell Bryce about all this." He already had enough going on with work.

"You should call him right away." Tessa nodded. "You need a strategy to keep Wendy from stalking you."

And Liberty knew the strategy. How to approach it, however, required prayers.

WHAT A LONG DAY! NOT wanting to think about her morning, Liberty had taken Myra to visit a client who always loved seeing Myra and kept a whole room of toys specifically for their visits. After that, Liberty returned home for lunch exhausted and managed to get Myra to take a nap. She'd fallen asleep with her daughter beside her and had woken up to Iris calling, wanting to know about Wendy's visit. Iris, even more furious than Tessa, had wanted to call Wendy to give her a piece of her mind.

That wouldn't end well. So Liberty calmed her down and diverted the conversation by asking about her meeting. Thankfully, Iris started talking about the new plans she was drawing for a commercial skyscraper.

For the afternoon, Liberty took Myra to meet a couple of moms from church. Since their kids were almost the same age as Myra, they all swam together in the recreation center's kiddy pool.

Liberty had held off on calling Bryce since he'd had meetings. Tonight, after getting Myra to bed, would be a good time to talk without interference. That conversation required concentration. Still, Liberty dreaded replaying her morning. Just thinking Wendy was entertaining the idea of taking Myra away from her still made her sick to her stomach.

As they exited the recreation center, the dim sun was sinking lower on the horizon. With the center closing in an hour, only a few cars remained in the parking lot.

It was almost six when she started the car and turned on Bible jams for Myra. Just then, her phone rang, and she reached for it from her bag.

She responded to Bryce's call by pressing the earpiece as opposed to video. She'd just let him know she'd call him back as soon as she got home.

But he spoke first. "Why did you call the police on my mom?"

At his terse voice, alarms rang in her head, and she turned down the music. "Wow, hello to you too." Her nerves tensed, and she turned off the car. Her new car that Bryce had gifted her on Christmas. Apparently, now was a better time to talk about his mom after all. "I take it Wendy called you."

"She was very upset. I've never heard her cry like that, not the way she was on the phone."

Liberty bit the insides of her cheeks, tempted to remind him of Wendy's fake tears and the conversation he'd shared of her crying when he refused to remove his wedding ring after Liberty left him. But now was not the time.

"Why are you putting a restraining order on her? Don't you see how complicated that would be?"

Who was this man speaking right now? His accusatory tone chilled her.

She glanced in her rearview mirror at Myra, sitting quietly, tugging on one of the toys dangling from her car seat. Swimming always relaxed and calmed her, so Liberty might manage this conversation without Myra wanting out of the car seat.

"What Wendy didn't tell you is that she ambushed my house this morning. Were you, by any chance, the one who told her where I live?"

"I have no idea how she found out, but a restraining order..."

Wendy must have guessed a restraining order was Liberty's only hope to keep her off their case. Save for the fact that Wendy had no clue how the police had shown up. If Wendy was in her position, she'd get a restraining order on Liberty.

"I didn't tell her I was going to get a restraining order, but I'm considering it." Grinding her teeth, Liberty shared Wendy's threats.

"Liberty, there are other ways you could handle this than leaping for restraining orders."

The muscles in her back tightened, and her heart rate kicked up. But Myra was in the car. Not wanting to upset her daughter by raising her voice, Liberty closed her eyes and counted backward from three to one before talking. "If she keeps stalking me and threatening to take Myra, I'll protect my daughter." Whether Bryce was with her or not.

He exhaled heavily. "I understand that—"

"You're doing it again."

"Doing what?"

She felt her blood pump, sensing the enemy who came to steal and destroy sneaking into her marriage once again. She ached as she rested her head on the steering wheel, then whispered, "You're taking your mom's side." Accusing her like he did years ago when Wendy gave him the local paper with that photo of Liberty and her uncle. Instead of asking her about it, Bryce had accused her of cheating on him. So many other times he'd sided with Wendy.

"She just told you her side of the story." Liberty rocked her forehead against the steering wheel, shaking her head as if surrendering even when he couldn't see her. She was so tired and spent over Wendy's games. Why did Wendy's tears matter to Bryce when Liberty's didn't? Wendy faked a few and added a false story, and Bryce believed her—every single time. "You made your conclusions before you called to hear my side."

That's if he wanted her side at all.

"That's not what it is—"

"Then what is it you're trying to say, Bryce?!" she snapped, grinding her teeth while ignoring the song in the background warning the little tongue to be careful of what it said.

She was so done with this conversation. "I never told you to choose a side, but we're going back to where your mom always comes first. Does it even matter what I say?"

"A restraining order is something you might regret."

What was it with him about the restraining order? "I'm done!"

"No. Don't hang up. Please, talk to me. What exactly happened?"

Seriously? She massaged her temples, wincing at the onset of a headache. She wasn't in the mood to explain anything, not when he'd started off accusing her. Whether she was wrong or right, she expected consolation from him, not accusation. Or at least him starting the call by asking her side. Instead, they'd circled back to the past she didn't want to revisit. "You're not a child anymore. If you can't see that your mom will always work to tear us apart, then I don't need you to drag me into that."

Her voice was now shaking, her headache intensifying with each word that sounded like she was ending things. "You're not ready for us to be together."

"I am." A sudden urgency cracked his voice. "I'm—I *love* you."

How foolish she was to not understand what love was. "We need to take a break."

She should've known it would come to this the moment she saw him at the cabin.

Bryce's frustration groaned through the phone.

"No! Dimples—"

It was too late for his panic to sway her. They weren't teenagers anymore. "I have a child to take care of." She sat up straight and pressed the button to end the call. Could this day get any worse?

As she peered through the window to the darkening sky, a real cloud of darkness took residence in her heart.

Her phone rang. It pained her to ignore him, but she put the phone in the bag. Thankfully, Myra was humming whatever song was playing. Something about being happy, but Liberty was far from it.

She started the car again and kicked up the volume. Perhaps the bright-as-sunshine music would dry up the melancholy now drowning her.

Tears blinded her view of the road, and she didn't feel like going to her house. Not with Bryce's conversation and Wendy's visit and threats still raw on her mind. She wanted to call Mom, but she felt too unstable driving, let alone making a call while driving. She'd just show up at Mom's house, perhaps stay the night and sleep off today's events.

Her phone rang a few times during the drive. But it had to be Bryce, and he was the last person she needed to hear from right now.

She felt like laughing at her foolishness as she navigated the interstate. She loved and trusted him with her life while, more than once, he'd proved a stranger she should never trust.

Yet the thought of not having him in her life brought an actual stab of pain to the center of her chest. *Oh no! Did I just break up with him?*

A wave of nausea hit her so intensely she felt her body weakening as her head throbbed. She needed to pull over and throw up. So confused with everything, of course, she was playing a role, once again, in ending her marriage. *Lord, what have I done?*

CHAPTER 20

Angry and confused, Bryce spent over an hour on his penthouse terrace, pacing back and forth as he kept punching Liberty's name, then listening to the ring until it went to voicemail. He was such an idiot to assume she'd answer, such an idiot for how he'd handled things.

He'd been walking out of his office when Mom called, wailing, and caught him off guard. The restraining order had shocked him. It wasn't Liberty's nature to seek such an action, and he knew she'd regret it if she went through with it.

"Whew!" Pocketing his phone in his dress pants, he ignored the frigid January air seeping through his button-down shirt as he walked over to the balcony and gripped the railing. His chest tightened while he peered at the city lights reflecting on the Hudson, a scene he'd normally find appealing.

What had Liberty done in the hour since he'd talked to her? Perhaps he could try calling again. But deep down, he knew she wouldn't respond and he had to come to that realization. He'd been there before when she'd broken up with him last time. He clenched his teeth and twisted his grip on the cold balcony railing. His fault then too.

After she'd shattered her phone and left it at the cottage, he'd had no way of reaching her except for calling Rhonda. Liberty's mom only told him to wait until Liberty called him. Liberty never did.

The thought of having a repeat made him cringe. Pain shot up his chest, and he pushed away from the railing. Raking his hands through his hair, he resumed pacing. Just how could he fix things? *Why* had he thrown Mom in Liberty's face?

He'd have to wait until tomorrow to let her cool off, then call her again. He closed his eyes, and Myra's little face flashed in his mind. Love hurt so badly, and now pain was crashing him like a market sell-out, pulling him under.

When he went to bed later, he tossed and turned, reaching for his phone from under the empty pillow next to his. A space Liberty should be occupying, but the bed and penthouse were a temporary home for him. Soon, he'd be moving to Pleasant View, to a home with his wife and daughter—he could only hope Liberty would take him back.

He turned, flopped to his stomach, and typed a text. *Please don't give up on me. I need you. I love you.*

After the simple text and minutes of no response, he knew whatever chance he had with her was over. His heart squeezed tight, and an emptiness hung thick.

Since he'd kept on his night-light, he sat up, attempting to pray to end the sorrow emotionally bankrupting him. He was going to talk to a God he doubted would listen to him. Why would He when Bryce continually doubted His existence?

Staring at the wall of floor-to-ceiling windows where he would normally see Central Park whenever he felt like it, Bryce spoke what he assumed was a prayer. "If what I read in the Bible about those miracles is true, please help me clean up my mess."

What else was he supposed to say? Last time he'd just said the words on his drive to the cabin, and miraculously, Liberty had shown up. What were the odds that this time Liberty would forgive him again?

His cellphone rang, and he grabbed it so fast he didn't even check the caller ID. "Dimples." He breathed her name and gritted his teeth when a deep male voice responded.

"I wish, pal." It was just Logan.

Bryce groaned. Not that he didn't want to hear from his best friend, but he'd wanted his wife's call. The last time he'd checked the time on the phone it was twelve thirty. "Why are you calling this late?"

"Ask that to Iris. She didn't think sleep was important to me." Logan's voice was hoarse as he explained why Iris forced him to call Bryce, warning him of the dumb incident Bryce was responsible for. Thankfully, Bryce didn't have to relay his conversation with Liberty. Logan knew everything from Iris. Actually, he knew more than Bryce, who hadn't listened to Liberty's side. His muscles tightened, and he was shaking when Logan said Myra had hit the emergency call button while Liberty and Mom argued.

"I don't even know what I'm supposed to tell you, but long story short, Iris is ready to throttle you."

Bryce stood and walked with unsteady legs to the windows. He braced a hand against the cool glass, leaning into it as he overlooked the city's bright lights. He never gave Liberty a chance to say anything, and he'd started out with what sounded like an accusation. All this after his mom had threatened his wife and invaded her privacy. "Is Dimples okay?"

"I'm sure she's fine—if you mean physically."

In other words, Bryce wounded her emotionally. He raked his fingers through his hair, tugging at the roots. "What should I do?"

Logan was silent as if thinking of an answer. Then he huffed. "You're asking the wrong person here. Have you ever wondered why I'm still single?"

"You mean because you break up before things get serious?"

"That, for one, but I don't have what it takes not to mess things up." Logan cleared his throat. "You and Liberty have what it takes. You're crazy about each other, always have been."

Bryce stared through the city lights, soaking in Logan's comment. Central Park, while lovely in the day, was too far from his penthouse to see in the shadowy light. Maybe because his life felt like a shadow and all the light Liberty reignited was fading once again. With his legs feeling weaker, he lowered himself to sit on the cool tile that seeped through his pajama shorts.

"Do you think she'll come around?" Logan might know what Iris thought.

"Hmm…" Logan's hesitation wasn't good. "See, I went along with Iris's plan to get you back together because I believed you'd never let your mom come between your relationship again."

That didn't answer his question at all, but Logan continued. "I'm not good with romance and all, but it doesn't take an expert to know your wife should always come first. You're a team. Whether she's wrong or not, you have to defend her—no matter what. I would think that's what love is."

As Logan gave him a load of lessons about love, Bryce wondered why his friend wasn't married yet. "For someone who's not in a relationship, you sure know a lot."

"I watch my parents." Pride rumbled in his deep voice. "They say that, without God running the show, their relationship would be in shambles."

Logan had a rough childhood before he was adopted into a loving home. Whatever hang-ups he still harbored had to do with the years before his adoption. Perhaps being part of a godly home had helped him with his childhood trauma. Not that Logan talked much about his faith, but Bryce knew he went to church. Resting one forearm on his knee and his back against the glass, Bryce asked about his friend's relationship with God. A conversation they'd never had before.

"Finally, we talk about faith." Logan chuckled through the phone. "The hardest people to talk to about your faith in God are the ones closest to you."

"Why's that?"

"If you get into a deep argument, that relationship could end up in flames."

Bryce had never thought about an argument interfering with a friendship or any relationship. Could that be why Liberty didn't talk much about her newfound faith unless he asked?

He told Logan about the spiritual books he'd been reading and his research about faith and truth. "Did you know the Bible is the most read book in the world?"

"Because so many people are using it," Logan said. "If it's of any comfort, I don't have all the answers. I think that's why I'm always terrified to talk about my faith. I'm afraid I won't deliver the facts well enough."

The more Logan shared about his faith and his doubts at times, the lighter Bryce's heart felt, and the smaller his inability to have all the answers where God was concerned seemed. "Bottom line, we're all sinners. God created a perfect world for humans, but the first man and woman ruined that for us when they disobeyed and ate the one fruit they were told not to eat."

Bryce had read all about creation in Genesis, and it made sense as Logan broke down the meaning of sin and God's redemptive plan to save everyone by sending His Son, Jesus, to die for each person's sin. "If you realize you're a sinner and need redemption, that's when you believe in Jesus, and voilà! You surrender and let God run the show in your life."

"Run the show like you say He runs your parents' marriage?"

"You've got that right, bro."

"And Eric's life." A life he'd come close to losing due to an illness out of his control.

"You should talk to Eric. Aren't you meeting with him on Friday?"

Bryce gripped the front of his hair. He'd almost forgotten his meeting in San Francisco with Eric. "I will. Thanks."

"He knows more about God than I do," Logan said. "I won't be here when you come." Logan talked about the leadership training he had to lead in Paris for Stone Enterprise's European branch managers. Eric wisely chose to let Logan run the company while he spent time with his family. "But keep me posted on how things go with Liberty."

"I'll need all the prayers." *What?* Bryce jolted. Did he just ask for prayers, rather than luck?

Logan had just connected the dots between Jesus and God. He'd also helped Bryce understand why he needed God more than anything. Sin. Now he needed to figure out what sin was. That was his next topic to study.

Bryce hung up, motivated to call the pastor. He needed to confirm their virtual counseling session for the last week in January, but he also had a couple of questions to ask him—questions on things he needed clarifying from what he'd read. He'd saved Pedro's number in his phone. The first two counseling sessions were both scheduled for next week and would be virtual. When Bryce returned to Pleasant View, they'd meet in person, but after his conversation with Liberty, he'd likely be alone at the marriage counseling.

Grateful for Logan's call distracting him, Bryce pushed off the floor and crossed the tile to his bed. He flopped onto it and draped an arm over his eyes. With Logan's words playing in his mind, he was able to fall asleep until a female voice awakened him.

"Good morning, darling."

Bryce blinked once or twice at the end of the bed where a figure stood, light streaming in around her through the drapes he hadn't shut. He jumped. "Mom?"

He sat against the padded headboard, frozen and fuming as he stared at her. Her flowy pants covered the back of her heels while she picked up the clothes and shoes he'd worn to work yesterday.

The last person he needed to see was Mom. Not today, not when she was the wedge between him and Liberty. What had she been thinking when she went to Liberty's house in a rude intrusion and cruel attack on his wife? As those questions lingered, he had no idea what to ask first or how to approach the subject without having to kick her out.

"What are you doing here?" He forced his voice to stay calm, grinding his teeth after the words as his insides burned with something he had no right definition for.

Mom waved his shirt in the air. "What a silly question. I'm here to see you."

Her heels clicked as she carried his shoes to the walk-in closet and then walked to the bathroom where she deposited the dirty laundry.

Adjusting her white blazer, she marched toward his bed. "I was hoping we could catch breakfast this morning."

For someone who'd been sobbing on the phone yesterday, her eyes looked clear without a remnant of swollenness. "You flew all the way from Colorado to catch breakfast with me?"

Her brows drew together, and she crossed her arms while standing in the center of his bedroom. "I do this all the time. Why so surprised?"

Maybe because it's my wife who should surprise me this early, rather than my mom? Maybe because you trampled over my wife and dragged me down with you?

His stomach tightened into a knot.

"I have to work." He bit the inside of his cheek to avoid grinding his teeth again. "You know I have a job right?"

"Yeah, the kind of job you can take off whenever you feel like."

He placed his hands on his legs, flattening them on his thighs rather than fisting them. "I have a conference." He was the opening speaker at an entrepreneur's conference—although addressing eager entrepreneurs would be challenging while he didn't currently have any business enthusiasm.

"I'll let you get showered and dressed." She walked away. "I'll go make you some coffee."

"I don't need coffee!" He spat the words out over Mom's back as she walked out of the door. He desperately needed the coffee, but only with Liberty.

He'd been okay with Mom's intrusion for years, and she had the code to let herself in. So it would be awkward if he asked security not to let her in. She'd chosen the luxurious condominium for him, even though he insisted on paying the rent without her help for the last two years.

He now realized how far from resourceful he was. All that money could be going toward building a house for his family.

After showering and dressing in a button-down shirt and khaki pants, he met his mom in the kitchen. The smell of coffee wafted through the house. Seated on the barstool with her back to him, she sipped her coffee. Her gaze seemed intent on the marble waterfall behind the sink, or maybe she was staring at the gleaming skyscrapers beyond the window? Either way, she seemed lost in thought.

Despite his argument against coffee, he poured himself a cup and pulled out one of the six barstools from the island to sit across from her.

She peered at him, opening her mouth, then closing it as if she wanted to say something. So he pushed his coffee along the white marble counter and leaned on his forearms, peering at her so he could address what needed to be said.

"You forgot to tell me you waltzed into Liberty's home."

Mom tapped her red manicured fingernails against the mug, her face not giving anything away. "I wanted to give my granddaughter a present."

"And you thought showing up unannounced was the best way to do it?" Clasping his hands together, he kept steady eye contact, wanting to grasp her motives once and for all. "Then you threatened to take Myra from her?"

Mom's ears flared red, and she sat taller. "You're not going to believe her lies, are you?"

Heat burned his chest. "Mom!" He pounded his fist on the counter. "You're the liar!"

She gasped, her eyes widening, and her hand flew to her gold necklace. Yes, they both didn't see that coming, but Bryce didn't feel sorry at all, not now. He didn't hear the recorded interaction of Mom's visit, but Logan relayed what Iris told him.

It was time to say it. "After what happened at the Christmas party, I didn't want to talk to you again."

Mom shook her head, her eyes shining, but who could say if they were real tears or the fake ones again?

"Liberty insisted I needed to talk to you because you're my mother." Bryce told her about all the times Liberty insisted she didn't want to come between him and his mom. He told her about Myra's photo book Liberty made and how she'd included Mom, even when she didn't have a reason to. The more he spoke, the harder his heart for his mom got. His jaw tightened, and he spoke through gritted teeth. "From now on, if you come near me or my wife or my daughter, I'll be the one to get that restraining order."

Her gaze narrowed on him. Her face was drained of color. Her voice sounded so cold. "Surely, you don't mean that."

"You'll never accept Liberty, but she *is* my wife." Or at least she was until Mom ruined everything—again. "I don't want to see you for a long time."

For good measure, he explained her role in ruining his marriage. Perhaps Liberty was right. Perhaps Mom needed counseling to get over whatever she had. "I'm going to get counseling. You should too."

Mom was sniffling and swiping at the blackened tears that mixed with her eyeliner. Again, Bryce didn't care to find out if she was genuinely hurt or acting. He stood with his mug and dumped the coffee in the sink. It had lost its appeal.

"Did you know... your dad wants a divorce?"

Flinching, Bryce spun around. Did he hear her right?

"You both can't leave me."

So, Dad had finally gotten bold. Although surprised it had actually happened, Bryce had seen it coming.

Still, he had to act surprised as he returned to the barstool he'd vacated. "When did he tell you this?"

Mom cleared her throat. "After Christmas. When I came back from my mini vacation."

Was it possible she still loved Dad? She certainly hadn't shown it before. And she must have seen the divorce coming too. He hated to see divorce as their last resort, but Dad had endured her abrasiveness and control too long already. Either Mom didn't care, or she didn't know she was disrespectful.

Maybe she loved Dad in her way. Whether she was faking tears or not, Bryce reached to touch her hand. Her palms were soft, no doubt since she never worked hard a day in her life—except for giving campaign speeches when she ran for mayor, but even then, someone wrote those speeches.

"Are you surprised he wants a divorce?"

She frowned. "Do you know something I don't?"

"Well, you spend more time messing around in my life than going out with your husband." He found himself expressing all the things he'd observed while growing up. The disrespectful way she spoke to Dad and the multitude of friends she spent time with, even during Dad's visits when she ignored him. Yet Bryce enjoyed spending each moment with Liberty and would drop any friends as long as he spent time with his wife.

"Was it necessary for you to take a trip on Christmas and leave your husband behind—*alone* for the holidays?"

Mom touched her head and threw it back. "You weren't talking to me—"

"That's what I'm saying, Mom!" He didn't mean to let his voice rise. He took a deep breath and pressed his palms to the cold marble before continuing in a cooler tone. "You need to stay out of my life and focus on yours and Dad's."

"Your dad never said he wasn't happy!"

Bryce chuckled at her naivety of her relationship, then reminded her of her overbearing personality. She never took no for an answer. "Do you love Dad?"

She shrugged, which was not a convincing answer.

Either way, Bryce wrapped his hand around hers. "If you love him, you're going to get some counseling."

Her hand jerked in his grip. "I don't need counseling!"

"If you don't, you can say goodbye to your marriage." Unclasping their hands, he glanced at the digital clock on the refrigerator screen. It was almost nine. He needed to head out and told her so. Slipping the top button in its hole, he said, "I love you."

He meant it, and Mom's lips curled into a sad smile.

"But I meant what I said. I can't live my life without Liberty, and I can't fix my marriage when you're constantly interfering. Please, I need space from you."

Being that direct hurt, but as much as he hated to choose, he was left with no choice but to choose his wife unapologetically.

CHAPTER 21

Midmorning Friday, Bryce sat in Eric Stone's office overlooking the San Francisco skyline.

Eric was standing by the window, staring at the city as he spoke on the phone with his wife. He'd asked Bryce to stay when Bryce offered to give him privacy.

Making himself comfortable, Bryce stood from the sofa and crossed the velvety brown area rug to the opposite side of the room. Abstract paintings, art Eric's wife had painted, brightened the office's muted browns, tans, and creamy white tones. As Bryce approached Eric's desk, he studied the photos there—Eric's kids with toothless grins. Bryce didn't have to pinpoint and count to know there were eight kids. He tilted a picture of Eric and his wife toward him. Joy was staring at Eric with such affection Bryce almost winced from the punch of reality to his gut.

Liberty always looked at Bryce like he was the best thing that ever happened to her. Yet she was the best thing that ever happened to him. And he'd blown it.

He hadn't heard from her since Tuesday, and he was coming to terms with the fact that he wasn't ready for her or Myra. He didn't deserve them. How many times was he going to fail his wife? Perhaps a shrink would help. Then, when he was a responsible adult, he could earn Liberty's love and trust again.

He'd had a long conversation with Dad on Wednesday, the evening Mom left his house. Dad wasn't seeing anyone, but he wanted out of his stifling marriage.

"I don't want you taking the kids by yourself." Eric's conversation pulled Bryce from his thoughts, and he turned toward Eric, who was now walking around the sofas with his face flushed. "I'll come as soon as I finish this meeting. I can send Terrence to help, and I'll meet you guys there."

He chuckled at something, then told his wife he loved her. His relaxed posture and glowing face confirmed his words.

When Eric placed the phone on the table and sat, Bryce joined him, taking a seat on the other off-white sofa across from Eric. Bryce nodded to the chessboard laid out on the table and was about to ask how often Eric played when Eric adjusted his tie and apologized for interrupting their meeting. "It doesn't matter what I'm doing when my wife calls"—he spread out both his hands—"I have to answer."

In other words, his wife came first above his job and anybody else. "Don't mind me." Bryce understood, especially since Eric came close to death a few years ago. Joy had been his caregiver, and they'd fallen in love.

"Are Joy and the kids here in San Francisco?"

Eric crossed one leg over the other, and a smile relaxed his lips. "For any trip that will take me over twenty-four hours, I take my family along."

It made sense. Eric had stepped back from his role as CEO of Stone Enterprises. He'd let his younger brother, Logan, run his financial company so Eric could spend more time with his family while also focusing on his charities.

Bryce asked about his kids, resuming the conversation they'd started before Joy's call.

"Little Dustin is just like his mom, so adventurous and quite the artist." Eric's eyes gleamed as he spoke about his children's unique personalities and the gifts they each had. "Except for the twins waking us up in the middle of the night, I can't complain."

Those hazel eyes were kind as his gaze searched Bryce's. "Enough about me. How are you adapting to your new role as a dad?"

His genuineness indicated he wasn't aware of Bryce's dilemma. If anyone portrayed godliness, it was Eric. Several years older than Bryce, Eric was one of the most selfless people Bryce had ever met.

Bryce leaned back, resting an arm on the leather armrest, and blew out a breath. He couldn't lie to Eric—he would know he'd been lied to. He was too wise and the kind of man God would speak to... if there was such a thing.

So Bryce cleared his throat. "I... messed up again."

Eric scratched his clean-shaven jaw. "I'm sure it's not that bad."

Ashamed of ruining things so soon, Bryce rubbed his palms on his khakis, wrinkling the fabric beneath his sweaty skin. "You have no idea."

"You want to talk about it?"

He didn't want to take up Eric's time while he had his family waiting for him. "We better discuss the business proposal—"

Eric held up a hand. "If things aren't going well with your family, no business proposition is going to satisfy you. Success in the office can never supplant success in the home."

Then Eric leaned further into his seat and raised his elbow to the armrest, his chin on his palm, clearly waiting for Bryce to talk. After all, Eric had experience with loss, family, and marriage.

"It's my mom again...." While Bryce told Eric everything that had happened on Tuesday, Eric remained silent and closed his eyes, something he did while absorbing information or thinking. Perhaps it was his way of listening to God.

"You can see why I'm terrified. Liberty won't forgive me this time."

"With God... all things are possible." Eric whispered the words, his eyes still closed.

Hmm! Was that the anthem line for spirituality? Liberty's plaque, the Christmas message, and now Eric. "What is with that quote? I'm hearing or seeing it everywhere lately."

Eric slowly opened his eyes. "Maybe God is trying to tell you something." He told Bryce about the different ways God spoke to people, through music, the Bible, and the pastors who taught His word. "There could be a message for you in those words."

With God all things are possible. The words echoed in the back of his mind, and the memory of the week before Christmas shone bright like the guiding star of Bethlehem in those Christmas songs and stories. *With God all things are possible.*

His heart rate picking up, Bryce whispered, "I asked God for a miracle, for a way to bring Liberty back into my life." He raised his gaze to Eric's knowing one, but he had to finish. He had to admit the miracle. "I got to the cabin, and... there she was."

Warmth ran through him as he remembered how he'd touched her soft face, how his heart had raced, and how he'd found it hard to believe Liberty was standing in front of him.

"That's not the only miracle you mentioned God fulfilling."

Bryce blinked, trying to remember if he'd ever asked for a miracle in front of Eric.

"It was almost a dare when you came to visit me with Brady, Ryan, and Lucas. Remember that day? You said, 'If Eric ever recovers from this blow and still clings to this God, then maybe, just maybe, I might believe there's a God.' " Eric wagged a finger at him. "Those were your exact words."

The words niggled his memory. Bryce rubbed his hands on his thighs again. "I remember the argument with your buddies the most." They'd become his buddies as well during that visit. Some of the neatest guys he'd love to hang out with if they all lived close to him.

Eric shifted in his seat, leaning forward and bracing his elbows on his knees and his chin against his clasped hands before he spoke with clarity. "I prayed then that God would heal me, if not for me, then for you to see that He is the God of wonders and miracles. He could do anything because He created the universe and everything in it."

As Eric spoke, everything became surreal, fading beneath the words *all things are possible*. The miracles God had made, the sin Logan had talked about, and the need for redemption. Bryce had looked at the meaning of sin, and he didn't think he was evil or immoral until he read the Ten Commandments in Exodus. Coveting, not loving God, swearing, and you name it. God had a standard, and Bryce was far from it.

"I've been looking for evidence...." Perhaps Eric could shed more light on his research. Bryce shared the books he'd read recently and the Bible. "It seems to make sense."

"God always makes sense."

When Bryce talked about the laws complicating things, Eric told him how simple God's ways were but how it was in human nature to assume everything had to be hard and complicated. "The Ten Commandments are there not only to be our moral compass, but also to show us how righteous God is and how much we need Him to purify us daily." Eric continued highlighting the need for God. "When we allow God to work in us and through us, our abilities to sense, to learn, and to understand, to create and to manage life's resources are powerfully expanded."

"So, in other words, when I give God control of my life, He will deal with my problems?"

"Yes. That also means, you step back and pray and wait." Eric was specific in reminding Bryce that his life wouldn't be easy or perfect just because God had his problems, but Bryce would be freed from his burdens, knowing God was responsible for the end results of every circumstance in his life.

"Since you're searching, you're already there." Eric spoke about faith being like a mustard seed. "Even the little bit of faith you have is all God wants. He doesn't want you to be perfect, but He wants you to try."

Eric used an example of investing that resonated with Bryce. "Sometimes we take a chance and invest in entrepreneurs without knowing if their company will take off or not, but—"

"Through taking risks, we learn what works and what doesn't," Bryce said as it all made sense now since he was compelled to invest in Javir. Liberty's words flashed in his mind. "But it takes... a leap of faith."

"Exactly. It's the same way with faith and trusting God." Eric nodded, a ghost of a smile lifting his face. "You believe in what you can't see. Believing in God or not, it still takes a leap of faith. Even in our disbelief, we take a leap by having faith that God does not exist."

Just like Liberty had said when she spoke about faith.

"When God forgives your sins, you're securing your eternal home."

As Eric talked about death and the world being a temporary home, Bryce realized he hadn't ever thought about what would happen to him after he died. A burning sensation consumed him as conviction flared in his chest. He wasn't sure of his next words, but they flew off his tongue and felt right. "I want to give this God a chance. How can I ask for forgiveness?" He'd promised to believe in God if Eric ever recovered and if Liberty returned to his life. She wasn't at the moment, but Bryce was to blame for that.

There was no harm in believing or trying as long as God didn't expect him to be perfect. "I want to be a good dad and husband. How can I do that?"

"Oh, Bryce!" Eric beamed as he stood and walked to Bryce's side, slapping him on the shoulder. "Since you're seeking God first, talk to God. Even if we can't see Him, He can see us and can hear everything."

Bryce had no doubt about God hearing everything.

"Love God with all you've got and leave the rest to Him."

Eric offered to leave in case Bryce needed a moment to talk with God, but Bryce asked him to stay and pray with him and for him.

When Eric clamped a hand on his shoulder, Bryce's mouth opened, and he spoke instead, praying if that was what it was. "Please forgive me, God. Come into my heart." The more he prayed, the more emotional he became. Now his throat felt like he swallowed glass; he was shaking and sobbing, yet his heart felt light as if he were flying. He felt free of guilt; he felt loved and forgiven. It was as if a light shone into his soul for the first time.

Eric's hand squeezed his shoulder. Bryce had almost forgotten someone else was in the room.

Somehow, everything was going to be okay. He couldn't control or undo the damage he'd done, but God who had healed Eric, God who had brought Liberty back into his life once again, He'd do it again somehow. Bryce had no choice but to believe all things would work out the way they were meant to be.

By the time they talked about the startup investment, Bryce understood where he wanted to put his investment from there on. In learning more about God, praying hard, and doing whatever it took to be ready for whenever his family came back into his life.

CHAPTER 22

Even as Liberty tried to talk to her mom about the revelation from her tests, Myra's toy piano drowned her out. Standing by the coffee table, not too far from the couch where Liberty and Mom sat, Myra hummed "Who Built the Ark" as she slapped her fingers on the toy. The thing was too loud, and Liberty reached for it and turned down the volume before facing Mom again.

The afternoon light streaming through the window lit Mom's brown eyes as she waited.

"Like I was saying..." Liberty pulled out a Ziploc bag from her purse to display the evidence—three plastic strips she'd used over the last three days. She'd missed her January menstrual period, and it was already the second week of February. Far too late to expect her period to show up.

Mom snatched the bag out of her hand, her focus intent on the strip where two colored lines were still visible.

"I'm going to have another grandchild." Wonder whispered through Mom's awed words, and Liberty wished she'd felt the same excitement. Even now, she was still indifferent. Mom frowned as she touched Liberty's shoulder. "You should be happy."

"I know." Liberty scooted further onto the couch and leaned her head back, closing her eyes. She would love her child like she loved Myra, but... "Why do I always have to be pregnant whenever I end things with Bryce?"

"Maybe the pregnancy hormones get the best of you, and you leave your husband as soon as you have an argument."

She blinked to peer at Mom, basking in those eyes, so kind and full of wisdom. Even though she knew the answer to her question, Liberty still asked, "Do you think I overreacted?"

Mom's gentle face relaxed with her smile. "You already know the answer to that. You have to remember the devil will take advantage of everyone's weaknesses and use it to his advantage. He knows Wendy makes you lose control, so that could be his weapon against you in your marriage."

Mom was right, especially when she reminded Liberty she must always talk things through with Bryce before she resolved to break off with her husband. Mom had been wise in not saying anything until now, and letting Liberty go through the motions since her debacle last month.

"I just want Bryce to stand up for me." An ache stirred in her chest, a longing, as she told Mom about Bryce's calls she'd ignored. The times Myra had reached for her phone whenever it rang since she expected her dada to call, but Liberty thought it best to cut Bryce out of their lives again. Now he'd stopped calling. He'd probably given up on them, and she didn't blame him.

"My dear girl..." Mom cupped one hand to Liberty's cheek and smoothed down Liberty's hair with the other, a gesture familiar from childhood. "Bryce was a mama's boy when you met him. He may not know how to deal with his mom yet, but his love for you is something Wendy will not take away from him."

She moved her hand from Liberty's hair, now framing Liberty's face with both hands. "Do not doubt his love for you. He's called me every night for the last two weeks to see how you and Myra are doing."

Guilt gnawed at Liberty, unease twisting through her all over again.

Myra moved to the couch and pulled out a container of Goldfish from Liberty's bag—technically Myra's as well since it served as Liberty's purse and Myra's diaper bag.

"I guess it's a good thing I've decided to go to counseling."

Mom nodded. She'd come over to watch Myra while Liberty went to meet with Pastor Pedro. She'd already figured out she needed to work on herself before she blamed Bryce each time Wendy came between them. Although it was supposed to be marital sessions, Liberty planned to ask the pastor what was expected of her as a godly wife.

She had to chuckle about her usual reaction. "I'm the Christian in this, yet I'm acting like one who doesn't know God."

"You're showing Bryce that being a Christian doesn't make you perfect." Mom opened her mouth when Myra shoved a handful of Goldfish toward her face. Most of them fell on Mom's lap.

As Liberty drove to church for her meeting with Pastor Pedro, her mind worked on ways to make things right once again with Bryce.

If he hadn't changed his mind about moving to Pleasant View, he should have moved back to town last week for their first two in-person sessions with the pastor.

She had canceled their two online sessions and the first in-person sessions, but when she'd called the pastor requesting a meeting, he was still available to meet at three on Wednesday as planned.

She pulled into the church parking lot and parked. Since the white steepled building wasn't large, the church had three services on Sundays to accommodate its growing congregation.

When she walked inside the building, she wrinkled her nose at the smell of coffee. Once pleasant, now it didn't smell so good. She turned to the left and walked down the hall to the receptionist's desk.

"Liberty!" White hair wisping over her forehead, Dorothy moved her wire glasses down to her nose as she looked away from her computer. Her smile was always kind.

Liberty greeted her. "I have an appointment with Pastor Pedro."

"Of course. He's expecting you." Dorothy picked up the phone and informed the pastor that Liberty had arrived. She then gestured for Liberty to head on in.

Liberty walked past two doors down the hall. To the right was the pastor's office. The door was wide open. He usually kept it that way whenever he was doing his counseling sessions. What made her pause was the familiar figure propped in the chair before the pastor's big maple desk, with his back to her.

Liberty's heart started racing, but before she could follow through on the idea of backtracking, Pastor Pedro waved her forward, beaming. "Liberty, come. Have a seat, please."

Bryce jumped from the chair to stand, turning his head and looking directly at her. With his blue plaid shirt unbuttoned, he appeared relaxed and casual in the white T-shirt underneath it.

"Hi, Dimples." His gray eyes softened, the way they always did whenever he saw her. "I didn't know you were coming."

Bryce being polite, apologetic even, made her feel worse. He shouldn't have to apologize for their encounter.

"I–I didn't either." With her legs as weak as her voice, she managed to enter the office.

As she eased through the doorway, the pastor peered back knowingly. "Bryce never canceled the sessions," he said in his thick accent. "You wanted to meet, so what better day than today?"

"Would you like to sit?" Bryce pointed at his chair, and the pastor walked around his desk to pull up another folding chair that he set next to Bryce's.

Bryce seemed so calm, relaxed, and apparently not weighed down by her absence. Seeing that he didn't seem to have lost the sleep she'd lost almost bothered her. But she knew one thing as she accepted the offered seat. If she walked away now, she may never have her husband back.

"I'll leave you two. You need to talk."

She kept her gaze on the desk as Bryce sat next to her. The door swishing closed behind them indicated the pastor's exit.

Liberty stared at the water bottle and family photos on the pastor's desk, alternating with looking around the room. By now, she should have memorized all the Bible verses on the wooden plaques hanging on the grayish wall. Bryce's joggers brushed against her tights as he bounced his knee, seemingly lost in his own thoughts too.

With her heart beating so hard, surely he could hear it. Unless his off-and-on exhales drowned out the noise from her chest.

She broke the awkward silence by clearing her throat and turning to look at him. A few days' worth of scruff dusted his jaw. "I'm sorry—"

"I'm the one who's sorry." His voice was hoarse, and his face fell before he reached for her hand and entwined their fingers. His palms were moist against hers. He lifted their entwined hands to his mouth and kissed the top of hers. "I failed you and Myra. That's why I needed to get counseling before I could bother you again."

"You don't bother me."

"I made my peace with God."

Sweet chills shivered down her spine. She touched his face, the scruff prickling her flesh. No wonder he didn't appear restless. "You did?"

"I feel like my life is just starting." A smile crinkled up his eyes. "I went to see Eric about the proposal...."

Over the next several minutes, Bryce shared his visit with Eric. Eric had agreed to go in with Bryce and help with the starting costs of Javir's company. Eric also told Bryce to consider the investment a donation. Many starter companies never took off.

"That's good advice," Liberty said, more thrilled about his new life with God.

He rubbed his thumb across the back of her hand. "My lease in Manhattan is up in two weeks. I'm not renewing it. I'll be working from here, in Pleasant View, and flying to New York whenever necessary to attend certain meetings."

His thumb stilled, his whole body seeming to still. "I'm backtracking, but the transition began when you refused to answer my calls."

"I shouldn't have done that."

He ignored her response as he continued to share the agony he'd been going through the week he'd met with Eric Stone. Despite everything, his mind kept replaying the stories he'd read in the Bible and the research about truth he'd learned. "Eric said God didn't expect me to be perfect or to have everything figured out."

"I don't think I'll ever have everything figured out." Liberty's voice was shaky with tears of joy threatening to take over. "But that's why Jesus died for me and you. So that He can figure out the rest for us."

"I like that." With his free hand, he touched her cheek, his fingers trailing and leaving goose bumps in their wake. "My mom came to visit me...."

Liberty's muscles stiffened at the mention of Wendy, but that was just what they needed to talk about.

"I'm getting counseling somewhere else," he said. "I know I have other issues to deal with."

Her heart felt heavy when he told her that he wasn't talking to his mom for the time being. "At least until I'm in a good place with you and Myra."

Wendy might be mean to Liberty, but Wendy loved Bryce. And the soft way she'd interacted with Myra hinted a gentleness hiding in her somewhere. However, one thing didn't make sense. "How are you staying at her house if you two aren't talking?"

He slid his hand away from her cheek and set it on his legs. "I'm staying at Eric's house for now. I even threatened to put a restraining order on Mom if she came anywhere near me or my family without my permission."

Oh my! Liberty slapped his leg, giggling. "I shouldn't have given you that idea."

"Actually, Mom gave me the idea." His face turned serious, and a hint of sadness etched his drawn brows. "I'm torn between being happy for my dad and sad for my mom."

"Why's that?" Liberty kept her gaze on him.

"Dad's leaving her."

That depended on whether Wendy wanted to stay in the marriage. She always got what she wanted and that included Charles, if the money was keeping her in the relationship. Liberty sighed out the sudden weight on her chest. "What does Wendy think about the divorce?"

"I talk to Dad every so often. He says Mom asked him to give her some time to seek out counseling."

If Wendy was coming to terms with counseling, perhaps there was hope for everyone, including Liberty and Bryce. "Where's your dad now?"

"He's in the Hamptons. He wants to retire in a couple of years and move here to be with us. He doesn't want to miss out on being part of his granddaughter's life like..."

Her heart constricted as his voice fell away, the unspoken "like he missed out on mine" lingering between them. She sniffled, fighting tears.

"Don't cry, sweetheart." Bryce bent slightly and wiped her tears with the back of his knuckles.

She reached for a tissue from the box on the desk. Blowing her nose, she spoke through the snuffling noise. "Mom thinks the pregnancy hormones make me cry and overreact."

Bryce cupped her chin and turned her face so she'd look at him. His gentle gray eyes seeped into hers. "Did you just say you're pregnant?"

When she nodded, he beamed and looked down at her blue sweater by the stomach. "You don't look pregnant."

She felt her body relax when his hand fell from her face and he helped her stand. His grin stretched so wide she imagined it pulled at his mouth as far as it possibly could while he touched her stomach. "Does it hurt?"

He was so adorable, and her heart warmed at his excitement.

"I'm only like four weeks I think." She hadn't had time to count or get a pregnancy app. "Unless the three tests are wrong."

"I hope you're pregnant." He pulled her into a warm embrace, tucking his chin atop her head and rocking her in a slow dance. "Have you gone to the doctor?"

Only if she wanted to confirm her pregnancy, she doubted she needed to go to the doctor anytime soon. "It's not necessary."

He eased out of the hug and looked at her with so much love her knees weakened. "I want to be there with you, Myra, and the baby." He kissed her cheek, sending a shiver coursing through her nerves. "I want to be at every doctor appointment for the baby and Myra from now on—"

He stopped himself, then blew out a breath. "After you forgive me."

Taking his hands in hers, she said, "God has forgiven you." That was the most important part. "I don't have anything to forgive. I'm not innocent in this." He'd already made the sacrifice of moving from his usual comfort zone, to a small town. He'd shown up to the counseling sessions even if she hadn't followed through. "Myra misses you."

"I miss her, too."

"And I missed you. Please come home." Once again.

"I first need to work at being perfect." He leaned in and brushed his lips against hers.

"Let's work at being perfect together."

The way he looked at her determined her next action. Stepping up on her tiptoes, she gripped his collar, pulled him to her, and planted her lips on his.

Bryce took it from there, moving his fingers to thread into her hair. She savored the warmth of his lips against hers and the oh-so-familiar feel of his closeness.

"I–I love you, Bryce." She spoke breathlessly when they caught a breath between their kisses.

"I love you too, Dimples."

She wrapped her arms around his waist, and as he hugged her tight, his chest rumbled with the tremor in his words. "Don't leave me again."

She breathed in, then out, unable to contain the unexpected sweet outcome of the day. "I don't ever want to leave you again."

They clung to each other as he sniffed at her neck, his warm breath teasing her.

Mom was right. They'd almost let an enemy destroy their marriage twice, but they wouldn't let it happen again. Rather than shutting Bryce out, Liberty would work hard and talk things through, all while knowing he'd stood up to his mom enough to prove to Liberty he would defend her and choose her. Bryce being here today and seeking counseling proved he was just as committed. They'd both matured, and unlike before, they could now build a marriage with God as their foundation, taking their troubles to Him in prayer.

EPILOGUE

Tessa Richardson stood by the kitchen window, staring at the gently falling rain as she listened to Liberty's instructions to care for her twenty-one-month-old. "Bedtime is at—"

"Seven. Your husband already told me." Turning around, Tessa leaned against the counter to face Liberty, who was snapping open the lid of a glass container.

Tessa had met Liberty when they worked together in a mutual client's home. Liberty had been pregnant with Myra then and starting her business while Tessa was also starting as a physical therapist.

"She can stay up later if you want, but she's not been napping lately." Liberty closed the container and opened the fridge to put it back. "She's not too fond of peas these days, but that's all the veggies I had."

"She can eat the pasta. We'll be fine." Knowing how her friend emphasized her daughter eating only healthy meals, Tessa nudged her with an elbow. "On second thought, she might prefer the Hershey's I brought her for dessert."

Liberty closed the fridge too fast. "No! Having sugar this late will disrupt her sleep." She then pushed her hair to the side. Styled in waves, it fell over her elegant belted long-sleeve dress.

Tessa had no experience with little ones, except for Myra, whom she watched now and then for no more than two hours at a time.

"As long as Myra won't tell you what we eat in your absence." Tessa reached to adjust the drop pendant on Liberty's diamond necklace. "You look stunning, by the way."

Liberty's dimples deepened when she smiled. "Thank you."

And Tessa's chest warmed. Seeing her friend having her family back—and knowing she and Iris had a hand in their re-union—cheered her every time. "Where's Bryce taking you tonight?"

"It's a surprise." Liberty peered through the kitchen doorway to the living room where Bryce had plopped in Myra's little chair. Dressed in a blue button-down shirt and dress pants, he beamed as his daughter put a princess crown on his head. "He might change his mind and cancel this date." Liberty smiled, her hand touching her stomach. Although she was pregnant, the baby bump wasn't visible yet.

As if aware of his wife's gaze, Bryce lifted his head, and a secret smile just for Liberty crinkled up his eyes.

"He won't change his mind. I can assure you of that." It was as if they were newlyweds. Tessa doubted Liberty heard any of what she said since her friend was biting her lower lip before she touched her cheeks with both hands and turned to Tessa.

Tsking, Tessa laughed and shook a finger at her friend. "You should leave before I change my mind."

Liberty walked over and embraced her. "Thank you so much for watching her."

"I'm getting free practice if I ever have a family someday." Or never, if she kept her hopes on the military guy who may not even be alive.

"You're tense." Liberty moved out of their hug and gripped Tes-sa's shoulders. Warm brown eyes the same color as Tessa's searched hers. "You haven't talked about Chad in a while."

Tessa drew out a breath, and as much as she'd wanted to keep her concerns from Liberty and Iris, perhaps it was time to say something. "We haven't talked yet this year." They were supposed to have a video call on New Year's Eve, but he didn't call. "He hasn't even responded to my emails."

Liberty's brows lowered. "There has to be a reason why he hasn't called."

"That's what scares me." Panic roared in Tessa's brain, and she tried to shake her head to brush away any fears. Just because her dad died in the Army, it didn't mean Chad had the same fate. "He probably just got bored with me."

That should be a consolation, but it wasn't at all.

"That's not true." Liberty tightened her grip on Tessa's shoulders, more confident than Tessa. "You guys have been friends and stayed in touch for almost a year, he can't just ghost you."

She hoped so, but talking about him dying or not wanting her dampened her spirits. So she put on her best smile to assure her friend she was okay. The evening light streaming through the window was getting darker. "You should get going."

Liberty dropped her hands and kissed Tessa's cheek. "God's got this."

Tessa knew God had it, the same way God had decided it was Dad's time to die.

Bryce and Liberty hugged their daughter and kissed her good night before heading to the garage. Bryce slipped his arm around his wife and kissed her on the neck. Then Liberty kissed him back on the cheek. The journey of their love life was bumpy, but they were insanely in love with each other. The gentle curve of Liberty's baby bump had just started to show. Tessa longed to have that kind of love someday.

Not only had Bryce moved back to Pleasant View, but he'd also set tight boundaries with his Mom. Last Tessa had heard, Wendy was getting counseling to save her own marriage.

Charles, on the other hand, FaceTimed often to talk to his granddaughter. Although Bryce feared he would lose money by moving to Pleasant View, he had a steady enough stream of income from the companies he'd invested in—and he surprisingly volunteered to teach trading at the Business Institute twice a week. His way of giving back to the community.

"Princess." Myra's little voice reminded Tessa of her duty, and she snapped from her thoughts to look at the crown Myra had been putting on Bryce's head.

Tessa's heart squeezed at the cuteness. Myra looked so adorable, so beautiful in her fluffy purple dress with her hair in pigtails. "Would you like to dress up like a princess?"

"Yes!" She flashed her tiny bright teeth. She had another upcoming tooth on the lower row.

As Myra waddled to her room, Tessa followed her to the basket overflowing with dress-up clothes. They were all recycled clothes Liberty had bought at the community garage sale last summer.

As soon as Tessa finished dressing up Myra, her phone rang from the kitchen. She hoisted Myra up from the floor and set her on her hip. She couldn't ignore the call because the ringtone sounded different and her heart was racing—okay, her heart raced whenever the phone rang lately. So she was grateful she'd not let the call go to voicemail.

Her finger shook as she slid her hand on the screen to answer.

"Hey..." said a number of voices, and it took her a few seconds to locate Chad from the group of guys on the screen. Most of them were dressed in white T-shirts, except for the one guy in camo. And the man lying on the bed with a bandage wrapped around his head. She gasped and dropped the phone on the floor.

Setting Myra down, Tessa murmured, "Sorry, sweetheart. Let's go and sit." She scooped up the phone, thankful she hadn't lost the call yet. "What happened?"

On weak legs, she walked to Liberty's lime-green couch and dropped onto a faux-leather cushion. With Myra now eager to get the phone from her, Tessa held onto it tight.

"My buddies wanted to say hello." Chad's voice was hoarse as he attempted a smile. "Okay, guys, say hello to Tessa."

They hadn't defined the nature of their friendship—in fact, they were friends—but she felt drawn to him and wanted more. Her cheeks warmed while she imagined the handsome man behind the bruised face, and her chest tightened with an ache.

"It's me, George," said the man with a bandage on his left eye. "I loved the jerky you sent us."

"Next time can you send some Goldfish?" asked another soldier.

One by one, the six men introduced themselves. She'd only heard Chad talk about two of them from his unit. They each had a visible injury, but they didn't look as battered as he did. She frowned at the cast on the hand he'd propped on the bed rail.

Her friendship with Chad had started when she sent packages to the soldiers in the Middle East where Dad had died. When Chad mailed her a thank-you note, it started their interaction and friendship.

Myra couldn't help herself, and since emotion lodged in Tessa's throat, she set Myra on her lap so Myra could look through the phone. After all, Tessa needed a moment to compose herself.

"Aww!" They all oohed and aahed as little Starlight shone for the camera.

"She's adorable," someone said.

Chad told Myra how he'd heard so much about her. Yep, Tessa had told him about her friends over their last two video calls. Content from the attention, Myra wiggled free and toddled to her toy kitchen. After everyone said their goodbyes and left, Chad exhaled as if he'd been using his friends as a buffer.

"Are you going... to be okay?" She cleared the lump in her throat. "What happened?"

"Hey, I thought I looked presentable." His tone was light, but the shadows under those green eyes couldn't hide a pain more emotional than physical. It seemed like he was avoiding talking about his injury. "I'm still counting on that triathlon this summer."

"You're coming home soon?"

"As soon as they clear me."

Once he'd learned she was a physical therapist and trainer, he'd wanted her to train him whenever he returned home. Although born in Virginia, he wanted to start in a new place when he left the Army.

Tessa just needed to know when he was returning so she could schedule a week off for his arrival and plan when he needed to start his training. Except, he didn't look in any shape for a triathlon. "When do you think you might return?"

His response was muffled, and the screen went dead. Just like that, she was left with a multitude of unanswered questions. What were the extent of his injuries? Was he getting physical therapy? Would he be coming soon? All those questions left her wishing she'd minded her own business when Chad sent that thank-you note. But no, she'd had to write him back.

Sending packages and praying for the men and women in service was safe as long as she didn't hear about their injuries and deaths. Setting the phone on the couch, she braced her elbows on her knees, fighting a sense of unease while she stared at Myra. As Starlight stacked plastic broccoli and carrots on a plate, Tessa remembered she'd better feed her real food.

As for Tessa, she had no idea if she should fall in love with a soldier or end things before they even started.

-THE END-

If you've enjoyed The Investor's wife, please leave your review on Amazon, Goodreads and Bookbub

Next in the Series is The Soldier's Trainer. You can order your copy on Amazon

Feel free to connect with me on Facebook[1] in Rose Fresquez's reader group, where I usually chat with my readers on a regular basis.

1. https://www.facebook.com/groups/243932449976110/?ref=pages_pro-
file_groups_tab&source_id=435344610252020

Next in the Series...
The Soldier's Trainer

He's given everything to the Army. The Army has taken everything from her. Can they possibly find everything in each other?

Career soldier Chad Whitlock doesn't expect a victory in his life's battles. After his wife divorced him during one of his deployments, the Army's all he has left. But when a mysterious stranger sends packages and an inspirational note to his unit, Chad's response enlists him in a new operation—friendship with Tessa. Now, a mission gone wrong brings him face to face with death, but losing Tessa might be more terrifying than risking his life.

Physical therapist Tessa Richardson is more comfortable rehabilitating her patients than probing her wounded heart. Since her dad died in combat, her sending packages to support the soldiers seems safe... until one writes her back. A year later, eager to meet Chad in person, she wasn't ready for him to sweep her into an unexpected—and *incredible*—kiss at the airport. Now, how's she supposed to train this charming soldier for a marathon while caught in a crossfire between her fears and hopes?

Even if Tessa could risk loving another soldier, she's trained to rehabilitate people's bodies, and the healing Chad needs is in his heart and soul. He's fought for his country, but will he be brave enough to fight for his girl? And will she realize love is worth surrendering her fears?

Order your copy on Amazon.

A NOTE FROM THE AUTHOR

Thank you for reading *The Physician's Helper* It's always a blessing to meet new readers. And to those who have read all my stories, thanks for giving me another chance and for your reviews and notes of encouragement.

I can never forget to thank God who enables me to create these stories. Thank you Lord!

You can connect with Rose on Facebook or email her at rjfresquez@gmail.com

ABOUT THE AUTHOR

Rose Fresquez is the author of the Buchanan -Firefighter series, Romance in the Rockies, The caregiver series, two short stories and two family devotionals.

She's married and is the proud mother of four amazing kids. She loves to sing praises to God. When she's not busy taking care of her family, she's writing.

OTHER BOOKS BY ROSE FRESQUEZ

The Buchanan Series

1. First Site
2. Something Right
3. New Light
4. Bright Side
5. Short Sighted

Romance in The Rockies

1. Complex
2. Choices
3. Beyond Repair
4. Stand Out
5. Crystal Clear

The Billionaires' Reunion

1. A Legitimate Date
2. A Sudden Romance
3. A Necessary Compromise
4. A Genuine Disguise
5. A Marriage of Convenience
6. A Surprise Rescue

The Caregiver Series

1. The Doctor's Nanny
2. The Entrepreneur's Nurse
3. The Physician's Helper
4. The CEO's Companion
5. The Investor's Wife
6. The Soldier's Trainer
7. The Realtor's Attendant

TRUST ME (A group project)